Chronicles
The Crystals of Time

Stephen Moore

ISBN: 978-1-0685573-1-6

I reminded myself not to look down on someone
you see talking to themselves. It's simply
a reflection of a vivid imagination.

Stephen Moore
Author

N
W
E
S
Malware Island
Drakonia
The Fortress
Volcanis
Pinnacle of Hope
Nebula Ore
Amber Leaf
Verdantis
Dragon Forge
Twin Peaks Hills
Datadome City
Arbitration Land: Motherboard City
Lumania
Glimmerhaven
The Waterfall Cavern
Valaria
The Never Ending Forest
The Royal Palace
Emberfall Village
Sahelian Springs
Untamed Land
The Salt Flats
The Withered Bleach Tree

Personal Reflections

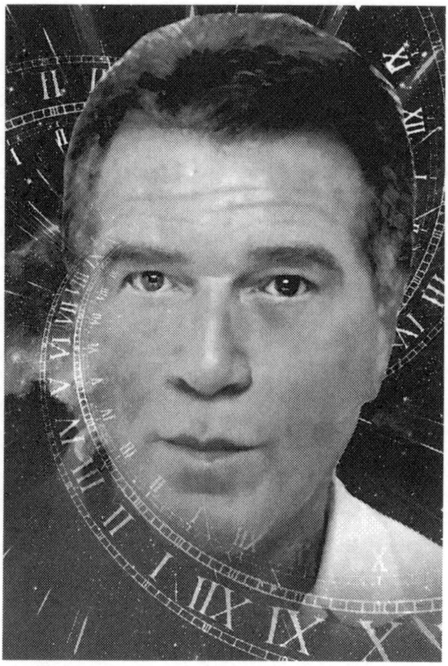

Having surpassed the retirement age, I still derive great satisfaction from my work with Chevron Traffic Management on the highways. The company's unwavering commitment to employee safety and training is exceptional. I am married and a father of four, and while I hold no favouritism, I have chosen my grandchildren Max and Mia, whose names and characters perfectly reflect the spirit of this story.

However, I dedicate this book to everyone who has experienced the "life gets in the way" syndrome and to all grandparents, whose wisdom, love, and support enrich our families and guide the younger generation through life's challenges.

Acknowledgements

I extend my gratitude to Kyra McDonald. I am truly indebted to this hardworking young mother of two. Kyra, your relentless support and encouragement in bringing this book to fruition has been invaluable.

A huge thank you to Tommy Cunningham for his vision and artistry in crafting the map of Cyberia

To Chris Moore—no relation—whose expertise in preparing and formatting books for publication has been invaluable.

Preface

A tale took root in a time when legends whispered secrets. It held a wondrous mystery from the heart of Southeast England. But legends are fickle companions, often masking the line between reality and fantasy. Is this tale true or woven from the threads of imagination? Two young siblings set on a quest, armed not with swords or scrolls but with digital amulets. They sought to unravel the unknown, a challenge that would test even the most creative mind. With a touch of their amulets, the world would warp and dissolve. They would enter a realm where time flows unrestrained, unlike on Earth. Yet, the bestowal of their digital amulets steals the limelight. It is fitting to delve into the heart of this extraordinary gift, which shimmers with the potential to become one of the most amazing tales ever recounted, whether to the young or old.

General Titanous

Contents

Chapter 1

Cyberia Farm
Writtle
Chelmsford
South East England

A young family's life in Chelmsford suddenly transformed when they learned that an elderly spinster had left the father an old workers' farmhouse and a few acres of land. Taken aback by the unexpected inheritance, the father was eager to learn more about the spinster's life. However, the acting solicitors were instructed to provide only her name. The parents felt a mix of emotions. Would the farm feel like home? Would the quiet of the countryside be a welcome change or a lonely retreat? They recalled their town life—the constant noise and hurried pace—and experienced relief and apprehension. The thought of selling or renting the property tugged at their heartstrings, but the idea of waking up to the sound of birds instead of traffic was too enticing to ignore. Despite its disrepair, the parents boldly decided to move to the farmhouse.

On removal day, they set out from the nearby bustling town. In the backseat of their parents' car, siblings Max and Mia felt their thoughts drifting like the wispy clouds overhead. With each passing mile, their worries began to fade as the scenery gradually transformed from the concrete and asphalt of urban life to the serene embrace of the countryside. Small trees lined the road, their branches forming an archway that filtered the sunlight into dappled patterns on the ground. Green and yellow fields stretched out on either side, dotted with wildflowers. A glimpse of a distant barn or a grazing herd of cows would break into view, standing against the backdrop of rolling hills. A smile crept across their faces, and they felt a sense of belonging wash over them for the first time. At the farmhouse's entrance, a timeworn sign swayed in the breeze, its weathered surface revealing the words—Cyberia Farm.

The car's tyres crunched over the gravel of the uneven driveway, a reminder of the many repairs the family faced. The Georgian farmhouse, built from sturdy red bricks, was a typical example of English rural architecture. A cobblestone path led to the front door, giving it an inviting appeal. The double-bayed front of the farmhouse featured a lean-to garage on its left, while a single-bedroom dormer window peered out onto the world above. Framed by aged wooden shutters, it added an element of elegance to the exterior, though time had left its mark with cracked, faded paint. At the back of the farmhouse were two bedrooms with weathered cream-coloured shutters. Beyond them lay a spacious garden filled with wildflowers and overgrown greenery.

Climbing ivy sought to claim parts of the structure. Like their first visit to the farm, the youngsters reacted dismayed as they gazed upon the dilapidated scene. Yet, the building's spirit seemed to resonate with memories. Max, a 16-year-old with a mop of dark hair and eyes the colour of charcoal, stood next to his 15-year-old sister. He possessed an insatiable curiosity and a boundless imagination.

In contrast, Mia had a unique passion for gadgets, especially computers. Her hazel eyes were always focused on the intricate world of technology, and today, they had more time to explore.

Their exploration led them to a wooden door that creaked as they pushed it open, revealing a staircase spiralling down into the cellar. Flicking on the light, they began their descent. The air turned cooler and mustier, infused with the scent of aged wood and damp earth. It was as if they could almost hear their father's voice echoing in their minds, recounting stories of the farmers who had depended on these cellars to preserve their food through the sweltering summers and cold winters.

At the bottom of the stairs, they entered a vast space lined with dusty bookshelves. The pages of the books were yellowed with age and filled with handwritten notes and recipes. It was a valuable collection of history, providing a window into the past that connected them to the age-old traditions of the farm. Amidst the dust-covered boxes, something draped in a sheet caught Mia's eye. Curiosity piqued, she gently pulled back the cloth, revealing a peculiar computer unlike any she had ever seen. Its sleek design was devoid of logos or manufacturer markings. A wave of questions flooded her mind: Why had it been abandoned in the cellar? What stories lay dormant within its memory? Her mind raced with the possibility of reviving its memories as she noticed the power cord plugged into the socket. With a mix of anticipation and excitement, she pressed the power button. Max stood back, arms crossed, watching her disinterestedly, seemingly unconcerned about whether the machine would spring to life. Suddenly, the cellar door slammed closed.

They stood stunned as a cacophony of electronic tones and an eerie hum filled the cellar, reverberating with a loud, pulsating frequency. Static crackled, intensifying the atmosphere with an electric charge. Panic began to grip them as the noise escalated, drowning out their thoughts and leaving them struggling to comprehend the unfolding chaos. The screen lit up with a bright, unexpected surge of energy. The radiant light illuminated their faces, revealing expressions of disbelief and shock. In the centre of the cellar, a tiny sphere materialised, seemingly from thin air, pulsating with an otherworldly glow. The sphere expanded rapidly, its radiance intensifying into a white brilliance that hovered and pulsated with energy; its final form resembled a portal straight out of a sci-fi novel.

On the brink of the extraordinary, their fear was overshadowed by shock as an apparition emerged from the emptiness. Its features looked human yet suggested a depth of existence that transcended their understanding. Draped in a brilliant white robe, the unsettling figure emanated an overwhelming aura. Its eyes shimmered like stars, radiating a calm as if it had foreseen this moment for eons. They recoiled as a mist-like hand extended and swiftly retracted in the blink of an eye. Its touch ignited a cascade of emotions, stripping away their defences and leaving their souls vulnerable to its watchful gaze. A charged silence fell, and time itself appeared to pause. The entity smiled and vanished, leaving them captivated and confused.

An irresistible force pulled Max toward the portal. The force clung to him like a magnet when he attempted to step back. Panic washed over him as he fought against its powerful embrace. With no time to think and seized by the terror of losing her brother to the unknown, Mia reached out to grab him, but the powerful force engulfed them both. Frantically, she shouted for her dad. The pull intensified, drawing them inside a void that defied the rules of physics. They felt a strange trembling sensation and a popping sound in their ears as the portal sealed shut. Underfoot, a glowing, transparent floor radiated an ethereal light, creating a weightless sensation as if they were treading upon the essence of time itself.

Crafted from crystal, the arch above them glowed with a soft, ever-changing spectrum of shimmering blues, vibrant greens, and fiery yellows. Majestic figures flickered in the reflections, leaving one to wonder: were they illusions or the guardians of the portal's secret? Surrounding Max in this mystical conduit were strange, chanting whispers that only he could hear, resonating with memories of the past and unfulfilled events yet to come, drifting far beyond the limits of his imagination. Silence fell as the portal gateway opened to an unfamiliar place.

Hesitantly, they stepped out of the portal into a realm alive with a kaleidoscope of colours beneath the vast blue sky. The terrain resembled Earth, yet the Luminara ferns stood twice as high, their glowing stems arching in the soft wind. What rooted them to the spot were the captivating creatures resembling animals from home: winged rabbits and glowing squirrels darted through the foliage while birds with crest-like crowns and ribbon-like tails soared above. Tiny birds with glittering feathers chirped their tunes, only to be drowned out by a piercing noise as the portal rapidly contracted and vanished from sight.

Overwhelmed by the uncertainty of their situation in the vast unknown, Max struggled to find the right words. "We should take a deep breath and approach this one step at a time," he said, trying to reassure his sister.

Faced with three divergent paths, they chose the widest one, marked by a signpost that read, "Welcome to Cyberia." The uncanny coincidence of Cyberia sharing the name of their farmhouse was too striking to ignore. They both wondered how such an extraordinary connection could even be possible. As they walked, the ground beneath their feet felt soft and mossy, the path unfurling like a ribbon of dreams through a landscape alive with vibrant energy. Towering trees with iridescent leaves arched gracefully overhead, their branches weaving together to create a natural canopy that filtered sunlight into a dazzling kaleidoscope of colours.

Overhead, data packets composed of light pulses artfully masqueraded as fireflies. Mia gasped in surprise as lively, glowing squirrels danced around their feet. Their spirited antics helped to soothe her nerves until the squirrels vanished as quickly as they had appeared. Max decided to share with his sister the continuous flow of whispers he had heard resonating from the portal, hinting at the high-tech names they were about to encounter.

Among the whispered exchanges, the name "Pathfinder" echoed with significance, suggesting a reason for their presence. With various tidbits swirling in his mind, Max chose not to alarm his sister about the danger they might face. He decided to keep it on a need-to-know basis—and she didn't need to know. While Mia remained oblivious to the whispers, her brother's words struck a disheartening chord.

As night fell, they stumbled upon a campsite settled beside a stream. Illuminated by the flickering blaze of a campfire, two canvas sheets, each pitched separately beneath the canopy of trees, served as sideless yet protective roofs against the elements. Above the crackling flames of the campfire, a cooking pot emitted savoury aromas that mingled with the scent of burning wood. Despite their hunger, they resisted the urge to eat, fully aware that the food was not theirs.

Mia welcomed the comforting warmth of the fire while Max cautiously inspected the canopies. Under one, he found two makeshift beds crafted from compressed leaves. The other contained a much larger single bed. However, only one set of fresh footprints led to and from the tent's entrance. Under the moon's glow, the mystery of his unease deepened. He joined his sister, shifting the cooking pot from the fire to prevent the food from spoiling. Hunger and exhaustion eventually drove them to eat what tasted like beef.

Opting to rest under the two-bed makeshift tent, Max took the watch while Mia slept until his eyelids grew heavy, and he succumbed to sleep. A tug at his toe jolted him awake. A forceful cough roused Mia. The two siblings froze as they caught sight of a towering figure. Vulnerable and filled with dread at the unknown intruder, they felt his piercing steel-blue eyes probing their very essence as their minds raced with thoughts of imminent danger.

Towering at seven feet, the giant's silver-grey locks framed his human face with an air of distinction. Draped in a half-shoulder tunic decorated with bright patterns of flowing streams of binary code, it barely concealed his bulging biceps and finely toned muscles, reminiscent of a colossal gladiator ready to enter the fray. The firewall spear he wielded was the pinnacle of design, fusing the qualities of a javelin with the soul of a sword, its metallic blade pulsating with electrifying brilliance. The spear symbolised the stranger's solemn duty as the protectorate of Cyberia. Overwhelmed by fear, Mia clutched the covers tightly, pulling them to her neck. The fabric felt like a frail shield against the encroaching terror. Her wide eyes flickered between the towering figure and her brother. Max lay frozen, unable to muster any words.

The giant's voice shattered the silence but did not carry the menacing tone they had anticipated. Instead, it was a soothing and unexpected contrast. "Welcome to Cyberia. I didn't mean to startle you. I'm General Titanous. I've been anticipating your arrival," he declared, his smile radiating friendliness.

Having never spoken to or been in the company of a general, Max nervously asked, "How could you have known of our arrival? We were oblivious to this until we encountered a computer in our cellar."

"The explanation will come in due time, but not from me," replied the general.

The mention of the cellar filled Max with panic once again. "Our parents! They must be worried sick about us disappearing like this."

The general dispelled their concerns by elaborating on the unique time system used in Cyberia, assuring them that such a situation wouldn't arise. "On Planet Earth, time is a construct created by humans. Who's to say that other planets in your universe adhere to the same definition of time? In Cyberia, we certainly don't. Our time runs at a baud rate of 86,000 bits per second. To capitalise, one second here equates to 23.88 hours on your Earth."

"But that's impossible!" Mia asserted, her eyes widening in astonishment, aware that the baud rate is the data transmission speed.

"Impossible? Yet, here you stand, defying such an impossibility," the general remarked casually, flashing a wide smile. "In Cyberia, our baud rate calendar is different. A year is a Dion, a month is a Chronoray, weeks are Splintrills, and days are Glitchmarks. The smallest units are Pulsarbits and Ticksparks, aligning with your minutes and seconds." Mia thought utilising baud rate speed as a timepiece was mind-boggling and expressed her amazement. "Planet Earth, known as the blue marble, doesn't lag in speed either," the general continued. "It maintains a rotation of three different speeds within your universe."

"Three rotational speeds? I don't quite understand what you mean," Mia replied.

"Your blue marble rotates on its axis at a speed of 1,037 miles per hour. Simultaneously, it orbits the Sun at 18.5 miles per second. The Milky Way Galaxy containing your planet travels 372 miles per second through the cosmos. Impossible? No! Fact! Never forget that 'impossible' is 'possible' with a negative twist."

To grasp the magnitude of such speed, Mia imagined travelling from England to Germany in the time it took to blink. "Wow!" she exclaimed, any apprehension she once felt fading.

Gathering his resolve, Max dared to ask, "General, are you human?"

The general, aware that this question would be forthcoming, answered, "My appearance transcends your conventional understanding. In essence, I am who I am. And who I am is of no concern to anyone but me."

Mia chuckled and then posed the same question from a different perspective. "Our parents are our origin. What about you?" Surprisingly, the general divulged more than she expected as she listened to his bizarre explanation.

"I was called Titanous by the Pathfinder. It was the zenizens of Cyberia who hailed me as a general. I fight against evil and the self-replicating viruses that infiltrate software by inserting their duplicates into the host code."

"Who is the Pathfinder?" inquired Max. "I caught whispers of this name within the portal, yet I cannot recall any mention of zenizens."

"The Pathfinder is as enigmatic as the passage of time itself," explained the general.

"Veiled in power and mystery, he communicates solely through me. Though I hear his commands, his physical form remains unseen. Until the Pathfinder decrees otherwise, this arrangement will persist. The zenizens of Cyberia are what you would call citizens on Earth. They revere the Pathfinder as a mystical entity, whispering his name in trepidation. Come! Let us gather around the campfire so I can rest and enjoy what's left," he smiled.

"Can I ask how you earned the rank of general?" Mia questioned as Titanous prodded the campfire to rekindle the flames.

"Through a gruelling and unyielding struggle with my arch-nemesis, Malice Malware."

Mia cocked her head. "Malware is a name we use for a computer virus back home. I'm intrigued. What does this person look like?" she asked.

"It's good that you've asked. If your paths do cross, you'll instantly recognise him. Malice Malware is toweringly tall and exudes great strength; he possesses a chest with stomach muscles that ripple as robustly as my own, but his face carries the burden of hostility. His skin, to gaze upon or touch, has an icy pallor—chilling as the whitest frost one could envision. Malware's hair is fiery, and he sports a straggly beard adorned with red and black beads, enhancing his distinct and villainous appearance. He wears gold hoop earrings with charms and trinkets such as tiny anchors, coins, and seashells. Around his neck, he carries a silver pendant with two symbols of a compass—there and back!" Max chuckled. Not quite finished, the general added, "His boots clank like chains as he walks, leaving a trail of corruption wherever he treads. Long-winded," he teased, "but I thought it best that you should know. His trail of action is mostly on the cyber seas."

"Cyber seas?" asked Max.

"This phrase captures the essence of cyberspace, much like sailors traversing the open waters. Malice Malware is the leader of feared cyber pirates!"

"Whoa," said Mia, interrupting. "You did say 'cyber pirates'!"

"Mia, the word the general used was 'feared,'" Max replied, knowing that there were no more secrets to hide from his sister.

"Malware sails through cyberspace aboard his malevolent ship, The Infector. The ship is an ominous sight adorned with menacing spikes and shadowy sails that absorb light for its flight. Wherever it sails, he hatches evil schemes to infiltrate and disrupt. He emulated my title by proclaiming himself an Admiral, not just an ordinary Captain," he scoffed. The general's tone shifted from belligerent to reflective as he discussed his enemy. "Despite his villainous nature, Malice Malware is a peculiar creature. Some claim he was once a brilliant coder who succumbed to the temptations of power and darkness, while others adhere to the myth that he arose from a rogue computer bug that gained awareness. Others, like myself, entertain a simpler interpretation: he came into existence embodying nothing but pure wickedness."

Max said, "General, I'm confused. Is this world some kind of virtual reality? Back home, we have games that immerse you in a digital simulation while wearing a headset. Being here feels both real and unreal," he mused.

The general replied, "Now isn't the moment to ponder such divergent intricacies that are more a part of the Pathfinder's understanding. Your thoughts should centre on returning to your world. Tomorrow holds more to digest, so rest for now." Acknowledging that delving further into what he had to foretell could lead to a restless night, he bid the siblings goodnight and retreated to his makeshift tent.

A modest breakfast was set before them in two bowls in the early morning. Plump, ruby-red berries gleamed like precious gems, their innate sweetness delivering bursts of flavour with each mouthful. The berries had been freshly gathered from thriving wild bushes deep within the forest's heart. Beside the vibrant berries, a pile of golden-hued oats, each grain toasted to a perfect crunch, had been harvested from the countryside.

Mia was the first to express her thoughts. "General, can you tell us why we were chosen among millions of others? And who built the Sphere—the Portal," she corrected, "to bring us here?"

"The Portal is the Pathfinder's creation, and it is due to him that you find yourselves in Cyberia. Why? Only he can answer that question. Perhaps the Pathfinder intends for you to unravel his identity eventually. However, that time is in the future. Currently, your focus should be on earning your Transportal Digital Amulets. This endeavour will demand immense courage from both of you. Though it may take time, I hope you will succeed."

"Transportal Digital Amulets! What are they?" asked Mia, intrigued by the technical undertone.

"Yes! And what is their purpose?" Max asked curiously.

"The Digital Amulets are similar to wristbands but are made of gold. They respond to the touch of those destined to wield their extraordinary powers. The key to activating them lies in your belief. This faith will allow you to independently travel between the blue marble and Cyberia. Moreover, the amulets are enhanced with an integrated sensor, enabling the Pathfinder to pinpoint their precise location at any moment. Once set in motion around your wrists, these amulets transform into an impenetrable shield, defying all efforts, even the most forceful, to detach. The sole authority to reverse the operations of these artefacts rests exclusively with the Pathfinder."

"So, with these amulets, we can come and go to Cyberia without relying on the Portal. How do we go about earning them?" Mia asked warily.

"You must venture to the town of Glimmerhavan in the province of the Never Ending Forest. In the heart of the town stands your purpose: The Great Tree Clock, frozen in time by Malice Malware. Its towering presence surpasses even the loftiest trees. Reinstating the clock to its former glory is your quest, which carries profound importance. Its rhythmic beats sustain the very fabric of existence in five of Cyberia's seven provinces."

"Reinstate a clock? The fabric of existence?" Max said. "This makes sense to you, but we haven't an inkling about either."

"Your challenge is to hunt for the sacred map that will reveal all the answers you seek. If you succeed, the map will remain with you until all its mysteries are uncovered. However, only one of you will have the ability to unravel its secrets. All will become clear when you reach the town of Glimmerhavan. I will guide you in the right direction. Beyond that, I cannot provide you with any more assistance. The Pathfinder has forbidden me to do so."

"Jeez, why can't we just turn around and go back home?" Mia sighed, feeling deflated.

"Because this is your destiny," the general replied frankly. "The road ahead is laden with formidable challenges that will evoke homesickness. Unless the Pathfinder alters his stance, the path to your home remains closed. From this moment onward, your future rests in the hands of a select few chosen by the Pathfinder. It is imperative to proceed with caution and avoid underestimating any potential adversaries. Malice Malware is aware of your presence. During times of our separation, it is crucial to maintain a vigilant stance."

For Max, the general's words somehow offered him the strength to continue. In contrast, Mia remained entirely unconvinced. When the general began describing the friendly creatures they would encounter on their journey to Glimmerhavan, they provided a significantly more joyful contrast to Malice Malware, bringing a smile back to her face.

Chapter 2

Motherboard City
Arbitration Landed

In Motherboard City, in the heart of Arbitration Land, the Grand Tower Stack rose, where delegates from every province gathered to prevent potential conflicts from erupting into devastating wars. Here, their disputes found resolution in the wise chambers of impartial arbitrators, esteemed for their profound grasp of law and order. Not classed as a province, Arbitration Land became an emblem of unity and collaboration, where foes evolved into friends through respectful dialogue.

In its conference hall, an assembly was poised to commence under the leadership of the venerable GranMother, Thalassa Starling. She had earned her title of GranMother through a legacy of wisdom and benevolence, drawing loyal followers from all but one of the governing provinces. Stepping onto the stage, holographic projections and pulsating lights showcased her remarkable achievements as the crowd rose to their feet in enthusiastic applause.

Adorned in robes that seemed to catch the light in a soft glow, her age-defying features were complemented by flowing silver hair that glimmered like moonlight. Her complexion was as dark as the night sky. Her eyes, profound and inscrutable as the deepest depths of the sea, bore the knowledge of countless generations. In the audience, there were distinguished individuals from various sectors of the digital world, including royalty, nobility, local leaders, AI experts, and those with civic duties of lesser rank. Thalassa Starling's warm and authoritative voice resonated throughout the hall as she addressed the assembly. She praised their achievements and celebrated their ingenuity in shaping the realms they inhabited.

Thalassa Starling had always avoided mentioning General Titanous or the Pathfinder by name. Both possessed a mysterious mystique akin to the very inception of time, but none more so than the Pathfinder. Her concerns came directly from her meeting with the General to discuss the gold Digital Amulets kept within the confines of the city's vaults. Their teleportation capabilities had never been tested and lay dormant, poised for an eventual awakening. Confident that this awakening had begun, as indicated by the faint, rhythmic glow from the amulets, she warned the General; now she had to reiterate his response.

Inhaling deeply, she addressed the assembled crowd with what she had learned. "Two beings, known as humans, have crossed the digital expanse into Cyberia, exposing themselves to grave peril. From the information gathered, these humans are on a bold quest to assist and restore the Great Wall Clock within the Never-Ending Forest. Should they falter in their endeavour, the repercussions would usher in an unparalleled level of tumultuous disaster, affecting three-quarters of Cyberia's ecosystem.

Honoured guests, prepare yourselves. General Titanous has informed me that the Pathfinder has sought your endorsement for your intervention," she provocatively proclaimed. The members let out a collective gasp, a reaction she had foreseen. The very name held a mystique that had remained tantalisingly out of reach. Like a chameleon caught between the guile of truth and myth, his name was tempered like no other due to his elusive form. The audience was hooked upon this unveiling, particularly as she divulged the motive behind the Pathfinder's intervention—the Digital Amulets.

She proposed granting the powerful amulets to the humans to protect them against the evil force of Malice Malware and to guide them safely to and from their homeland. With her characteristic wisdom and judicious approach, she sought unanimous agreement from all seven provinces, a customary requirement before the law could be enacted.

"Each province will exercise its voting right, representing the unified consensus of Cyberia," she concluded, entrusting the provinces to contemplate the possible risks and rewards of granting the siblings the amulets. One province weighed on her mind—Drakonia. Should this region decide to abstain, all endeavours would be in vain. Drakonia, the most potent domain, stood tall with its formidable army, casting a shadow over all other realms with its imposing presence.

Throughout the debate, heated discussions unfolded as representatives from each province voiced their perspectives and apprehensions. Some emphasised the pressing need to safeguard the siblings, given the dangerous nature of their quest. Others raised their concerns about rewarding such potent artefacts to outsiders, given that no one seemed to know how they had arrived in the land. The GranMother had clearly stated that it was a mystery beyond her comprehension.

Following the deliberation, the votes were cast, culminating in a unanimous verdict. Cyberia, as a cohesive entity, acknowledged the importance of the siblings' mission and the potential benefits it could yield for their realm. However, one province asserted a condition: the humans must succeed in their endeavour first. Drakonia firmly insisted on this stipulation.

The GranMother pondered their reasoning behind the condition. Their military might always won them more concessions than they deserved. It wasn't the outcome she wanted for the efforts of the humans' noble cause. But her heart still swelled with pride, knowing that the unity of the six other provinces would enable the humans to face the challenges that could preserve the harmony of Cyberia.

Amidst the unfolding assembly, a lone figure known as Whispering Grass stood sharply attuned. Operating as a covert informant, he bartered his knowledge as a form of currency in the shadowy dealings with Malice Malware, reaping the benefits of his endeavours in shining gold. Like the notorious turncoats of ancient times, Whispering Grass was acutely aware that his invaluable information would advance the ambitions of the Admiral and fill his coffers with precious wealth for the information he had gathered. He alone held the ability to communicate this news to Malice Malware promptly.

Chapter 3

The Never-Ending Forest
The Sacred Map

Max and Mia followed the general, savouring the delightful scent of hyacinths and sweet peas until they reached the edge of the Never-Ending Forest. The general noticed that his words of reassurance had calmed their anxiety as he bade them farewell. The forest trees possessed an extraordinary quality, emitting neon shades that seemed alive as their leaves changed colour. The display unfolded like a choreographed dance of light among the canopy of aligned treetops. Both felt they had entered a realm where technology and nature blended, creating a tranquil and heavenly illusion.

The first gathering described by the general was the GiggleSprites, each gracefully mounted on their elegant deer, exuding an air of woodland majesty. With appearances reminiscent of gnomes, the Sprites possessed a delightful charm that warmed Mia's heart. Their leaf-patterned clothing blended well with their natural surroundings. Their chubby, angelic faces radiated mischief and benevolence; framed by locks of mossy hair, they appeared to twin with one another. Their eyes, sparkling like dew-kissed petals, retained a vigilant watch as one of the numerous guardians of the woods. With a humble stature, their presence radiated a timeless bond with the forest. Beckoned to follow their lead, accompanied by their infectious giggles, each stride they took atop their mounts seemed to resonate with the land's beauty.

The Sprites led them through the Earveer camp, positioned by what Max perceived as the most colossal dam imaginable. The wooden structure stretched across the river, resembling a bridge as wide as a six-lane highway. The Earveers shared similarities with beavers but with an intriguing twist; their enormous ears served a purpose similar to those of hummingbirds. This unique flight adaptation allowed them to address leaks by mimicking the hummingbird's behaviour, enabling them to inspect or mend a leak from considerable heights. Though stout in stature, these creatures assumed the role of other unforeseen forest guardians, their sharp teeth, heightened senses, and unquestionable loyalty also establishing them as formidable protectors.

Continuing their journey, they encountered Flutterflies with wings glistening like myriad stars. Their graceful fluttering produced a gentle, melodic sound, contributing a magical symphony to the breathtaking landscape. Resting by the Lotus Ponds, they were unaware that the calm waters that mirrored the moonlight whispered truths to any question asked of those with pure hearts. When dusk marked the gradual darkening of the sky, their path was lit by luminous fireflies. Like digital lanterns, they led the way into Glimmerhavan.

The town of Glimmerhavan was a masterpiece of homely structures integrated into the surrounding trees and foliage. The homes shone softly from their candlelit windows, bathing the surrounding area in a warm, delicate light. What truly captivated them was the Great White Clock, a magnificent tree rooted in the town's heart. The clock's colossal size defied imagination. Its massive trunk soared upward like a titan's tower. Its glowing branches, with intricate patterns of symbols, were distinguished by its Carrara white bark, which stretched out in every direction.

Max guessed the clock's face was seven metres in diameter. The clock's four hands gleamed with a metallic sheen, once moving with precise mechanical clicks but now frozen in perpetual stillness. The elaborate dial featured three distinct sections: the sun's radiant path, its companion moons, and a barometer that had started to decline in pressure.

Housed within the timepiece was the lineup of two figures called Glimmer and Havan. Having once emerged from a window box positioned above the clock, they now remained frozen, no longer echoing the pulsating rhythm of time. Max and Mia felt a deep sense of humility as they understood that they had become integral to something far greater than themselves. The Great Tree Clock surpassed being a timekeeping instrument; it stood as a unique representation of Cyberia.

In the lively square, the chubby, grey-haired Elder MossFoot, the town's Mayor, awaited. Elder MossFoot held the dual roles of town leader and being the most senior and prudent among the tree dwellers. Radiating a serene smile and possessing a voice that resonated across the entire square, he extended a warm welcome to the siblings, expressing gratitude for their presence in Glimmerhavan. With a single snap of his fingers, the town burst into activity, orchestrating a magnificent celebration in honour of their guests. Invited onto a podium, it afforded an overall view of the town's surroundings. Wooden tables were readily laid with colourful bouquets and lanterns, while an exquisite array of fruits, pastries, and other delicate delights was placed on the tabletops.

The GiggleSprites captivated the audience with acrobatic feats and jovial dances, prompting enthusiastic applause. Under the canopy of stars, which grew more radiant as the night progressed, the luminescent Flutterflies created an enchanting light show. Their wings pulsated in harmony with the music played by a group of skilled tree dwellers on unique, handcrafted flute instruments.

Spurred by the Mayor's invitation, Max shyly stepped forward to address the gathering. Initially faltering, unsure of what to say, the Mayor encouraged him to unveil the wonders of royalty beyond their own. The zenizens listened intently, captivated by his words, as Mia sat transfixed at the levitating, shapeshifting dinner plates that adjusted to accommodate a small or large appetite.

The emotion that evoked the strongest groan of sorrow and cheer came as Max recounted the beloved Queen Elizabeth II's passing. He stated how her reign spanned generations, leading to the climactic moment of her son's coronation—an event that etched itself as an indelible milestone in their kingdom's history. Finished, Max looked at the Mayor and shrugged before resuming his seat.

Elder MossFoot sprang back into motion, causing a profound silence to settle over the crowd as he began his speech. "Although Glimmerhavan has extended a heartfelt welcome, we should now concentrate on the reason for your presence. The Great Tree Clock distinguishes itself from conventional timekeeping devices familiar to our honoured visitors. Our guests have shared that their land uses a system of hours, minutes, and seconds." The puzzled expressions on the faces of his audience prompted him to shift his focus. "Malice Malware, a cunning and evil foe, is a renegade who targeted the Great Tree Clock, responsible for generating the life-sustaining air in the Never-Ending Forest and four other provinces. With sinister intent, he released a powerful cyber virus, breaching the clock's intricate workings, a task previously thought unachievable. The Five Crystals of Time, the clock's most precious jewels, were corrupted and shattered, forever losing their infinite, radiant sparkle."

Mia struggled to comprehend that five crystals in a solitary tree were critical for preserving an ecosystem spanning five provinces. The Mayor turned to face the siblings. "To repair the damage inflicted by Malice Malware and restore the Great Clock to its former glory, a daunting task lies ahead. Somewhere within the seven provinces lie five additional Crystals of Time, the final lineage of their ancient ancestry. They must be found and integrated into the Great White Clock to rejuvenate the air we breathe and restore the spirit of our realm."

The siblings exchanged worried glances, their expressions revealing the enormity of the mission they were to carry out. "The culmination of the clock's restoration hinges on a pivotal requirement," Elder Moss-Foot continued, "it calls for the presence of an individual with a heart untainted by selfishness, pure in its intentions, to replace the tainted crystals with the new. That person is none other than you, Mia."

"Oh, my goodness!" Mia exclaimed, surprised by the daunting comment. Her voice quivered as she voiced her apprehensions to Max. "What if my best isn't good enough? What if I fail? What then?" She somehow managed to muster a half-hearted smile to the enthusiastic crowd.

"We mustn't dwell on failure," Max whispered back sharply. "The general or the Pathfinder may want to test our bravery. Despite the disheartening circumstances, we must maintain hope. Still, I wonder why the Mayor hasn't mentioned the sacred map that the general referred to." A combination of unease and amusement, highlighted by the sheer absurdity of the situation, evoked a wistful chuckle.

Without warning, the weather shifted dramatically, indicating an oncoming storm. The calm night sky, enhanced by a brilliant full moon, was now veiled by ominous, dark clouds swirling menacingly overhead. "It's Malice Malware!" the Mayor exclaimed, his anxiety evident as he paced back and forth rapidly on the podium.

"Max! This is not good," said Mia, wide-eyed and unsure of what to do or expect. Elder MossFoot's actions did little to alleviate her unease as he bypassed the steps and vaulted over the side railing, landing clumsily on the ground. The entire assembly promptly followed suit, disappearing in a matter of moments. The clouds parted, revealing the descent of the colossal flagship, the Infector. The pirate ship's sails gleamed with an eerie, supernatural glow, signalling the ominous presence of formidable power. Mia gulped, but Max couldn't help but stifle a nervous laugh as it hovered above the town centre.

The ship bore the unconventional appearance of a 500-year-old British war frigate, complete with worn and tattered flags, giving it an air of ancient and maligned history. The bow featured a fearsome figurehead of Malice Malware, which was exactly how the General had described him. The figurehead's expression highlighted a wicked grin, while the stern bore menacing carvings of snarling supernatural creatures. The floating fortress, bustling with a dedicated crew, radiated an air of menace and authority as they enacted every directive of their eerie commander, who strode confidently across the deck, his cloak billowing in the breeze. His piercing gaze surveyed the square below.

Max felt the gravity of the impending confrontation but understood that the fate of the five provinces rested on his courage. Gathering all his inner strength, he was determined to confront what seemed to be a horrendous nightmare. "Exercise utmost caution," a chilling whisper echoed from the obscurity beneath the podium. "Though the ship might resemble a bygone era, its cannons hide cutting-edge technology—not with grapeshot or cannonballs, but with lasers designed to slice through a tree."

Max narrowed his eyes toward the voice and glimpsed a silhouette of a face peering up at him through the gaps in the wooden floorboards. "Have courage," the female voice reassured. "Wait until I ascend the stage. You and your sister must stand directly behind me. Failing to heed my advice will put your existence in great danger."

"But how can I be sure you're helping us?" Max inquired, his uncertainty evident.

"You don't! But considering your situation, I don't believe you're in a position to negotiate. Do you?" she retorted impatiently.

"I guess not," Max admitted, recognising they had no alternative as the ship landed.

Over the Portside, a rappelling rope morphed into steps, providing a simple way to disembark. "That is so impressive!"Mia burst out nervously, marvelling at the advanced technology.

Max arched an eyebrow, his reaction starkly different. He watched in dread as Malice Malware descended the steps, holding what seemed to be a wooden staff. His confident stride towards the podium exuded arrogance, each step resonating with the metallic clang of his boots. Halting, his staff struck the ground with a resounding thud, morphing into a formidable spear-like sword. Resembling the General's weapon, arcane energy surged through its gleaming metal, emitting a pulsating glow. Brilliant arcs of electricity traced its length, casting a radiance that illuminated the surroundings. He struck the weapon against the ground again, reverting it to the staff's initial form.

Emerging from the space beneath the podium, a young woman appeared and gracefully ascended the steps. Aged around 18-20, with fair and coppery hair that flowed down to her waist, her warm smile revealed a dazzling set of pearly-white teeth, and her snug, tanned leather outfit complemented her sun-kissed complexion. What truly entranced Max were her vivid aquamarine eyes. In that fleeting moment, he felt his resolve soften under her gaze. When she turned to confront Malice Malware, he and Mia instinctively positioned themselves behind her as she'd asked.

Another figure emerged from beneath the podium. His robust physique stood firmly at the base of the steps. With arms crossed, Zenturion Valour exuded an authoritative presence. He was wearing a Roman toga, and the dancing flames from the surrounding stick torches cast flickering shadows on the wrist amulets he wore for battle. Valour kept his sword sheathed to avoid conflict, yet his eyes remained locked on Malice Malware, prepared to confront any threat that endangered the one he had vowed to protect.

"Well, if it isn't Princess Arabella and her devoted yet misguided Zenturion," Malice Malware remarked, offering a mocking bow.

Exuding authority, the Princess announced, "By royal decree, these humans are under my guardianship and shall benefit from the protection of my family."

Malice Malware interrupted, extending his palm as if halting a stampede of steeds, and directed his following words squarely at his opponents with a growling undertone. "Listen closely and take heed, humans. I embody wickedness, vindictiveness, cruelty, and deviousness, a wretch you will not encounter elsewhere." Sporting a wide smirk, he continued, "I can annihilate, devastate, decimate, and obliterate anyone I choose! Relinquish any thoughts of finding the Crystals of Time. Return to where you belong, or you may never return!"

Standing behind the Princess, Mia cautiously glanced at Malice Malware, her voice tinged with anger. "Why not confront someone your size, such as General Titanous?" she yelled, her audacity catching her off guard as she recoiled in amazement.

Malice Malware retaliated with a cold and chilling gaze, wondering how she knew General Titanous. He had always wrestled with a blend of begrudging admiration and simmering resentment every time his most formidable adversary was mentioned. Both had ascended to legendary prominence, their monumental conflicts leaving an enduring imprint on the digital realm, shaping the ongoing saga of cyber-warfare. "I offer you this one chance to escape Cyberia," he taunted. "Should you choose to remain to continue your fruitless journey on such an ill-fated quest, I will give a glimpse of the fate that awaits."

Foreseeing his impending show of power, Princess Arabella intervened. She directed his gaze towards the prominently placed statue of the town's mayor: "Regardless of your choice, spare the statue—a treasured gift presented to the esteemed Mayor by the zenizens of Glimmerhavan."

Malware ignored the request and barked an order to his chief gunner. The wooden ship groaned and creaked, echoing age as it tilted. Two starboard gun openings dropped, revealing the spouts of the cannons aligning with their intended target. Upon Malice Malware's command, the cannons unleashed a formidable energy at the statue. A surge of laser beams, akin to blazing white-hot arrows, burst forth. They etched a radiant trail through the stone with the precision of a sculptor's chisel. Sparks danced along the edges as shards of stone flew, transforming the once grand statue into a heap of debris. The young siblings could only watch in awe at the incredible demonstration of sheer power.

"Do you still believe in your ability to challenge me?" Malice Malware taunted, clearly enjoying the fear he was instilling. "Leave Cyberia while you can, or prepare to face the consequences!" With a menacing presence, he turned and walked decisively towards his waiting vessel. The frigate commenced an ascent, gradually accelerating and vanishing with an uncanny, almost supernatural speed. Max and Mia grappled with the gravity of the situation, realising the impending peril if they defied his ominous threat.

From his hidden refuge, Elder MossFoot emerged with a slow, deliberate movement, the burden of grief evident on his face. Amidst the wreckage, he stood, a solitary presence encircled by the statue's remains that once symbolised his prominence and importance to his loyal patrons. Zenturion Valour gently ushered the Mayor aside. Undeterred by the scattered debris, he searched through the wreckage until his fingers felt and grasped a canister. Glowing like an Olympic flame, he held the elusive treasure of the Sacred Map aloft before presenting this newfound hope against the darkness of desolation to his Princess.

Princess Arabella turned to the siblings. "Sadly for the mayor, inside this canister is the sacred map," she stated, holding back a smile. "The clue to its location was passed on to me by my father. The clue was as follows:

In public places, I stand tall yet never walk. With eyes that never blink, I oversee all. In silence, I witness the ebb and flow, forever still, in grandeur, I bestow.

Malice Malware unwittingly spared us from dismantling the statue or persuading the Mayor that it was the right course of action to take," she explained, her delight evident as she handed the canister to Max. Bewildered, he asked about Malice Malware's choice not to initiate an attack against them.

"Firstly, he wouldn't dare to assault royalty, knowing it would trigger an unprecedented response from all provinces. Secondly, my skin is blemished with optical filters completely invisible to the naked eye. They can absorb, block, or even redirect laser light, preventing it from penetrating my body. To Malware's annoyance, I requested you to stand behind me—for your safety," she emphasised. "My father, King Osred, places your safety above all else, which is why he assigned me to accompany you until your mission in Cyberia is fulfilled."

Max now understood that the Princess and her guardian were the select few General Titanous had mentioned to assist them. He repeated the question he had posed to the General. "But how did you know we would be here?" he asked, scratching his head.

"The tale of your destination and destiny is woven into the constellations," she stated. With such an unusual response, Max avoided asking further questions, knowing that any answer would lead to more perplexing or evasive responses. However, the Princess provided more insight into her status and kingdom. "I hail from a province called Valaria, where my father, King Osred, reigns supreme. The journey to Glimmerhavan was a challenging trek. Were it not for the determination of my guardian, Valour, I would have found it too testing to arrive here on time. Hopefully, our minor triumph over Malice Malware will be one he will forever regret."

"I'm finding it hard to keep pace with all of this; could you please remove the map from the canister, Max?" Mia pleaded. Max unscrewed the canister and unfolded the circular parchment on the podium table. The Princess and Valour stepped back. The sacred scroll was not intended for their eyes.

The map's unusual circular design made identifying a clear starting or ending point challenging. The parchment displayed a captivating mosaic of mountains, rivers, and landscapes finely intertwined with the geography of several provinces. He recited the names of the other six regions: "Valaria, the Princess's province; DragonForge, Lumina, Drakonia, Volcanis, and Verdantis." His excitement quickly faded. The clues to the five Crystals of Time locations appeared in a hieroglyphic form, a text he couldn't understand. He could do no more but stare at the scroll in disappointment. The text on the scroll seemed to blur, prompting Max to shake his head in frustration and rub his eyes. To his astonishment, the hieroglyphics changed into legible text, leaving him bewildered.

"I'm as confused for not having the same insight as you," Mia said after Max explained what had happened.

Max shared the same thought: if Mia had the task of dealing with the Crystals of Time, why was he the one able to decode the complex map? He shrugged. "The upside is that at least one of us can decipher it." With a finger placed on the Never-Ending Forest, he focused on the text and read it aloud for the Princess and Valour to hear.

"I'm often found in oceans deep, Where waves and whispers softly sweep. In the sky, I dance with grace, A tranquil hue, a calming space. What colour am I?"

"I believe the colour is blue," said the princess without a second thought. To Max's disbelief, the map reformed into another riddle and recounted what he had just seen.

"Search for a blue sapphire bathed in an ethereal glow which captivates the beholder with its mesmerising facets. Its surface ripples with internal energy, like elusive spirits within its crystalline structure."

Mia's jaw dropped. It seemed as if the situation had transitioned into an awful, inescapable dream. Her dire expression did not escape Max's notice. "Look, Mia, let's just focus on the whereabouts of the blue crystal."

"Okay," she said, braving a smile.

Max studied the map. "The key to discovering the first crystal is selecting the correct direction to begin the search. Yet, adding to the intrigue is the curious omission of a compass rose, leaving no indication of north, south, east, or west."

Words began rearranging into another riddle, guiding them toward the first crystal like a phantom orchestrating their journey. Max wondered whether the other four crystals would unveil themselves one by one after securing the first. Yet again, he read out what he saw.

"The Great Tree Clock casts a shadow that points in a particular direction."

Shadows become visible at night, particularly with a bright moon or under specific conditions, but they lack the sharpness of those in sunlight," Valour stated as they all looked up at the colossal clock.

The Princess focused on the distinctive face dial, where four hands stood frozen, and a spark of inspiration struck. "I think I've unravelled the riddle," she said thoughtfully. "Observe the four motionless arrow hands! Beneath them, the shadows converge, all pointing towards the north. Surely, this indicates the direction we should take."

When Max saw a new riddle replace the old one, he knew the Princess had to be right. With a better understanding of how the map operated, he eagerly shared the updated riddle.

"I slither silent, where few dare tread. In shadows deep, I make my bed. With scales of ebony, I blend well in a realm of solitude where secrets dwell. I'm not in gardens or forests fair but in a land untouched by stare. In the heart of darkness, I find my home, a place so remote, you'll never roam. What am I, dwelling in this lonely space, with scales that shimmer in a hidden place?"

"You could go through the alphabet of creatures with scales," said Mia. "The first thing that comes to mind when I think of 'scales' that shimmer is a snake," which made her shiver.

The mayor interrupted. "To the north, there lies an encampment near an area devoid of gardens or a thriving forest: the Sahelian Retreat," he exclaimed. "I recall hearing a story about a snake in that area, though the specifics escape me, as tales often do."

The Princess was familiar with the Sahelian tribe residing in that area. Max examined the map and pinpointed the Sahelian Retreat. His jaw fell open as he gazed at a warning that had suddenly appeared below the final symbol. Mia saw his shocked expression. "What's the matter, Max? What did you see?"

"Nothing," he lied. This was another secret he had to keep from his sister, but this would be the most significant. It became clear why he and not Mia had the insight to read the map. Interrupting his thoughts, the elderly Timekeeper of the Great White Clock mounted the podium. His round face resembled a watch dial, a testament to the dions he had devoted to overseeing the intricacies of timekeeping. His neatly trimmed white beard contributed to the aura of authority that enveloped him. Valour questioned the Timekeeper about the operation of the clock's mechanism.

"The mechanism intertwines with the pulses of digital energy from the Crystals of Time. Once the harmonious gears and cogs fell victim to Malice Malware's insidious infection, it spread to the fuel-lined crystals where time faltered and froze. The chaos unleashed a maelstrom of detrimental underground waves that will continue to wreak havoc upon the natural order by squeezing its ability to generate life-sustaining oxygen for five of the seven provinces. Zenizens will no longer exist. Trees, once teeming with vitality, will wither and gasp for breath. Rivers, once clear and vibrant, will turn sluggish. Creatures of all kinds, from majestic to humble forest critters, will not survive in this tumultuous upheaval."

Detailing the foreboding account offered a fresh perspective on the vital importance of the crystals the group sought. It was the Princess who broke the ensuing silence. "Timekeeper, how much time do we have?" she asked with a deep frown.

"Until the snow season begins," he replied. "After that, it will be too late to reverse."

"Which are the two provinces unaffected, and why?" asked Max.

"My province, the kingdom of Valeria and Drackonia," answered the Princess. "Our unique geographical features ensure the sustainability of its ecosystems without the need for external resources."

The TimeKeeper added a twist to the mayor's earlier words. "With all five crystals gathered, the individual with the purest heart must ascend the Great Tree and place each crystal in its assigned position. Any misplacement will result in the crystals inevitably shattering. Only the sacred map can decipher the alignment pattern. The clock's magic will be restored when the last crystal is inserted. General Titanous has assured that Malice Malware won't be able to repeat this grave act of lunacy twice."

"Haven't you got police? Prison is the place for him," emphasised Mia harshly.

"Police? Prison?" Princess Arabella's eyes sparkled with intrigue as the continuous unfamiliar words cast a spell of fascination. Her reaction when told was one of astonishment. "Oh, my stars! Earth is a whirlwind of bewildering chaos. In Cyberia, we do have dungeons, which is a futile endeavour. Scarlet, the Siren of Deception, is the only pirate who has been caged. General Titanous allowed her to go free. No one knows why, and no one has dared to ask." Mia felt the urge to inquire about Scarlet, but there was already an overflow of concerns to cope with.

Trotting into the square, a group of four WhiteTail deer, mounted by GiggleSprites, stopped at the podium. Max regarded the majestic WhiteTails as similar in size to a thoroughbred racehorse, their powerful legs poised gracefully beneath them. Each WhiteTail stood tall, their elegant necks arched, and their large, expressive eyes sparkled with intelligence and mischief. The luminous coats, shimmering like liquid silver, seemed to dance in the soft light of the square, captivating the attention of all who gathered.

"The GiggleSprites, known for their playful nature, had chosen to gift these creatures for a reason. They are imbued with a spirit that resonates with the magic of Cyberia," declared Elder MossFoot. "In the realm of Cyberia, these WhiteTails are unique entities, bred from a lineage unlike any other," his voice resonating with pride. Mia imagined riding one of these extraordinary beings, feeling the wind rush past as she galloped through the forests, their hooves barely touching the ground.

Princess Arabella's eyes sparkled with gratitude as she addressed the mayor, her voice soft yet commanding. "Please convey my heartfelt thanks to the GiggleSprites," she implored, her expression earnest. Opting to wait until dawn, they were invited to stay at the Treetop Inn.

Enveloped by the tranquillity of the forest, their accommodations were perched high among the trees, connected by wooden walkways and swaying suspension bridges. Inside the lodges, glassless windows allowed Max to admire the breathtaking view of the moon, enhanced by the gentle rustling of leaves and the soothing hoots of an owl. The lodging was furnished in a blend of rustic and modern styles. A bowl on the table held an assortment of exotic fruits. Max chose one that resembled an apple in both appearance and taste. The leaf bed, shaped like a mattress, looked well-compressed and comfortable. Rainwater was collected in a large overhead tank that captured the deluge of rain to serve the Inn's needs. His thoughts delved into a whirlwind of emotions and reflections as he grappled with feelings of uncertainty. He considered Mia's choice to turn on the computer and become trapped by the portal in the cellar, but it was too late for regret.

Amid his anxiety, he wished that with each hour passed, he would find clarity and a renewed sense of purpose, prepared to tackle whatever came next. Looking toward Mia's lodge, he noticed her with her hair wrapped in a towel. He waved and mouthed, "Good night, Mia." Responding with a tired smile, she silently mouthed, "Good night, Max."

Chapter 4

The Blue Crystal
Sahelian Springs

Mia woke up before dawn, having spent a restless night. The arrangement of the seven provinces on the circular sacred map confused her—until it reminded her of the European Union's map. She pictured substituting France with the Never-Ending Forest as her starting point. Once she determined their locations, the other six provinces would represent European countries. The creaking of the rope bridge outside indicated the group was walking along the walkway. The prospect of riding a WhiteTail lifted her mood, prompting her to spring out of bed before Max knocked on her door, urging her to prepare to leave.

Nostrils flaring, the WhiteTails breath emitted wisps of mist in the early morning dew. Prepared with saddles, bridles, and a keenness to proceed, they pawed the ground eagerly while the GiggleSprites maintained a firm grip on their reins. Valour assisted the princess in mounting and adjusting her stirrups before aiding Mia onto her steed. Mia subtly adjusted herself for Bilko to accommodate her weight, and in that indescribable moment of connection, she sensed a reservoir of hidden courage lay dormant within his spirit.

Each WhiteTail carried packed provisions: water skins to quench their thirst, energy bars to fuel their bodies, and succulent fruits to savour. Seeing the mayor and a minor assembly gathered was a surprise, showering them with optimistic and enthusiastic best wishes. The GiggleSprites guided the WhiteTails to establish a rhythm before releasing the reins. United by a shared sense of purpose, the group embarked on their journey, venturing north through the dense forest towards Sahelian Springs.

Princess Arabella's WhiteTail led the group with its innate sense of direction, its silvery mane glistening in the dappled sunlight that filtered through the canopy of trees. Riding beside the Princess, Max became her companion while discussing the journey. Their conversation flowed effortlessly, weaving tales of adventure. Max couldn't help but admire the determination in Arabella's eyes. She spoke passionately about the lands they would traverse, the zenizens they would meet, and the challenges they might face. Her enthusiasm was infectious, igniting a spark of excitement.

At the group's rear, Valour rode with a vigilant demeanour, his presence a steadfast anchor amidst the unfolding adventure. Accompanied by Mia, who exuded a quiet strength, he kept a watchful eye on their surroundings. His keen senses attuned to every sound and movement, and his sharp ears caught the faintest rustle in the underbrush. He understood the importance of their mission and the potential dangers that lurked in the shadows.

The winding path guided them beneath the canopy of towering trees adorned with abundant foliage. With each stride, the WhiteTails trod on a soft carpet of emerald moss, cushioning their hooves as sunlight filtered through the verdant leaves. They had to navigate their steeds around fallen branches that blocked their path. Persistent vines tangled through the undergrowth, presenting challenging obstacles that required coordinated teamwork. Once in a clearing, they pressed on, the cadence of their strides propelling them nearer to their destination.

At sunset, they settled by a babbling brook and established their campsite. Gathered around the glowing flames of the campfire, they swapped stories, fostering connections. With the early dawn light, they continued through the forest, rejuvenated by the unrelenting promise of strenuous trekking, until they reached their long-awaited destination: Sahelian Springs. The twigs snapping under the WhiteTail's hooves subsided as the dense woods gave way to a visually stunning terrain. Eager excitement surged as they entered the awe-inspiring clearing—a natural sanctuary where the forest merged with the majesty of towering mountains. Their peaks, veiled in delicate wisps of clouds, framed the scene like timeless sentinels that appeared to ascend infinitely upward. Their slopes intertwined with a mosaic of emerald trees, cascading waterfalls, and rugged stone formations.

While they advanced, a disconcerting sensation heightened. An unsettling presence began to envelop Valour, a feeling of being constantly watched. The WhiteTails also displayed signs of unease, glancing warily in all directions. Max, Mia, and the Princess noted the concern on Valour's face, clearly indicating that something was wrong. Beneath their path, concealed figures hidden in leafy camouflage suddenly sprang from hidden pits. Their masculine, cloaked forms exuded a distinctive presence strongly tied to Arabian culture. Their boltholes disguised with elements of nature, with earth and twigs arranged to blend seamlessly with their surroundings. Like phantoms, they moved with fluid grace, each step purposeful and precise. Max instinctively tightened his grip on the map's canister that had guided them thus far. In this heart-pounding moment, his thoughts churned with questions. Who were these shadowy figures, and why were they lying in wait?

Chapter 5

The Fortress
Malware Island

With its dark legend, Malware Island had solidified its standing as a menacing location. Named after the notorious Admiral, it was a destination not for the faint of heart. Here, he had erected a fortified sanctuary that rendered him untouchable due to a formidable decree passed by Arbitration Land.

Malice Malware presented an imminent danger to digital existence, with the ability to cause chaos in computer systems with astonishing speed and efficiency. General Titanous proposed a solution to halt his evil spread, leading to a controversial yet vital choice: isolating him on an island shielded by virtual barriers and protected by complex algorithms. However, this idea had one flaw—Drakonia. Without warning, they retracted their agreement, perceiving it as an imposition of excessive regulations in the dynamic realm of cyberspace. With the firewall withdrawn, Malware roamed unchecked throughout the digital domain. General Titanous expressed his displeasure, but the decision from Arbitration Land was clear—to maintain a delicate balance between Drakonia and the other provinces. The Island still required the utmost caution and vigilance. It was a constant reminder of the lurking dangers and the unrelenting efforts needed to safeguard against the Admiral's potential threats.

The elusive spy, Whispering Grass, found himself in an unforeseen and intimidating predicament upon receiving a summons to the Island. The summons was no casual invitation but an unequivocal demand offering him no avenue for refusal. The urgency of the summons became evident when the Admiral's vessel, the fear-forged ship The Infector, unexpectedly materialised within the haven of his expansive gardens.

The vessel seemed to pulsate with a supernatural vitality as it hovered, readying for him to board. Despite his hesitation, he realised that the consequences of defying the Admiral's request would be far graver than complying with it.

Whispering Grass stood at an average height, neither too tall nor too short. His enormous feet immediately caught your eye, which seemed to glide across the ground, giving him the uncanny ability to approach without warning. He wore a long, tattered cloak over his broad shoulders that reached down to his oversized feet. His face was obscured by a wide-brimmed hat, casting a shadow over his eyes and leaving his full features hidden. It gave an eerie sense that he could pierce through the darkness with uncanny insight.

A crew member who resembled a cyborg guided him onboard to rest in the Admiral's cabin. A blend of advanced technology and ancient symbols created a disquieting vibe inside. The 500-year-old war frigate, a relic of a bygone era, stood as a striking testament to the fusion of ancient craftsmanship and cutting-edge technology. Its weathered hull whispered tales of conquest, yet as one stepped aboard, the disquieting vibe of the vessel became palpable, a contrast of history and futurism that left an indelible impression.

The frigate's bridge was a marvel of modern engineering, starkly contrasting the ship's timeworn exterior. Sleek, holographic displays flickered to life, casting a soft blue glow that illuminated the faces of the crew. Advanced radar systems, seamlessly integrated into the ship's design, scanned the horizon precisely. The hum of machinery blended with the ship's creaking, creating a sea-bound sound. Control panels, adorned with touch-sensitive interfaces and augmented reality overlays, allowed the crew to navigate cyberspace with unparalleled ease. Ancient symbols, once used for navigation and communication, were now reimagined as digital icons, bridging the gap between the past and the present. It was as if the ship's spirit had awakened, merging the ancient with the futuristic in a harmonious dance of technology and tradition.

Outside the bridge, the frigate's deck was equipped with state-of-the-art weaponry integrated into the ship's design. Laser cannons cloaked in the ship's historic aesthetic stood ready to defend against any threat.

The 500-year-old war frigate was not merely a ship but a testament to the enduring spirit of exploration and innovation, a bridge between the ancient world and the limitless possibilities of tomorrow.

The ship's journey to the Island involved a complex web of diversionary manoeuvres to avoid detection outside its safety zone. Stepping onto the upper deck on arrival, a feeling of unease embraced him. The Island was shrouded by a disconcerting mist, allowing it to materialise or vanish in a wisp. He knew this mysterious trait made it highly challenging for intruders to track or anticipate its whereabouts. The Island displayed an uncanny level of artificial intelligence, exposing and foiling any infiltration attempts.

Whispering Grass disembarked on the volcanic sandy shores to be greeted by contorted trees stretching to the horizon. In the distance loomed the fortress. Its ominous silhouette soared like a formidable sentinel, an impenetrable fortress that struck dread into those who even whispered its name. Built from hard, dark, glass-like volcanic rock, its rugged spires and ominous ramparts extended skyward, resembling the talons of a formidable creature.

A coalition of three brigades, known as the Triad, were composed of Trojans, Rootkits, and Botnets, who maintained its vigilant watch outside the fortress walls. While forbidden entry to the fortress, the Triad was fiercely devoted to its duty, ready to sacrifice all to thwart any intruders who sought false passage. Whispering Grass passed through the stronghold's sturdy iron gates, overlooked by grotesque gargoyles on the ramparts. The fortress formed an intricate network of interlinked hallways and tunnels, culminating in dungeons rumoured to conceal unspeakable horrors. Sinister-looking vines wove intricate patterns along the inner walls, alluding to its eerie essence.

The atmosphere bore a dense, acrid fragrance, a fusion of ancient manuscripts, prohibited experiments, and the faint trace of sulphur. Gazing upon the mystical artefacts adorning the walls and alcoves, he was transfixed. The crew member escorting him elucidated that those who touched these relics jeopardised their sanity. Legends spoke of the vault harbouring extensive libraries of mystical insights and ancient wisdom, watched over by spectral guards beholden to the Admiral's commands. Scarcely had anyone caught a fleeting glimpse of these mysteries, and those who managed such a feat seldom survived to recount the experience. Whispering Grass was led to the central banqueting chamber, where the Admiral awaited upon his throne carved from obsidian rock.

The chamber buzzed with a legion of devoted followers, each as devious and sinister as their master. Malice Malware's sharp, vigilant eyes never faltered as his spy approached the banqueting table and bowed in a display of respect. When Whispering Grass spoke, his soft and sibilant voice was a hushed murmur that floated delicately on the air like a faint echo. His preference for communicating in hushed tones drew others in like moths irresistibly drawn to a mesmerising flame and only deepened the mystery that shrouded him.

For Malware, Whispering Grass intensified his curiosity instead of challenging his patience. He granted him considerable leeway, acknowledging the distinctive quality that distinguished him from everyone else—his ears were finely tuned to capture even the slightest whispers that lingered in the deepest alleys and darkest corners of Cyberia. Two of his most loyal crew sat on either side of Malware. To his left sat Slade. His hooded robe concealed the pockmarked sores that oozed from his face—to his right sat Scarlet, the Siren of Deception. Whispering Grass had heard numerous tales of her beauty and captivating charm, but her looks still managed to steal his breath. Her skin was akin to the finest porcelain. Her hair cascaded over her shoulders like a waterfall of spun gold, with hints of silver and platinum. Scarlet's eyes were legendary, shimmering like precious gemstones from the deepest blue ocean, possessing a power capable of captivating even the most hardened of hearts. She dressed and embodied the spirit of a pirate queen and a legend among shipmates in open cyberspace. However, only one Cyberian had ever captured her heart—and it wasn't Malice Malware.

"Walk with me," Malware ordered and led him along a dimly lit hallway; the faint hum of machinery grew louder with each step. With a subtle yet commanding gesture, he placed his arm around Whispering Grass's shoulders. "The details you provided regarding the Crystals of Time the humans seek, and the reward of the Digital Amulets are undeniably captivating in the mystery of their intent. But the mention of the Pathfinder was a colossal mistake. The Pathfinder is a name that stems from myth, an unfounded supremacy that remains unseen by any. It matters not; the GranMother will say anything to capture an audience. I sailed to Glimmerhavan in the Never-Ending Forest and warned the humans to return to their realm. The path to replenishing the crystals is as daunting as walking the plank—they hold no hope of success. Do you have any idea of how they arrived in Cyberia? Or why Princess Arabella of Valaria was present and sworn to protect them?"

"Admiral, the GranMother hinted at insights beyond her comprehension, granted to a chosen few. Regrettably, there had been no indication of the princess's involvement. However, it does suggest she is among the chosen."

"If the humans decide to carry on regardless of my threat, it will be their undoing." Malware's mood swiftly shifted, and his words carried an authoritative tone. "You've been summoned with good purpose. Princess Arabella's brother Golen wields substantial influence—a pivotal figure who could open doors of utmost significance. You possess the power to earn his loyalty and the responsibility of ensuring that he aligns with our cause."

Intrigued by the involvement of Prince Golen, Whispering Grass wondered why the Admiral emphasised the terms' pivotal' and 'cause' without delving into the underlying reasoning behind his thoughts. He responded with a barely audible voice, grazing the Admiral's ears like the whisper of the wind. "Indeed, I have heard whispers of Golen's worries and wishes. The Prince carries the burden of uncertainties. He scrutinises the trajectory of his father's kingdom with caution. I believe there may be a chance to sway him towards your cause once unveiled," he added.

"Could the temptation of gold have the ability to enhance these perspectives?" Malware's query hung on more than the threshold of curiosity.

"Ah, gold! That spark might indeed be Prince Golen's Achilles. Gold can mould desires and reshape motivations. What other precious metal could do that?"

The response kindled a fire within Malice Malware's gaze, and his voice heightened in optimism. "The support of Prince Golen can be the bearing of my endeavour. I can sense the weight of his impact in the marrow of my bones. Your task is to explore how the gleam of gold harmonises with his values. If your whispers can truly penetrate his consciousness, it will be the force that tips the scales in my favour. How would you shape these whispers into a convincing manner?"

Whispering Grass uttered a solemn vow. "I shall weave Golen's troubles into the whispers of the wind he desires— wrapping him in a cocoon of support and inspiration while reminding him of the rich and echoing chorus of gold!"

"I embrace your optimism," admitted Malware; nevertheless, you must proceed cautiously, evading the traps of manipulation that might undermine our endeavours."

"Worry not; I shall bear nothing but truth and genuineness."

Malware heaved open a heavy oak door, revealing a scene that Whispering Grass could only describe as a workshop. At its core thrived Gadgeteers, an erratic but industrious breed of diminutive entities. Sporting lustrous metal frames, they scuttled across the floor like devoted labourers, unceasing in their efforts to salvage precious resources from discarded computers. Their tiny mechanical arms worked tirelessly, plucking chips, resistors, and other valuable components. The central processing units, memory chips, and connectors were the crucial components containing scrap gold.

Whispering Grass was convinced that this lucrative stream originated from the province of Lumina. Lumina's technological marvel had a peculiar stipulation. If anyone attempted to take their equipment outside Lumina's borders, it would become dysfunctional and funnelled through the black market to the Admiral. It was solely thanks to a network of unknown scallywags delivering the components to the Island, where Malice Malware coerced them into signing a contract binding them for multiple dions.

To Whispering Grass, it seemed a symbiotic relationship—the scallywags and Gadgeteers discovered a purpose while the Admiral harvested the fruits of their toil. The response kindled a fire within Malice

Malware's gaze, and his voice heightened in optimism. "The support of Prince Golen can be the bearing of my endeavour. I can sense the weight of his impact in the marrow of my bones. Your task is to explore how the gleam of gold harmonises with his values. If your whispers can truly penetrate his consciousness, it will be the force that tips the scales in my favour. How would you shape these whispers into a convincing manner?"

Whispering Grass uttered a solemn vow. "I shall weave Golen's troubles into the whispers of the wind he desires— wrapping him in a cocoon of support and inspiration while reminding him of the rich and echoing chorus of gold!"

"I embrace your optimism," admitted Malware; nevertheless, you must proceed cautiously, evading the traps of manipulation that might undermine our endeavours."

"Worry not; I shall bear nothing but truth and genuineness."

The Admiral caught sight of the glimmer in his eyes as he gazed at the mounds of gold nuggets. Stepping out of the bustling workshop, they emerged on the battlements. "Go to Prince Golen and share what you've witnessed; the truth will lend weight to your words."

"May I be so bold as to ask why Prince Golen is the key to unlocking doors of such great importance?"

"I want the prince to concentrate his support for me and to shift his family's allegiance away from Arbitration Land."

"Golen's father, King Osred, would never agree. It could be feasible, but solely upon the prince's ascent to the throne as king."

"Yes! The sooner, the better," he remarked, leaving his intentions open to interpretation. "Only then will I receive an open invitation to enter the province of Valaria."

Whispering Grass sensed the unspoken inquiry that the Admiral hesitated to pose. It seemed that the province of Valaria would soon crown a new ruler—Prince Golen; hence, he tactfully avoided mentioning King Osred by name. "In the realm of mystic concoctions and arcane arts, a potion known as the 'Ebonheart Elixir' is spoken of only in the darkest corners. This nasty brew, a sinister mixture of alchemy and sorcery, is designed to end an existence without a trace of foul play or telltale signs of betrayal."

"Pray tell me more," said Malice Malware, with an understanding smile.

"The Ebonheart Elixir has rare ingredients harvested under the shroud of the moon's eclipse, gathered from the most forbidden corners of Cyberia. The potion's base is an inky-black fluid. The elixir is flavoured like wine with the sweetest notes of elderberry. The taste, a velvety warmth, lures its victim into complacency. Once consumed by the unwitting recipient, it courses through their veins, seeking out the heart. But it cloaks itself in the semblance of a natural passing."

"How?"

"As the Ebonheart Elixir takes effect, the heart rhythmically slows, mirroring the cadence of a dreamless slumber. Their breath becomes shallow and tranquil, mimicking the gentle sigh of a peaceful night's rest. The face retains the tranquillity of a peaceful sleep, and the skin takes on a white pallor. To any who observe, it would appear as if the victim has succumbed to a heart that has naturally, and without malice, failed."

"And the expense of carrying out such a task?"

Whispering Grass's eyes widened with greed. "Gold in Cyberia is worth a thousand times more than any other mineral or metal."

"Golen's purse is fixed at 30000 gold coins to forgo any agreement with Arbitration Land. Your commission is 5000 gold coins to have him agree and make everything we discussed possible. Is that understood?"

"Of course, Admiral," he said, thrilled by the reward. Malice Malware nodded and smiled, pleased with the outcome. The pact was agreed upon without a single reference to King Osred.

Chapter 6

The Blue Crystal
Sahelian Springs

Valour acted quickly to draw his sword, but the group's leader raised a hand, signalling him to hold back as the attackers seized their reins. Ambushed and surrounded, he reluctantly followed the Princess's instructions and withdrew his hand from his weapon.

"You tread on sacred ground," the lead figure admonished. "State your purpose!" Princess Arabella responded with unshakable resolve, her voice steady. "We seek the Crystals of Time to unveil truths hidden within our hearts and to fulfil a destiny entrusted to us."

The strangers' eyes flickered with a curious mix of intrigue and hostility. Their expressions were inscrutable, yet the tension in the air was palpable. "You will come with us," he ordered, his voice low and commanding. The words hung heavily, prompting Max and Mia to share a glance that conveyed unspoken fears and steely resolve. They weighed their options at that moment, knowing that every decision could balance safety and peril in such grim circumstances.

Led to an encampment, tents of all sizes, ranging from simple to grand, dotted the landscape. Each was arranged in an orderly layout resembling a small town with interconnected pathways. A crowd gathered as they approached the royal pavilion, watching intently as the captives dismounted. Clad in long, loose-fitting white robes, two imposing guards stood tall and vigilant at the entrance.

Within the luxurious pavilion, a realm of splendour revealed itself with the rich aroma of fine incense. Exquisite carpets covered the floor. A grand divan decorated with cushions in striking royal blue and deep gold showcased the rich artistry of Arabian culture. The Chieftain sat regally upon the divan, radiating authority. His red robe symbolised his status. His eyes held the wisdom of leadership, and his cascading silver beard gave him an air of distinction. By his side sat his wife, Isolde, whose silver hair mirrored her husband's. Her welcoming smile conveyed a depth of kindness cultivated throughout shared joys and sorrows.

Their captor, whispering in The Chieftain's ear, stood upright and announced, "Allow me to present Chief Elden, leader of the Caelumar tribe."

Max sensed that Chief Elden's eyes exuded a gentle yet commanding presence as the Chieftain rose from his seat. "Princess Arabella, your presence graces our region with honour. The wind's whispers suggest that you and your companions seek a hidden treasure within our domain."

The Princess replied courteously, "Your graciousness is renowned for embodying the enduring spirit of your tribe. Your name is spoken with reverence and admiration in royal circles."

Chief Elden smiled, his words resonating with respect. "Your youthful appearance belies your profound wisdom that has reached my ears. Please forgive my lack of manners." He made a sweeping gesture, and large cushions with backrests were swiftly arranged on the floor. Max and Mia sat on either side of the Princess while Valour stood ramrod behind them. While her husband turned his attention to the Princess, prompting her to elaborate on her noble quest, his wife ordered food to be served. Servants quickly brought platters laden with an array of delectable dishes, each offering a compelling blend of flavours and aromas. Exotic spices infused the air as succulent grilled meats made Max's mouth water. Fragrant, golden and fluffy rice offered a delightful accompaniment to the savoury dishes. The Princess gestured for Valour to join them at the table. His initial hesitation faded, and sat down beside them to share the meal.

Enveloped in the warmth of the gathering, the Princess embraced the sense of unity nurtured by the meal and the quest she shared. Impressed by the compelling argument he heard, Chief Elden told the haunting tale surrounding the blue gem. "According to ancient myths, the guardians of the Crystal are indeed serpents. Some resemble delicate vines; others are as thick as an arm or leg. Their eyes are said to gleam with intelligence. Each scale bears a unique pattern, which serves as a warning to their potent venom honed over countless ages of hunting. It is said that one force dominates all others: The Devourer. Her size is said to be a sight to behold. Her body coils like a mountain, and her jaws can unhinge dagger-like fangs. Legends claim that her strength is sufficient to crush and consume a Goliath with remarkable ease. The Devourer stands as the supreme ruler, evoking both awe and fear.

"I'm done," Mia declared. 'I've heard enough. If I hear another word, I might just be sick."

"Mia. With the greatest respect to Chief Elden, prophecies, folklore, and reality often diverge," said the Princess calmly. I am confident that whatever lies ahead will not be as dire as foretold."

"I truly hope your optimism is well-placed," Max whispered, seeking to boost his sisters' and his spirits.

"I have been informed that your WhiteTails exhibit an unparalleled uniqueness." Chief Elden commented. "Our customs revolve around negotiating a fair price for such creatures. Would you consider wagering the WhiteTails for the Crystal of Time's whereabouts? I suggest a race between one of my prized stallions and the girl with the flowing hair on her WhiteTail." The terms were clear; if Mia lost, they would relinquish their WhiteTails and perhaps the whereabouts of the Crystal. "I'm afraid it's a calculated risk. Not one you could afford to dismiss," Chief Elden smiled confidently.

Princess Arabella mulled over the request, her face betraying no emotion. Her teachings taught her to counteract negotiations. "I agree to your terms, but on the proviso that if Mia loses, you reimburse us with four good horses. After all, if we cannot proceed with our task, Sahelian Springs will no longer exist after the coming of snow." Mia was rendered speechless by the boldness of the acceptance. Sure of her impending defeat, she couldn't help but feel a sense of disbelief at the sheer absurdity of the bet.

"I believe that the apocalypse you describe will not occur," the Chief exclaimed. "Why? Common sense will prevail where the wonders of nature will override such a disaster." He gestured for the leader of their captors to step forward. "Regardless of the outcome, I will permit Isaiah to lead you to the Crystal you seek. One addition to my terms: Isaiah must remain out of harm's way."

Max and Valour's tent had a simple design, starkly contrasting the lavish quarters the Princess and Mia shared, with furnishings highlighting her esteemed status. Kneeling on the parched grass outside their tent, Mia, unable to hold back her frustration, engaged in a lively exchange with the Princess, who remained resolute about the bet; her expression only emphasised her determination. "Princess, you need to realise that involving me in this race is a recipe for disaster!"

"I agree," chimed in Max, his concern for his sister's safety evident. "Could you at least explain the reasoning behind your decision?"

With a heavy sigh, Arabella's eyes wandered to the distant horizon. "As a princess, it often feels like living in a gilded cage. While I've experienced luxury and privilege, I'm burdened by expectations. I continually strive to discern what is right and to make choices that reflect that."

Max voiced a different opinion. "The pressure you live under is something I can't even imagine. However, I wouldn't have taken this risk with the odds so heavily against Mia winning the race."

"I suggest you see it from my perspective. What other option did I have?"

After listening to their conversation, Valour decided this was the right moment to interrupt. His eyes sparkled with a combination of loyalty and reason. "Mia, like you, the Princess didn't choose this path. If I may continue, Your Highness?" Arabella nodded. "The bedrock of strength needed to pursue this race is your faith. No matter the speed, twists, or seemingly impossible obstacles your WhiteTail will face, you and Bilko will come together to mesmerise the crowd. You will sense a connection as if you have been companions for eternity. In that instant, there will be no one in whom you would have more trust. When this emotion takes hold, Bilko will charge forward with the speed of a raging storm. Only then will you see that triumph is within your grasp."

The sibling's mood had lightened when retiring to their tents, but the apprehension on Mia's face still looked visible. Following a turbulent night of broken sleep, the first rays of dawn began filtering through the canvas walls and casting a haze over the campsite. Had it not been for Valour's trust, the urge to grab her brother's hand and vanish like fugitives at night would have been too irresistible to resist.

Finding Valour awake was unexpected but fortuitous as he guided her around the race track, navigating its challenges while patiently addressing her questions. Wanting time alone to reflect, she went to the WhiteTails stables. When Bilko heard her voice, he instinctively rolled his lips back, exposing his teeth in a gesture of greeting. Mia stroked his head, and despite an effort to speak plainly, her voice quivered with emotion. "Bilko, I can only hope you understand my words. Today, you and I must compete in a race we must win." Her arms encircled his robust neck. "When we step onto that course, it will challenge our strengths. If we fail, we risk losing each other, a thought that I find unbearable. I need your heart to help me face my uncertainty. Please guide me through each step of this journey." Mia's grip around his neck tightened, her voice softer but filled with hope. "Please, Bilko, help me believe." She placed a soft kiss on his forehead before turning and walking away.

The magnificent Sahelian stallion took its position at the starting line, its muscles glistening beneath the warm sunlight. Its coat possessed a lustrous ebony colour so deep that it absorbed and radiated light in equal measure. The steed's presence was regal and authoritative, every movement exuding an aura of self-assuredness and untamed vigour. The chosen rider steered it into position. The stallion arched its neck, holding its head aloft with dignified pride. Beneath its glossy coat, intricate patterns of veins testified to the life force coursing through its robust frame. With each breath, its chest expanded and contracted in a powerful rhythm. The steed's dark eyes, large and expressive, showed intelligence and an undeniable spirit, sparkling with a blend of mischief and fierce competitiveness, as if the horse were acutely aware of the competition that awaited. Bilko stood beside the stallion, a striking contrast to the spirited thoroughbred. His coat shone an immaculate shade of ivory, untouched by exertion, glistening like freshly fallen snow beneath the brilliant sunlight. With a poised stance, he held his head high, his ears pert to the world around him. His brown eyes had a serene confidence that spoke volumes.

Unlike the stallion, whose muscles coiled in anticipation, Bilko's chest rose and fell steadily. His hooves maintained a firm connection to the ground, conveying a serene trust to his rider. Valour grasped Bilko's reins and imparted the last nugget of wisdom to Mia. "Sink comfortably into the saddle, allowing your weight to settle. Keep your knees softly against the flaps to aid stability. Sustain a steady rhythm. Stay alert to Bilko's snort patterns to ensure he doesn't empty his lungs too early. Only you will know the right moment to unleash his full power to surge towards the ultimate goal — the finishing line."

The flag appeared poised to descend. The stallion's hooves scraped the earth, creating a delicate cloud of soil as if impatient to release its limitless vitality. As anticipation grew, the steed elevated onto its hind legs, presenting a breathtaking exhibition of its power and agility. His forelegs descended, exhibiting an awe-inspiring prowess of precise control. The assembled audience erupted in enthusiastic cheers, captivated by the undeniable magnetism of their extraordinary stallion. Bilko's unusual composure made Mia feel something special for the first time. She truly believed he was a natural champion of speed, and it was a moment she would forever remember: the flag dropped, and the crowd roared.

The stallion's mighty legs propelled him forward in a thunderous gallop, his hooves pounding against the earth like a primal drumbeat. Beside him, Bilko moved with unflinching grace, his lithe form bounding effortlessly with Mia's hands clutching his reins with unshakable trust. The racecourse transformed into a heart-pounding labyrinth of unforgiving challenges, demanding a fusion of focus and coordination. Fallen logs and tangled thickets strewn across their path required lightning-fast navigation, with Bilko's body stretching with a supernatural fluidity. His muscular power propelled him to overcome the five-foot hurdles effortlessly, while the stallion's swift agility allowed him to soar over the obstacles just as gracefully. Mia's heart raced as she sensed Bilko's power surge beneath her, an unrelenting rhythm of strength that seemed boundless.

Max's fervent cries of encouragement pierced the air as they approached the Chieftain's enclosure, filling Mia with a surge of determination that drove Bilko onward amidst the exhilarating chaos of noise. The tiny gap separating the two steeds vibrated with the palpable energy of unbridled competition, saturating the riders with electrifying intensity. They charged through the race's midpoint in a whirlwind of speed, a pivotal juncture that beckoned more challenges. With a subtle shift of her weight and a gentle yet commanding nudge, the wind swept through Mia's hair like a wild gust as Bilko launched himself over the fallen logs and deep pit holes to land with a fluidity that belied the daunting nature of the obstacles.

The crowd's cheers and gasps of amazement were a distant echo as her focus remained solely on the path ahead. Her determination was a force unto itself, thrusting Bilko forward with an intensity that matched his raw power. The challenges kept unfolding, putting their agility to the test, yet their connection provided the guidance they needed through every twist and turn. As the finishing line loomed ahead, Mia felt her heart surge with anticipation and exhilaration as the stallion raced four lengths ahead.

The sight of the white banner fluttering in the breeze was a beacon, a reminder of the goal they had been hurtling toward. With a burst of energy, Mia entered the final stretch with Valour's words ringing in her ears. She knew the moment was right and yelled, "Go, Bilko, go!" She felt they'd become airborne as he majestically glided through the air at an uncanny speed that left the stallion in their wake as they thundered past the finishing post. Breathless but ecstatic, Mia screamed delight, punching her fist in the air. She watched the Princess and Max wrapped in a joyous embrace, leaping up and down with excitement.

Valour sprinted toward her, his expression radiating pride. In a whirlwind of emotion, he hoisted her from her saddle and set her down on his broad shoulders. With Bilko in tow, he guided them back triumphantly to the enclosure with an electrifying smile that the Princess had seen on no other.

Greeted by thunderous applause, Isolde, the Chief's wife, amazed by the unlikely outcome, gifted Mia with the most exquisite and lavish perfume from a rare musk enclosed within a dazzling jewellery box. With a warm smile, she shared, "For you, a reminder as you grow never to forget this remarkable event." As pledged, her husband instructed their captor, Isaiah, to commence their journey when they were ready to depart for the Oasis of the Withered Bleached Tree.

Princess Arabella acknowledged the name of their destination with a gracious nod. "We'll be ready as soon as my friend Mia," she emphasised, "finds her second wind."

Isaiah confidently entered the Princess's tent, his lean frame moving gracefully through the entrance. His olive-coloured skin glowed softly in the dim light, a testament to his heritage and the sun-kissed days spent outdoors. The contours of his face were defined and angular, giving him an air of strength. His striking crystal-blue eyes set him apart, a rare hue that accentuated his sharp features, making him an unforgettable presence in any tribal gathering. Isaiah's hair, dark and tousled, framed his face, adding to his nomad appearance. He wore simple yet functional clothing tailored for mobility and comfort, but even in such attire, he exuded an undeniable charisma. His movements were fluid, and each gesture portrayed a sense of intent that drew the eye.

As he elaborated on the journey to the elusive Crystal, his voice was calm and measured, resonating with a quiet authority. He spoke of the terrain they would traverse, the obstacles they might encounter, and the two moons it would take to reach their destination. He exuded an air of purpose with every word, embodying the spirit of adventure that resonated within him. In that moment, it was clear that Isaiah was not just a guide; he was a reminder that even the most elusive dreams could be within reach if one dared to pursue them. "As directed by Chief Elden, I will accompany you until I must turn back. I have added extra provisions of oil-soaked fire sticks that should cast a generous amount of light in or around the serpent's territory."

Mia and Bilko, rejuvenated from their rest, set forth from the encampment under the guidance of Isaiah. As Chief Elden watched them go, he was uncertain whether they would ever return.

Chapter 7

The Withered Bleach Tree

They forged ahead through the challenging terrain, their mounts cautiously stepping over the uneven ground beneath them. They stopped at a shallow stream, its crystal-clear waters ripping as it flowed over pebbled stones. The glistening waters reflected their tired expressions as they dismounted and cooled their faces while their mounts eagerly drank the refreshing liquid. They gave themselves a brief respite from the prevailing dust and heat and led their mounts across the flowing stream.

The uncanny landscape transformed, shifting from scattered shrubbery to towering rock formations. The temperature dropped noticeably, creating a stark contrast to the earlier warmth they had experienced. A cutting wind swept through the surroundings, tugging at their garments and prompting them to gather closer for warmth. Their exhaled breaths materialised into misty clouds in the frigid air as they encouraged their mounts to press forward.

Isaiah paused before a cave, a sanctuary he used for rest and solace from the elements. He had never encountered weather of such intensity and severity throughout his journeys along this route. The thought crossed his mind whether this might be a foreboding sign urging him and the others to reconsider their path and return home. Darkness clung to every corner of the vast cave. Valour sparked a fire stick, its flickering light prancing across the rugged surfaces. Shadows receded, unveiling a grim sight. Before them lay a macabre exhibition of nature's relentless cycle. The ground, strewn with the skeletal remnants of creatures that had succumbed to their fate, was a sombre testament to the unyielding predator creatures that ruled this secluded domain. Its walls bore the marks of clawed battles, offering additional testimony to the struggles that had played out.

The cave provided ample space for their steeds to feed and rest. Isaiah built a fire using flint and dry brush, skillfully coaxing the flames to crackle and dance to life with the help of broken twigs and branches. The warm glow pushed back the chill of the surroundings, providing comfort as a large vent allowed the smoke to rise and blend with the outside elements.

The tethered steeds shifted restlessly at the sound of heavy paws thudding against the ground outside. The mountain bear moved deliberately, efficiently navigating the terrain while conserving its strength. Valour and Isaiah placed their fingers to their lips, signalling the others to move to the back of the cave. As they drew their weapons, they positioned themselves on either side of the cavern entrance, ready for whatever might come. Isaiah's hand gripped a dagger with a curved, single-edged blade that tapered toward the tip. The sharp edge gleamed with purpose. The hilt, embellished with intricate bone carvings, exuded an air of prestige, resting at his side as a symbol of honour and distinction. Valour brandished a sword distinguished by its compact blade, intentionally designed for use in confined spaces. The sword featured a double-edged design, measuring approximately eighteen inches long, a deliberate choice that emphasised its agility and effectiveness in close-quarters combat.

Max wondered why there were no firearms in Cyberia but he had witnessed Malice Malware's battleship, "The Infector," its cannons converted to laser beams. It was one of the numerous questions that required an answer. He envisioned the bears' sharp claws, capable of shredding their prey. Their powerful jaws could deliver deep, painful wounds. The animal's immense strength also allowed it to grasp, crush, and shake its prey until hope was lost.

Princess Arabella seized the lit torch as the creature edged inside the cavern. She advanced boldly, thrusting the torch repeatedly toward the animal's head while letting out an ear-shattering scream. Her actions prompted the creature to retreat. Valour's expression reflected his concern for her perilous act, yet secretly, he swelled with pride at her astonishing bravery as they took turns on guard duty at the entrance.

During their meal, Max took the opportunity to talk with the Princess. He was surprised when she inquired about their knowledge of General Titanous. She listened to how Max and Mia had met the general, each striving to tell their perspective of the tale. "Throughout my existence, I once encountered General Titanous in the Royal Gardens, where he visited my father. I vividly recall this formidable figure scooping and twirling me through the air like a toy."

Max found it peculiar that "existence" was used instead of "birth" or "life." Were they coexisting in a realm of reality or a fabricated illusion? His mind swirled in confusion. It appeared that only one individual held all the answers. He hesitated before asking if she had ever seen the Pathfinder. The question surprised the Princess, and she responded genuinely, stating her belief that nobody had ever encountered the enigmatic figure.

Mia, on a different wavelength from her brother, said, "The place we originate from shares many similarities yet differs from here. We have horses and bears. However, no Gigglesprites, WhiteTails, or structures like the Great White Tree Clock exist. And I'm only talking about the Never-Ending Forest. Who knows what exists in the other six?"

"I do," smiled the Princess. "Excuse me for saying, but your world does sound rather bizarre," she admitted.

Max considered inquiring about the invisible optical filters embedded in the Princess's skin, which were invisible to the naked eye and blocked laser light but deemed it too personal.

Isaiah settled beside them. "Your bravery in facing the bear, and Mia's with Bilko, demonstrated true courage." At the mention of his name, Bilko glanced over, evoking a playful giggle from Mia.

"Courage is something I sometimes wish I had more of," Max openly admitted.

"Max, your moment of true courage will come," said the Princess. "I'm confident that when it does, you'll show unmatched bravery among us. Hold onto these profound words that have meaning in your realm—if only I could. For whatever reason, they were inscribed in the cosmic expanse to pass on to you. But let's rest. We face another challenging leg of our journey when the sun rises."

In the quiet moments before sleep claimed him, the words — "If only I could" — resonated in Max's mind. He came to terms with it as yet another puzzle he aimed to solve.

Isaiah's guidance led them through treacherous and rugged terrain, demanding physical endurance and mental resilience. The weather hung heavy with searing heat, and the ground radiated the sun's relentless intensity. With each step, they stirred a cloud of fine dust, and the actual challenges began to unfold. The terrain transformed into a trail of unforgiving rocky outcrops, their surfaces jagged and unrelenting. They struggled to navigate the rugged landscape and were forced to dismount. Their path led them through an expanse of salt flats, where the ground resembled a fractured mosaic stretching endlessly toward the horizon. The intense sunlight reflected blindingly off the salt crystals, blurring the line between where the earth met the sky. Isaiah explained that these were the remnants of a long-lost lake, gradually evaporating to leave a crust of salt forming the unique landscape they now travelled. The mirage-like distortion played tricks on their minds, sowing seeds of fatigue and disorientation. Isaiah's guidance proved indispensable in this challenging terrain, as he skilfully followed ancient markers and natural formations to keep them on the correct course.

Max relied on his best subject at his private school—geography. He recalled the vast salt flats in America that covered parts of Nevada, Utah, Idaho, Oregon, and California. Although similar, he understood that Cyberia was a different world altogether.

The landscape underwent another transformation, morphing into a rocky gorge flanked by towering cliffs. The path snaked narrowly, demanding cautious manoeuvring to avoid becoming wedged between the imposing walls. Their trusty steed steps resonated off the rugged rock surfaces while Isaiah's voice provided steady and calming instructions, ensuring they navigated the twists and turns of the gorge precisely. They skirted the outskirts of a desert where the ground seemed to swallow their every step, causing the stalwart Bilko to pant with exhaustion. Isaiah's pace and determination became a spring of inspiration, urging the group to endure the harsh conditions. At last, their destination loomed ahead. The Withered Bleached Tree stood as a haunting sentinel amidst the desolate expanse of sand, appearing as though it had been deprived of life by thirst in the face of an unrelenting environment. The tree's twisted branches arched toward the sky, bereft of leaves or any sign of life. Its gnarled trunk bore the weathered scars of time's passage, a silent witness to the ages. For Valour, what added to the tree's extraordinary dry nature was its proximity to an oasis where palm trees were fertile. The water shimmered invitingly, extending a welcoming invitation amid the starkness of the surroundings.

The Princess entertained the notion that the oasis could be a mirage. She questioned the serpents' extraordinary ability to thrive beneath the scorching sand where the sought-after crystal lay embedded. "Some serpents hibernate during colder months or unfavourable conditions, surviving for several months without nourishment," Isaiah explained. "The oasis preys on unsuspecting creatures that drink here, primarily targeting migrating birds or the occasional desert fox. The creatures are seized while they drink or swim, caught off guard by the astonishing speed with which the serpents strike from the depths of their abyss. If you succeed," Isaiah continued, "your journey back will prove just as challenging. I've chosen to stay in the gorge to await your return. If you do not appear within two lunar cycles, I'll journey back to my encampment alone."

"Isaiah, your honourable commitment to wait means a great deal," the Princess conveyed, expressing her surprise and appreciation for such a noble pledge.

Mia's voice trembled with concern as she pleaded, "Isaiah, we need you here. Please stay. Don't go! I wouldn't hesitate to do the same for you."

Arabella intervened gently. "Mia, let it be. Isaiah is already going above and beyond."

Isaiah guided his horse, avoiding direct eye contact with Mia as he began to ride away. As if drawn by an unseen force, his horse gradually slowed to a halt, turned, and retraced his path back. "Isaiah?"

the Princess asked, her expression betraying a sense of understanding, while Mia smiled knowingly at her side.

"I returned, Princess because my pride couldn't bear the constant weight of bowing my head in shame and regret."

"I salute your honourable thoughts," said Valour, grateful for another warrior's company.

Seeking shelter from the scorching sun, they found shade beneath the clustered palm fronds surrounding the oasis. Amid the barren landscape, the oasis's shimmering waters resembled precious jewels, beckoning them with their alluring glow. They engaged in thoughtful discussion, aware of their limited options.

"Despite their harshness, deserts can conceal secrets beneath their fiery sands," Isaiah explained. "It is said that the creatures that inhabit this oasis protect an entrance to a connection—a complex labyrinth of underground streams that maintain their existence. Remember, be it a serpent or a plant, wherever water finds its course, the potential for all existence will prevail. This oasis, like others, does not appear out of thin air. These subterranean rivers are a complex interplay of geological forces involving hidden aquifers and water tables with caverns housing air pockets. It's an unseen world where the laws of existence differ." Max questioned the source of the water supply.

"From the mountains, whether rain or snow falls on the ice-capped peaks, it seeps and travels through the soil and rocks. Although this desert seems arid, deep beneath its surface, it is not."

Max joked, "This crystal might emerge like Excalibur from the lake." He proceeded to recount the English legend, but his reference to King Arthur's sword and Camelot only elicited blank stares from the group. "The point is, Excalibur is fantasy, not reality."

"While that may be the case," the Princess conceded, "we should err on caution and test the water beforehand. Just entering the water, let alone diving beneath it, would be foolhardy. We do not know its depth or where to start looking for the crystal."

Valour's resourcefulness took over as he approached the Bleached White Tree and cut a branch of appropriate length and straightness to serve as an improvised rod. The Princess and the siblings watched as

Isaiah, understanding the concept, took the branch and carved a small niche at one end with the tip of his knife. The niche was tailored to accommodate the fishing line, enabling it to dangle just above the water's surface when weighted. From the pouch on his saddle, he retrieved a reel of twine used for pegging down a tent and cut the length required for a line.

Cottoning on, Max assisted Isaiah in finding a weight while Valour rummaged through their meagre supplies to lure a serpent's appetite as bait. With limited options, he settled on Ful Medames, a food item known to endure days without refrigeration while preserving its taste. Comprising cooked and mashed fava beans, it was a popular snack in Isaiah's region. Max found a small pebble with a hole in the centre—the right size for the line to fit through—to use as a flyweight. Unbeknownst to them, the tiny pebble had aided a migrating bird in digesting its food. The bird's stomach muscles used the pebble to break down the food, making it simpler to digest while it travelled.

Valour secured the tightly balled bait to a hairpin provided by the Princess. With cautionary steps towards the water's edge, Isaiah cast the bait, gripping the fishing rod in one hand and holding his dagger at the ready in the other. Beside him, Valour stood, sword drawn, as the bait dipped beneath the water's surface. The serene facade of the ripple-free oasis shattered abruptly as a black serpent erupted from the depths with lightning-like speed. Sunlight danced off water clinging to its scales, casting shimmering reflections in the harsh daylight. Its curved body straightened and propelled through the air in a haunting display of muscular power. With an eerie luminosity, its eyes gleamed, revealing its predatory nature. Its arched, bifurcated tongue flicked out, tasting the scent of its prey, while poised fangs awaited a deadly strike. The abrupt, explosive movement caught Isaiah off guard, causing him to stumble backwards and collapse onto the sandy surface.

Mia's piercing scream reverberated as multiple serpents swiftly emerged, executing the same manoeuvre with equal speed, their predatory gaze fixed on Isaiah as they hastened towards the water's edge. Valour sprang into action. With two quick, precise strikes of his weapon, he decapitated two approaching serpents. Grabbing Isaiah by the scruff of his neck, he yanked him away from imminent danger while slicing through the air with his sword. As Isaiah scrambled to his feet, he sighed in relief after narrowly escaping a snakebite that missed his ankle by a hair's breadth.

The serpents' remains became a gruesome feast for their companions, transforming the once serene oasis into a chaotic battleground filled with red-tinged froth and furious aggression. Max, frozen with horror, watched helplessly as one of the decapitated heads continued to exhibit reflexive motions, writhing, twitching, and snapping toward him. Instinctively, Valour seized the head from behind and hurled it into the oasis, provoking another burst of frenzied activity among the creatures.

Maintaining a safe distance from the tumultuous oasis, they all exchanged looks of disbelief. Isaiah shook Valour's hand in gratitude, and Mia embraced him for saving her brother and Isaiah. The disturbing sight left them struggling to process what they had just witnessed, wondering about the location of the enormous serpent, the Devourer, and contemplating whether they could continue their journey.

"At least we found this out the easy way and not the hard way," the Princess said. "We exist to tell the tale!"

"I can't wrap my head around this at all," Max exclaimed. "No one could survive paddling, let alone swimming in that oasis."

"Max, you bring up a valid point," the Princess conceded. "Our focus on the oasis might have been too narrow, neglecting the possibility of an alternative entry point."

Mia raised her hands in despair as she surveyed the desolate landscape. "Another entry point? But where?" she wondered aloud.

"It's undoubtedly beneath our feet, but where exactly?" Max retorted, frustration evident in his voice. "There's no marker guiding us beneath tons of exposed sand."

Isaiah interjected with a contemplative tone, "You do have a marker. The bleached tree could serve as our compass. What other reason could sustain its existence?"

"An astute observation, Isaiah," remarked the Princess. "I believe our focus should shift towards the tree. Let's excavate beneath it. Regrettably, if that endeavour proves futile, we may have no alternative but to return home."

The group's gaze settled upon the solitary tree. Its skeletal branches were seemingly pleading for a drop of life-giving moisture. The Princess's words resonated in their minds as they converged around the tree, hope blending with uncertainty. Using their fingers, they excavated around the tree, exposing the dead, gnarled roots gripping firmly to the arid ground. The sun hung high above, casting shadows from their bodies as sweat dripped from their brows as they worked feverishly. A metallic glint emerged from beneath the exposed roots; their hands quickened in pace. Driven by determination and trepidation, they uncovered a tarnished ring below the gnarled wood. A shiver of recognition coursed through the group that this was no ordinary tree. They enthusiastically began clearing around the edges of a hidden trap door. Hesitant, Valour yanked at the pull ring of the wooden hatch. The creaking panel echoed as if the tree released a long-held breath as it opened.

Valour ignited a fire stick and peered cautiously into the dark abyss. Strategically positioned footsteps allowed for a safe descent or a quick retreat. Isaiah ignited his fire stick and followed Valour into the vast void below. The Princess whispered for them to be cautious as their flickering lights gradually faded from sight.

The air grew cooler, and an eerie silence enveloped the two warriors. Their torches illuminated ancient inscriptions that adorned the walls, telling the story of the Devourer—a creature born of malevolence, destined to protect the crystal from anyone who dared to trespass on its domain. Their wary steps led to the heart of a clandestine chamber, where their hearts leapt at the sight of the Blue Crystal laid on a slab, casting a brilliant azure glow that illuminated the expanse of the cavern. It seemed to pulse with an almost transcendent beauty. Their brief reverie was shattered as the ground trembled with a deep rumble swiftly building into a deafening crescendo.

The chamber echoed with an ear-piercing hiss as the Devourer, its massive form resembling the stoutest of trees in length and girth, glided into its lair. Its fiery red eyes, shimmering with iridescence, bore into its prey with an unyielding stare, intensifying its sinister nature. Its venomous fangs protracted, causing Valour's hairs to stand on end as its scales gleamed with a deadly sheen, coiling and unfurling with predatory precision.

Isaiah and Valour had no other alternative but to confront the massive serpent as it writhed, ready to strike. Valour spotted carved footholds tracing the perimeter wall up to a lofty ledge. Dropping his torch, he ascended the steps. Isaiah scraped his blade against the stone wall, eliciting a cascade of sparks that captivated and diverted the creature's focus. Now, with no avenue for escape or concealment, Isaiah couldn't shake the certainty that his end was swiftly approaching.

Valour realised this was his sole chance, with Isaiah's fate hanging in the balance. Every sinew in his body stretched as he executed a daring leap, where his figure formed a striking silhouette in midair. His weapon gleamed like a shard of silver as he landed on the serpent's upper torso. It was sheer luck, rather than precision, that guided his sword into the nape of the serpent's spine, eliciting a guttural hiss of agony.

The serpent's tail swished to and fro, pulverising the cavern walls like fragile stone. Rock formations disintegrated, and boulders tumbled, engulfing the chamber in a whirlwind of dust and debris. Isaiah leapt over the thrashing tail as it recoiled to dislodge its attacker. Valour clung to the serpent's spine, his grip unyielding on the embedded sword as he fought desperately against the tumultuous currents of motion. The serpent again directed its focus towards Isaiah. The serpent thrashed with newfound zeal. Its jaws stretched wide, showcasing fangs that shone like dual fragments of obsidian. Isaiah's steady gaze held firm as his dagger arced through the air, meeting the serpent's gaping maw like a powerful jackhammer. The serpent's fangs snapped, crashing to the ground with a resounding clang.

Seizing the moment, Valour thrust his sword deep into the Devourer's heart. A thunderous noise erupted as the serpent's tail pounded against the rocky formation, sending shockwaves with each convulsion. The creature's struggles weakened, its once fierce movements faltering. The battle's climax neared, victory within reach. Withdrawing his sword, Valour leapt from the beast. Isaiah's swift reflexes saved him from the serpent's final throes, sending rocks and debris scattering like leaves in a storm. Dust shrouded the scene, obscuring the serpent's form. Gradually, the rage subsided. The serpent lay still, its eyes dulled, its fury beaten. Amidst the aftermath of the fierce confrontation, Isaiah and Valour stood, their breaths heavy with exertion, surveying the monster they'd defeated between them. Valour swirled his weapon back inside its sheath. Amidst the remnants of their clash, he and Isaiah shared a silent nod, a quiet tribute to their joint triumph. Valour beckoned Max to descend.

Uncertain of what lay ahead, Max cautiously circled the colossal serpent, his wide eyes taking in the enormity of the creature they had just killed. With each hesitant step toward the shimmering crystal, his heart raced, fuelled by the adrenaline of their victory. As he drew nearer, the crystal's glow brightened, pulsating with a warmth that seemed to acknowledge his presence as if it were grateful to be liberated from its long-held captivity. He carefully lifted the first Crystals of Time from the slab. Feeling its weight, similar to that of a solid gold ingot, he held it close to his chest. An overwhelming wave of euphoria surged through him, eclipsing all other feelings he had encountered in his short lifetime.

Emerging from the hatch, Max held the brilliant crystal high, its light radiating in all directions. Mia and Princess Arabella watched with broad smiles. The crystal's vivid colours reflected the cloudless sky, creating a mesmerising display across their features. Mia's excitement overflowed as she reached for the gem while Arabella looked on in wonder, her heart swelling with pride for the achievements of Valour and Isaiah.

With the hatch entrance sealed firmly, Valour pondered whether the serpents had retreated after their victory over the Devourer. He casually tossed some of their supplies into the oasis, watching the ripples spread and eventually subsided into a tranquil calm. A wry smile appeared as he decided against provoking any more speculation about their whereabouts.

Max positioned the radiant crystal into a pannier strapped across the saddle of his WhiteTail. Once their mounts were ready, he exchanged a firm look with Mia and the princess. They set off, riding away from the oasis without a backward glance. Though the road ahead was uncertain, their spirits remained unyielding, buoyed by the deepening bonds they forged. Each shared experience, every moment of laughter and challenge, wove them closer together, creating a tapestry of camaraderie that fortified their resolve. This connection ignited their courage in the face of the unknown, reminding them they were not alone in their journey. Together, they embraced the challenges ahead, their hearts intertwined with hope and determination, ready to face whatever lay in wait.

Chapter 8

The familiar cave appeared as dusk settled over the land. Mia and Isaiah worked together to light a fire, gathering twigs and kindling with practised ease. The warm glow filled the chamber when the flames finally emerged, casting flickering shadows on the stone walls. Princess Arabella arranged two firesticks at the entrance, creating a protective barrier against any other unwelcome creature that might venture too close. The comforting light of the fire wrapped around them, instilling a sense of safety as they settled in for the night beneath the sheltering rock.

Max retrieved the sacred map while Valour prepared their evening meal. With a hushed reverence, he recited the cryptic riddle that held the key to finding the elusive coloured crystal they sought next.

"I glow like the sun, but I'm not in the sky, a fossilised treasure, from ages gone by. Insects may linger, trapped in my light, what colour am I, shining with a warm delight?

Amber, Max suggested. "I was right, the Map is reconfiguring," and read—

"In facets gleaming, a guide so bright, to find its kin, follow its light. A crystal's touch reveals the way to another gem where secrets sway. What am I that points the course, guiding the seekers with its radiant force?"

The words echoed against the chill of the stone walls. Ideas were scarce, and exhaustion weighed heavily on them as they struggled to conjure a solution that felt just out of reach. They exchanged weary glances, acknowledging their fatigue, and resolved to refresh their minds and rekindle their thoughts with the arrival of a new dawn.

Amid the night's stillness, Princess Arabella awoke with a revelation. She held the crystal in her hand, its glow currently subdued, devoid of the shimmer described in the riddle. Her infectious excitement not only jolted the others awake but also solidified her role as the group leader.

"Observe," she said, repeating a portion of the riddle. *"What am I that points the course, guiding seekers with its radiant force?"* She rotated the crystal, aligning it with each cardinal point of the compass. The cave bathed in a dull radiance, ignited when she directed it toward the East. Her role in solving the riddle was clear. "That's the direction we must follow."

Max shifted his attention to the map. Once more, a new riddle replaced the one the Princess had just unravelled.

"In hues of amber, like sunlit gold, a shade of nature's sweetness, bold. Where in flight and honey reside, search for secrets none can hide. Where is this place, so warm and bright, where this riddle's answer takes its flight?"

Struggling against exhaustion, Mia stifled a yawn. "A beehive," she mumbled before drifting back to sleep. The group unanimously agreed.

"East is the direction of my homeland," the Princess said, gathering her thoughts. "A bee colony stretches as far as the eye can see. It is the only one I am aware of in Valaria. Do you agree, Valour?" she asked, seeking confirmation.

"Yes, Princess," Valour affirmed. "I hail from a village called Emberfall, situated on a journey of two lunar cycles from that very apiary. The villagers have dubbed it 'The Untamed Land.' The amber crystal would likely be within a solitary hive."

"The queen bee?" the Princess gasped.

"Indeed, Your Highness," Valour confirmed. "In childhood legend, she was notoriously known as the Killer Queen Bee. The very name of this monarch instilled fear in all who heard it. Her presence is said to rival that of three heads. Her venom deadlier than the darkest poisons, and her eyes gleam with eerie intelligence," he added solemnly. "The tales are not mere stories to frighten children. The legend speaks of her wrath; many have ventured to claim her head as a trophy of their courage. None ever returned." She is said to guard her hive with an army of loyal drones, each as ferocious as the other. They will not hesitate to defend their queen; we would be wise to prepare for a confrontation.

Mia stirred slightly; sensing her friend's unease, the Princess placed a reassuring hand on her shoulder as she furrowed her brow. "We will not face this challenge unprepared. We must gather knowledge and allies before embarking on this journey."

Max reflected on a conversation with a close friend of his grandfather, who tended to beehives, and remembered that a queen bee could live up to five years. This realisation led him to conclude that the queen bee they discussed had likely died. However, when he converted the timescale from Earth to Cyberian time, a disappointed sigh escaped him. The queen bee was probably still in her infancy.

Valour elaborated, "The Queen's ability to lay countless eggs is a testament to her dedication to the colony's prosperity. What truly distinguishes her realm is the awe-inspiring spectacle of her devoted protectors. Their swarms eclipse the combined might of our Valarian army. Such a queen, ruling over a domain of hives, demonstrates these creature's extraordinary power and resilience."

"The crystal's colour is amber," Max mused. "I can't help but wonder if the similarity in colour to honey is merely a coincidence?"

Valour shrugged. "Honey can exhibit a wide range of colours, from pale yellow to dark amber and various shades of orange. It depends on the nectar source of the flowers they visit."

While Max admired the alignment of their colour charts across different worlds, his fatigue was evident as he shifted the conversation. "I'm feeling so exhausted that my thoughts are getting jumbled."

Her voice laced with regret, the Princess said, "Excuse my enthusiasm, Max. I was so thrilled about deciphering our path that I unintentionally woke everyone up."

Max responded with a weary look. "Now that the riddle is solved, we can seek some rest," he reassured, allowing his eyelids to droop as he sought solace in sleep alongside his sister. Before closing her eyes, the Princess conveyed her goodnight wishes to Isaiah and Valour.

"It's your moment to find rest, Valour," Isaiah acknowledged, his words heavy with gratitude. "And once again, thank you for saving my existence."

Valour reciprocated the sentiment with a heartfelt smile. "Having you by my side in battle, Isaiah, was an honour," he conveyed. "It was our combined effort that defeated the Devourer. Goodnight, my friend."

"Goodnight, Valour," Isaiah whispered, taking care not to disturb the others.

Chapter 9

The morning sun bathed the landscape in a golden glow. The rustling of leaves intertwined with the soft whinnying of the steeds as the group prepared to depart from the cave. A hauntingly familiar sound, an eeriness reminiscent of the cellar back on Earth, shattered the tranquillity. In an instant, the steeds were thrown into turmoil, their eyes wide with fear. Isaiah's horse bucked violently, sending him sprawling to the ground. With quick reflexes, Valour seized the loose reins to prevent further chaos. The group swiftly dismounted, moving to soothe their startled mounts and offering gentle reassurances to restore a sense of calm.

The crackling of energy sizzled through the atmosphere, bridging the gap between worlds. All eyes were fixed on the epicentre of this disturbance as the portal emerged, mirroring the phenomenon Max and Mia had once witnessed. A huge apprehension spread throughout the others as the sphere expanded steadily. The cyberians stepped back as the humanoid figure appeared from the captivating vortex and spoke in a harsh, gravelly voice that reverberated like a fierce wind's relentless rasp: "O Gatherers of the realms. The fabric of your existence has intricately woven your fates together, binding them with the weight of your choices and the impending consequences looming."

Isaiah was engulfed by an overwhelming sense of awe, as though the being's words revealed the poetic secrets of time. Princess Arabella and Valour, acutely aware of the profound significance of the encounter, humbly lowered their gazes to the floor, paying homage to a being far grander than their wildest imaginations had ever conceived. The Princess contemplated whether this mysterious figure could indeed be the immortal Pathfinder. The mere thought of his name caused her to step back further instinctively.

Max and Mia exchanged glances filled with apprehension and curiosity, unaware of the significance of the encounter. The humanoid shimmered as he directed his attention to them, its contours blurring with the portal's energy. "To seek the WellSprings of wisdom," it intoned solemnly, "you must journey back to where you once came. The Crystals of Time will remain untouched until you envision your future as you perceive it. Deep within gleaming depths lie answers long sought and truths yet unspoken. Take this step, or you may never return to the place you call home." The cryptic words began to dissipate, fading like dew in the morning sun.

The group stood in contemplation, their hearts racing with wonder and uncertainty as they recognised that their journey had taken an unexpected turn. Princess Arabella voiced her concerns, revealing the source of her unease. Speaking gently, Mia sought to reassure her. "Princess, as far as Max and I understand, this humanoid is a messenger, not the Pathfinder."

Princess Arabella posed a question, her eyes carrying a poignant ache that mirrored the weight of their reliance on Max and Mia. "What does 'to seek the WellSprings of wisdom' mean? Will you return?" Her gaze held a plea for reassurance.

His voice tinged with uncertainty, Max replied, "I don't know."

Princess Arabella's tone turned urgent as she insisted, "Everything I see suggests the hand of the Pathfinder. You must heed his request." She gently plucked a blooming flower from the nearest branch and handed it to Mia. "Please, pretty one, do not forget us," she implored, her plea filled with sincerity.

Taking a bold step forward, Valour shook Max's hand firmly. Without hesitation, he leaned down to softly kiss Mia's forehead, causing her cheeks to bloom with colour. "May you both find the wisdom you seek," Isaiah offered, clasping their hands in a heartfelt farewell. Max and Mia stepped into the portal. Before the entrance was sealed shut, they turned and witnessed the sorrow etched on their friends' faces. In the next moment, they were gone.

The journey back home was sombre, and the whirlwind of all they had experienced unfolded before them in a rapid and captivating display that highlighted the many remarkable beings and places they had encountered: gigglesprites, glowing squirrels, winged rabbits, fireflies, General Titanous, Princess Arabella, Valour, Isaiah, and the Great Tree Clock, Then the memory of their encounter with Malice Malware, his battleship, the Infector, and the fearsome serpent.

Max noticed the tears streaming down his sister's cheeks as the portal revealed their world again. He knew the incredible race she and her WhiteTail won was foremost on her mind. His mind was in turmoil. He had to think straight. The WellSprings of wisdom. If only I could. What did this all mean? Each encounter, each challenge, and every choice made on this journey illuminated a facet of wisdom, teaching him that it wasn't a destination but a lifelong pursuit of his existence – he smiled at the Cyberian terminology meaning life. He understood that his youthful curiosity and willingness to learn were invaluable companions on this quest. The journey itself, filled with trials and triumphs, was the essence of acquiring wisdom, and he was still very much prepared to embrace it with an open heart and an eager mind.

Chapter 10

Cyberia Farm
Writtle
South East England

In the cellar, everything seemed just as they had left it. Mia turned off the computer and concealed it beneath a blanket. Ascending the stairs, they exchanged quiet words, sealing their promise to keep the Cyberian experience to themselves. They both knew their story would be met with disbelief even if they chose to confide in their parents. Nonetheless, when the next opportunity arose to be alone, they planned to strategise their next steps, whatever that may entail.

Outside in the lean-to, their mother carefully wiped the dust off a large, framed photograph of the farmhouse she had found in an old tea chest left by the previous occupants. "This photo must be 40-50 years old. If only it looked like that now," she sighed, her lips forming a slight pout.

"Give it time, and I promise it will, Kels," her husband assured her. "The other items, of old books and cracked crockery, don't even merit consideration for a boot sale", he added.

"I'm going to hang this photo somewhere in the house. The photo will be our goal, Mark, to restore the house to its original splendour." she declared and shifted her gaze to her children, who had just appeared, "You two have been quiet. What have you been up to?"

"Nothing," they both replied in unison, their voices echoing in the moment's stillness. But beneath their calm exteriors lay a profound shock. The general's words about Cyberia being "baud rate time" reverberated in their minds. Despite what the general had said, they had expected to be missed, yet weren't. Realising their absence had gone unnoticed felt like a cold wave washing over them.

"When you two say 'nothing,' that usually means something," kelly teased with a knowing smile.

"Dad," Mia began, "we stumbled upon a computer in the cellar." Max shot her a look. "Although most of the stuff down there seems like junk. I just wanted to ask if I can keep it. You know how I enjoy collecting and tinkering with things."

"Sure, that's fine," her father replied, having failed to start the computer himself, but believing it would help keep her mind off the separation from her friends. Mia stuck her tongue out at her brother, knowing her quick thinking ensured their parents wouldn't touch or move the computer.

Kelly propped the old photograph against the tea chest as the large removal van pulled into the farmyard. The bedroom layout had been prearranged on the top floor. Mia's room, with its dormer window, overlooked the courtyard, providing a slightly more spacious area compared to Max and her parents' rooms at the back. With the removal men gone and twilight casting its shadow over the skyline, Kelly made a quick, simple meal. Lost in her musings, Mia suddenly blurted out, "Dad, can I have a horse, please?"

"What?" he replied, taken aback. "You can't even ride a bike in a straight line. Just because we have a farmhouse doesn't mean you automatically get a horse. And where in your infinite wisdom would you even keep it? In the lean-to?" he chuckled.

"Wisdom is understanding that the dream of having a horse is as exhilarating as the ride itself, Dad."

"Wow! Where did that one come from, my little poppet?" exclaimed her mother.

"From the heart," Mia replied, pushing her plate aside. "Sorry, Mum, but I've lost my appetite with all the day's excitement."

"Me too, Mum," said Max.

"I'm sure your father will be able to finish it all," Kelly assured them, annoyed with his disappointment with the meal she had prepared. "Alright, you two," she said, "let's focus on the task ahead and unpack those cases in your rooms. Don't forget, we have your grandparents'

Ruby wedding anniversary celebration to look forward to tomorrow," she said, her tone full of encouragement.

Kelly drew a deep breath as she started arranging the furniture in the lounge. She remembered the farmhouse photograph, prompting her to bring it inside. Cradling the image, she considered the perfect location to display it and held it against the downstairs hallway wall, where a picture had once hung. A nail was already in place, and the outline fit the frame perfectly. She wondered if it had once hung there and could understand why. Its welcoming beauty would greet all who entered and left the house. On the back of the frame, she noticed an inscription in small, scrawly handwriting. Her brow furrowed as she squinted to decipher the fading words to Mark.

> *"To JJ, a steadfast Pathfinder on life's odyssey With love and memories that will last a lifetime and beyond"*
>
> Abby & Jenifer Grey

"Abby Grey is the elderly spinster who owned the farm," she said, still baffled as to why Cyberia Farm had been left to her husband. "I suspect that Jenifer Grey is or was her sister. This inheritance is wrapped in mystery, and I still can't help but wonder about the reasoning behind it."

"Yes, but as my dad always said, don't look a gift horse in the mouth," Mark replied, reflecting on the situation after receiving the solicitor's letter on behalf of Abby Grey.

"Your dad is probably right," Kelly said, finishing by straightening the photograph, which offered a satisfied smile between them. She went upstairs to check on Max and Mia. On reaching the landing, she heard hushed voices behind Mia's closed door. She distinctly heard two unfamiliar names; one had a royal title, leading her to surmise they were discussing a school play. Fuelled by maternal curiosity, she opened the door. Much to her surprise, the cases were still untouched.

Taken by surprise, Mia swiftly interpreted her mother's expression; displeasure was written all over it. "Sorry, Mum," Mia started, "we were just talking and—"

"About a school play, I presume?" her mother interjected, a playful glint in her eye, subtly suggesting that she might possess some psychic insights.

Max couldn't shake the feeling that she had overheard their conversation about Princess Arabella and the General. "How did you guess?" he asked with feigned innocence.

"There's nothing you two do that escapes me. Now, unpack the pair of you."

With the unpacking finally done, the house embraced an uneasy quiet as night swiftly descended, draping the rooms in a shroud of unfamiliarity. Max lay awake in his room, sleep eluding him as his mind whirled with thoughts of Cyberia until exhaustion pulled him into a deep sleep.

The rays of morning light streaming through the window woke him. The dregs of sleep clung to him like a fog as he rubbed his eyes and blinked. The sound of his parents' voices drifted up from the kitchen, pulling him from the warmth of his bed to dress. The distinctive smell of freshly brewed coffee and toasted bread guided him to the breakfast table. He poured himself a bowl of cereal and half-heartedly listened as his parents' ever-growing list of chores seemed to multiply with each passing minute. The sleepless night compelled him to step outside, so he excused himself and went to the backyard, where the sun shone brightly in a clear blue sky. Max strolled over to an old two-seater swing hanging from a robust oak tree, its ropes worn yet resilient.

As he settled onto the seat, he began to sway while contemplating the WellSprings of Wisdom. He couldn't shake the feeling that there was something profound waiting for him to uncover, a truth hidden just beyond his grasp. Max wondered if Mia had experienced the same restlessness during the night, if she too had been lost in her thoughts, pondering the mysteries that seemed to beckon them both.

Mia had spent the night tossing and turning, trying to figure out why the farm and Cyberia shared the same name. Lingering in bed, the weight of the unresolved thoughts pressed down on her like a heavy blanket. With a reluctant sigh, she swung her legs over the side of the bed, her feet meeting the cool wooden floor. She took a moment to regain her thoughts and began the slow process of organising her bedroom. She spent the remainder of the day meandering through the house, tidying up and finding small tasks to occupy her time. Getting ready for her grandparents' party brought her a sense of relief.

Ready for the evening's celebration, Max and Mia descended the stairs, their footsteps resonating on the wooden treads. Max stopped to gaze at the farmhouse photograph hanging on the hallway wall he had passed several times during the day. He stepped closer, captivated by the details of the small trees in the background. They had grown considerably since whoever had taken the photo. Mia joined him, tilting her head to admire the farmhouse overshadowed by a twilight sky. "It's beautiful, isn't it?" she said softly. Max nodded, feeling an inexplicable connection to the image, but was unaware of the aged inscription on the back of the frame that held past secrets.

Kelly, a non-drinker, was the designated driver for their journeys to and from various events. Her slender figure and flowing blonde hair radiated undeniable attractiveness that caught Mark's eye when they first met. His cropped, black hair defined Mark's look. He was a tad overweight but had encountered more victories than defeats in dieting. Dressed in a stylish light tan suit, Kelly thought he was still striking as she adjusted his tie in the hallway. Planting an affectionate kiss on his cheek, she was pleased they shared a common goal to cultivate family unity.

At nearby Hylands House, the sectioned car park buzzed with activity as families and friends gathered to celebrate the occasion. The outside entrance of the pavilion had a variety of different-coloured party balloons. A wall of sound greeted them as they stepped inside the venue. Madonna's lively voice resonated, capturing the spirited vibe of the eighties. Max's grandmother motioned for them to sit at her table, but his attention was drawn to a figure slipping through the exit doors that led to the rear garden. Acting impulsively, he beckoned Mia to follow.

In search of a tranquil moment outdoors, Benjamin Hayes, an eccentric 60-year-old beekeeper and a close friend of Max's grandfather, sat alone in quiet contemplation. His salt-and-pepper beard framed a face that told stories of a life rich with experiences, radiating a warmth and kindness that drew people in. With his round, pot-bellied stature, he embodied the quintessential favourite uncle, the figure anyone longing for such a presence would cherish. "Ah, well, if it isn't the dynamic duo! How tall have you grown since the last time I saw you? Time does fly. So, what tales do you have to share since we last crossed paths? I'm sure you've been up to all sorts of adventures. Your smiles tell me there's much to catch up on. How's school been treating you both? Are there any new hobbies or interests you've picked up? I know quite a list, but I'm known as a nosey Parker," he chuckled warmly.

Max started the conversation. "School's not bad," he said with a mischievous glint in his eye. "But we have been assigned a bee project," he continued, stretching the truth. "Considering your expertise in the bee world, we thought you'd be the best guide. The focus is mainly on the queen bee. How would you handle the situation if she became a serious threat?"

Benjamin Hayes leaned back in his chair, a smile gracing his lips. "Ah, the queen bee," he began, his voice carrying the weight of experience. "She's truly the heart of the hive, a vital force that dictates the harmony and rhythm of the colony. But, like any ruler, there are moments when even she can become a challenge." He paused, gathering his thoughts. "Dealing with a queen that poses such a threat requires a delicate touch. She can exhibit aggression due to various factors, from environmental changes to internal dynamics within the hive. One approach is to isolate her temporarily. Creating a separate enclosure can help to mitigate her influence on the rest of the hive while giving her time to calm down." He leaned forward, his voice dropping to a conspiratorial tone. "Working with bees demands patience and a strong mind. I say 'mind' because they can sense a human's anxiety or fear."

"Are they easy to kill, if needed, of course?" Max asked, his curiosity prompting a straightforward answer.

Benjamin Hayes' expression turned solemn as he considered the dire question. "Well, Max, it's important to approach beekeeping with a mindset of preservation and respect for these creatures that play a vital role in our ecosystem. To eliminate a queen bee is certainly not a preferred option." He leaned in. "It would disrupt the entire colony, leading to absolute chaos. That's why exploring alternative solutions is crucial before resorting to such drastic measures."

Recognising the complexity and responsibility of tending to bees, Mia felt a newfound respect for the delicate balance within a hive. "What's the tool beekeepers use to smoke out a hive?" she asked.

"It's known simply as a smoker," Benjamin replied. "It's a common technique used to manage the behaviour of bees, including the queen. The smoke disrupts their communication and triggers a response where they gorge on honey, making them less inclined to sting."

"Can their sting kill?" Mia responded.

"In general, a single sting is not lethal to most people unless they have a severe allergy to their venom. The allergy can trigger a potentially life-threatening reaction, causing difficulty breathing, a rapid drop in blood pressure, swelling of the throat and tongue, and loss of consciousness. For the majority, a bee sting results in pain, swelling, and itching. The symptoms usually subside within a few hours."

"What if a hundred bees chased you after agitating the hive by attacking the queen bee?" asked Max.

"That's the absolute chaos I warned about. The bees release alarm pheromones that signal other bees to defend the hive. If someone is stung by many bees, the venom injected into the body will cause a toxic reaction due to the volume of the venom. If you believe you've disturbed a hive and attacked, the best action is to seek shelter or a closed vehicle if available."

"If I can pick your brain on the final point, what is the best-recognised form of protection?"

"Well, Max, apart from a veil, long sleeves, long pants, closed-toed shoes, and gloves, avoid wearing brightly coloured or floral-patterned clothing and refrain from using strong scents like perfumes or lotions. If you're in an area with many bees, staying calm and moving away can help prevent provoking them."

"There you are, you two. I've been looking all over. Hi, Benjamin."

"Hello, Kelly," Benjamin chuckled. "No need to be alarmed. We've just been having a very engaging conversation about bees."

"Oh, that's interesting," Max could tell from his mother's expression that she didn't quite share the sentiment.

Returning to the hall, Max and Mia settled back at their table, immersed in their thoughts, absorbing all they had learned from Benjamin Hayes. The phrase *"If only I could"* began to replay in Max's mind, and he remembered Princess Arabella's foresight: *Hold onto these profound words that have meaning in your realm—If Only I Could. For whatever reason, they are inscribed in the cosmic expanse to pass on to you.* The realisation struck as the words perfectly matched the melody coming from the loudspeakers. The lyrics resonated throughout the dance floor, with the elderly dancing and swaying to its lively beat. Curious, Max approached the DJ to learn more about the song. The DJ disclosed that the requested tune was one of many that each table had written down to forward. He discovered that *"If Only I Could"* by Sydney Youngblood was released as a single in 1989. Its lyrics bore deep meaning—of making the world a better place—leading Max to ponder the enigma as he returned to his table, ignorant of the requester's identity and whether the underlying reason would ever come to light. Upon arriving home, Max and Mia agreed on their plan for the following morning: after their parents left to shop for new furniture, they would attempt to summon the portal.

After their parents had left the farmhouse, Mia powered up the machine, her heart pounding as the portal materialized, and the humanoid they had dubbed the Gatekeeper beckoned them onboard. Bolstered by Benjamin Hayes' information, they confidently stepped inside. Their ears popped as the portal travelled through the digital hub of time, unsure where it would materialise in Cyberia.

Their eyes widened in awe as they emerged from the portal into an unfamiliar landscape with the overpowering scent of wildflowers. A different sunset adorned the sky, displaying a spectrum of colours blending with the fading light of day. Their amazement paled compared to the sight that greeted them: General Titanous. This unexpected encounter left the siblings exchanging incredulous glances, unable to believe their luck—or was it? "You did it again!" Max exclaimed, his eyes wide with astonishment. "How did you know we'd end up here?"

"Ah, that's a delightful mystery, sprinkled with a touch of ambiguity!" the General replied, a playful smile on his lips. "Let's keep the suspense alive, shall we?" He gestured grandly around them. "You are no longer in the province of the Never-Ending Forest. Welcome to the realm of Valaria, the province of the Princess. Acquiring the Blue Crystal of Time is a commendable achievement," the General said, his tone serious and encouraging. "However, the next challenge, involving the Amber Crystal, will truly test the wisdom you now possess."

Max's mind raced with confusion. Was the General referring to their insights from Benjamin Hayes— the lyrics of *—If Only I Could—* or perhaps a combination?

"We encountered Malice Malware back in Glimmerhavan," said Mia, her voice filled with concern.

"So, I am aware," the General replied, seemingly unfazed by the comment. "I did warn that he was aware of your arrival."

"General, may I ask a straightforward question?" Max inquired. "Do you know the outcome of Malice Malware's antics or any other event?"

"No," he conceded. "Your road ahead is fraught with uncertainties. However, should circumstances take a dire turn, the Pathfinder has granted me the authority to offer assistance."

Max thought of the sacred map and the final symbol he was reluctant to reveal to Mia. A nagging sense of unease crept over him as he pondered whether this was what the General had alluded to when he mentioned a dire turn of events.

"I will take my leave now," the General declared. "You must wait for the Princess's arrival. I extend my best wishes for good fortune to you both!" He turned and began to walk away swiftly, his brisk pace taking on an uncanny speed that was peculiar to witness until he vanished from view.

The siblings remained transfixed by his departure until the joyful sound of their names broke through their thoughts. Riding their WhiteTails, the Princess and Valour held the reins of Bilko and Max's steed. To their surprise, Isaiah was with them. Hurrying forward, they enveloped their friends in warm hugs. Bilko's characteristic smile-like gesture marked Mia's return. Max questioned Isaiah about his decision to stay instead of returning home.

"I recounted the events at the oasis to Chief Elden, emphasising Valour's bravery in saving my existence. To uphold my honour, Chief Elden agreed that I should accompany you until the end of your journey, whether it concludes in triumph or defeat."

"An honourable gesture," said the Princess. "Valour indicated it would take two lunar cycles to arrive at his village, where we can rest and plan our next steps. I trust the WellSprings of Wisdom you sought will aid us. Tell me all that you have learned on our journey. Come! We must ride!"

Chapter 11

The Royal Palace
Valaria

Whispering Grass and his guide emerged from the palace's cool interior and stepped into the royal gardens, which sprawled like a verdant canvas beyond the imposing walls. The gardens were the epitome of nature's artistry, a harmony of colours, scents, green lawns, and vibrant flowers that swayed in the lightest breeze.

Prince Golen gestured to Whispering Grass to join him on the marble bench beneath the boughs of an ancient oak tree. A nearby fountain, its waters cascading harmoniously, provided a soothing undertone to their conversation. Whispering Grass's proposals were to be unwrapped layer by layer in this tranquil sanctuary. In the embrace of the gardens, they grappled with questions of loyalty, ambition, and the enduring struggle for power.

Whispering Grass reached the culmination of his proposal, his voice steady and imbued with passion. He clearly articulated his vision, each phrase designed to captivate and persuade. Prince Golen listened with keen interest; his brow furrowed in thought. Deep and blue like the tranquil waters of a vast ocean, his eyes sparkled with intrigue as he contemplated the significance of what Whispering Grass asked and the profound impact his decision could have on their destinies.

Seizing the moment, Whispering Grass produced an ornate box from the folds of his robe. A cascade of warm, golden light spilled forth as he delicately lifted the lid. Inside the box lay a tiny parchment inscribed with Admiral Malware's offer. But it wasn't the words that drew Golen's attention; it was the sight of the gleaming gold coins accompanying the document. The coins, a treasure of undeniable worth, were a tangible representation of the power and commitment behind the Admiral's proposition.

Prince Golen's eyes, previously weighed down by the complexities of decision-making, now lit up with astonishment at his percentage. Whispering Grass articulated the extent of the Admiral's generosity as Golen instinctively reached out to touch one of the many coins promised. The metal was cool to the touch, carrying with it the weight of potential. The fragrant breeze stilled, the birdsong softened, and time slowed as Golen's gaze remained fixed on the coins. The decision before him was profound, a crossroads that would shape his legacy.

In his role as messenger and strategist, Whispering Grass watched the Prince with a mixture of anticipation and respect. Finally, Golen's eyes lifted from the coins to meet his gaze. A subtle smile tugged at the corners of his lips, and a spark of determination ignited. The moment was a turning point. With newfound resolve, he nodded, and their agreement solidified and silently forged.

Prince Golen's following words sounded like a melodious tune to Whispering Grass. "Join us tonight as my esteemed guest for a grand ball. You'll have the privilege of sitting at the royal table, savouring a great feast and enjoying music played by our finest musicians."

"It would be my pleasure, your Highness." He could hardly contain his excitement. The plan to reach the King, which had always seemed like an impossible challenge, had undergone a remarkable transformation with a single stroke of fate's brush. He felt a quiet thrill of possibility as if the path to his elusive goal had suddenly become more transparent and attainable.

Whispering Grass embarked on a mission of betrayal as he entered the splendid banqueting hall. The gathering within the hall was steeped in riches, a heady mixture of power and extravagance that mirrored the kingdom itself. Glistening crystal chandeliers dangled from the intricately adorned ceiling, casting shimmering prisms of light upon the assembled nobility. Richly woven tapestries depicting scenes of legendary courage and mythical conquests adorned the towering walls. The banquet table, the centrepiece of this grandeur, stretched before him, embellished with a diverse collection of gleaming silverware, sparkling goblets, and porcelain plates. At the head of the table sat King Osred. To his right was Prince Golen, the unwitting accomplice in his nefarious plot.

The hood of his cloak masked his intent from the prying eyes of the courtiers and guards. Drawing closer to the King's drinking chalice, a finely crafted vessel of gilded silver, indistinguishable from the rest, would be the instrument of regicide. With calculated patience, he swayed gracefully, embodying the stealth of a shadow, waiting for the right moment to strike, and felt euphoric that he had escaped the notice of all amidst the animated chatter of the hall. With practised skill and agility, he covertly swapped the poisoned chalice for the King's untainted goblet, executing the treacherous manoeuvre with a swift flick of his wrist. He felt euphoric that the King remained unaware of the imminent danger. Prince Golen's voice echoed through the hall as he proposed a toast to his father's well-being.

Amidst the gathering guests' approving murmurs, the King, wearing a benevolent smile, lifted his goblet, his eyes fixed warmly on his son. A hush fell over the hall as all eyes turned to the monarch, awaiting his response to the heartfelt toast. King Osred raised the goblet in appreciation, bringing the chalice to his lips. The liquid, a deep red as rich as royal blood, flowed from the chalice to the King's mouth. He sipped, enjoyed, and tasted more as a ripple of applause coursed through the assembly.

Whispering Grass watched, his heart pounding in contrast with the King's steady breaths. To his relief, the King displayed no immediate signs of distress. His face remained serene; his demeanour unchanged. He maintained his composure, knowing that the poison's deadly embrace would not reveal itself so readily. The evening progressed, and the King's chalice refilled whenever it ran dry. His eyes never left the King, noting that with each replenishment, the poison's potency grew, like a serpent slowly tightening its grip on its unsuspecting prey. Amid revelry and merriment, it now became a game of patience and cunning as he awaited the inevitable, praying that his crafty hand had sown the seeds of the King's downfall before the sun next lit the skies.

Whispering Grass bolted upright in his bed amid the sounds of chaos. Servants scurried past his chamber door, their footsteps echoing the unrest that had gripped the palace. He dressed hastily, his big feet lightly grazing the chilly stone floor beneath. A cascade of silver hair framed his face as he swung open his door. In the dimly lit corridors, the devastating news of King Osred's sudden demise spread like wildfire through the labyrinth of hallways. Servants and advisors bustled with confusion, their faces etched with despair as they carried scrolls and hurried instructions. His presence ignored, he approached the Prince's bed-chamber, footsteps away.

The slightly open door unveiled a room enveloped in darkness, illuminated only by the solitary flicker of a candle. Prince Golen's face was a mask of shock and grief as he sat alone on the edge of his bed. His father's passing had come with the swiftness of a striking serpent, leaving him paralysed with disbelief. His strong jaw trembled, and his fingers clenched and unclenched in a futile attempt to grapple with the reality of the loss.

Whispering Grass cleared his throat, a deliberate announcement to signal his arrival. Prince Golen's head jolted upward. "Sire," he commenced, "I extend my most heartfelt condolences for the untimely passing of your father, King Osred." His words hung as heavy in the stone-walled room that surrounded them. Prince Golen, tears glistening in his eyes, nodded in acknowledgement. He somehow found solace in the wisdom and experience of Whispering Grass. It was as though he possessed an uncanny ability to understand the depths of his grief and the weight of the responsibilities that now rested upon his shoulders. He listened attentively as Prince Golen spoke.

"The physicians believe my father's passing to be a result of heart failure, a tragedy that none could have foreseen."

"Fear not, your Majesty, for you do not walk this path alone. If needed, I shall remain by your side, offering my counsel and support in these trying times."

In Prince Golen's eyes, gratitude and relief were evident. The burden of his father's legacy and the fate of the entire kingdom pressed heavily upon him, yet the presence of his new business partner introduced a glimmer of hope. The Prince silently extended an invitation that held profound significance; he gestured to a nearby chair, a simple piece of furniture of regal elegance. It was an invitation to stay, not just as a partner but as a trusted companion and confidant.

Whispering Grass accepted the invitation with a nod, sitting beside the grieving Prince. At that moment, amidst the turmoil and uncertainty, a new alliance was formed—one that would shape the future of Cyberia and offer hope to a young ruler thrust into the maelstrom of leadership. In the darkness of that chamber, a flicker of resilience ignited, heralding the dawn of a new era for Cyberia.

Chapter 12

Emberfall Village
Valaria

Emberfall Village began Valour's existence, a quaint and humble place among rolling hills and forests. He first learned the values of community and resilience here amidst children's laughter and the warmth of family. However, his journey to the Valarian palace at fourteen truly shaped him into the Zenturion he was destined to become. As he left the comforts of Emberfall behind, a mix of excitement and trepidation coursed through him. The path to the palace was fraught with challenges, each step a test of his resolve and character. He traversed rugged terrains and faced fierce storms, all while carrying the hopes of his village in his heart.

The grandeur of the Valarian palace, with its towering spires and intricate stonework, was a world apart from the simplicity of Emberfall. Yet, it was within those opulent walls that Valour meticulously honed his abilities, immersing himself in the intricate art of strategy and diplomacy. He encountered mentors who recognised his potential, imparting wisdom and skills to serve him well in the dions to come. Each lesson was a stepping stone, shaping his mind and spirit and ultimately forging him into a proud and formidable Zenturion.

Valour swelled with pride as the Princess honoured his village with her visit. Overhead, the towering trees created a natural arch, allowing dappled sunlight to dance on the ground below. The gentle rustle of leaves and the melodic chirping of birds provided a soothing backdrop as the travellers advanced out of the woodland. The path wound through narrow spaces until Emberfall Village appeared in the clearing beyond. Farmers tended to their crops in the fields surrounding the village, their hands working the heavy soil. The village exposed an aura of rustic charm. Quaint cottages with thatched roofs, each displaying blooming window boxes and colourful gardens. Children played in the streets, their laughter echoing as they engaged in games of tag and make-believe. At its centre was the marketplace, busting with villagers who bartered for goods and exchanged pleasantries while doing business.

The scent of freshly baked bread wafted from a nearby bakery, mingling with the earthy aroma of the blacksmith's forge. On the other side of the village, the scenery changed, exposing a magnificent vista of surrounding hills. Valour eagerly pointed out his parents' cottage in the far-off distance. His heart raced with excitement and nervous energy. He had been absent for a considerable time, and the overwhelming anticipation of reconnecting with his family consumed him. Princess Arabella sensed his emotions and offered a reassuring smile; it was the silent encouragement he needed.

Valour spotted his parents absorbed in their tasks tending to the front garden. The house stood amidst a patch of greenery, its white walls and thatched roof blending harmoniously with the natural surroundings. A picket fence bordered the barn property, giving it an inviting and idyllic charm. Facing the direction of the approaching steeds, Valour's parents took a moment to register that the rider atop one of the magnificent creatures was none other than their son. In disbelief, their eyes widened as his father abandoned his gardening tool, and his mother, hands rising to her heart, gasped in astonishment.

Princess Arabella and the rest of the group stayed mounted as Valour rushed towards his mother, lifting her into his arms and spinning her around with pure happiness. Setting her down gently, he embraced his father in a tight bear hug, a greeting so heartfelt that it engulfed his mother to tears. A cry of jubilant delight resonated from the doorway, and a young girl with lively eyes sprinted towards Valour in unrestrained excitement. With his arms wide open, she leapt into her brother's embrace, her laughter echoing the sheer happiness of the moment.

"Valour! Your home!" she exclaimed, her voice brimming with emotion. His parents stood back, observing the heartwarming reunion, their faces expressing a release of long-awaited emotions.

The family turned their attention to Valour's companions. Princess Arabella, wearing a bright smile, dismounted. Max, Mia, and Isaiah followed, ready for the introductions. Valour commenced with the Princess, prompting his bewildered family to respond with unexpected curtsies and a bow. Confusion showed on their faces; they wondered why a royal family member should grace their home.

Overcoming her surprise, Valour's mother extended a warm welcome. "Your Highness. While we may not be familiar with royal visits, our door is always open to guests of honour," she expressed kindly. With a gentle sweep of her hand, she motioned for the Princesses to enter their humble home.

"Kind mother, amid his exuberance, Zenturion Valour seems to have momentarily overlooked the names of his parents and sister," said the Princess with a teasing smile.

"I humbly apologise, Your Highness," Valour replied, "Please allow me to introduce my beloved parents, Elara and Thorian, and my dear sister, Seraphina."

Helped by his father, Valour and Isaiah secured their steeds in the small barn while Elara showed the Princess and the siblings inside the house. The interior of the three-bedroom cottage held an inviting warmth. The main living area consisted of artfully crafted wooden furniture, each displaying rustic charm. Sunlight filtered through the windows, casting an orange glow on the worn but polished tiles that covered the floor. The kitchen, although compact, exuded an air of culinary delight. The aroma of fresh herbs lingered from a pot simmering on the stove, promising a savoury meal.

The three bedrooms were simple yet decorated with personal touches. Valour's room showcased trophies and mementoes of his courageous exploits. Seraphina's room was a haven of creativity, with sketches and trinkets that reflected her spirit. His parent's room exuded a sense of well-read books lining the shelves. Overall, the home radiated a sense of belonging and family unity, each corner telling a story of shared experiences and cherished moments. When Valour expressed his wish to stay overnight, Elara promptly detailed the sleeping arrangements with a weight of concern. "I'm afraid our sleeping spaces are rather limited, Your Highness. Would it be agreeable for you to share a room with Mia?"

Arabella's immediate and resounding "Yes, of course" elicited Elara's contented sigh of relief.

"Excellent. Seraphina will join me in my room. Max can stay in Valour's room. My husband, son and Isaiah must make do in the lounge or camp outside."

Being asked to camp beneath the moonlit sky alongside his father stirred up many fond childhood memories for Valour. He promptly embraced the suggestion while Isaiah was equally satisfied to sleep on the comfortable-looking sofa to ensure father and son could enjoy some precious time together. Before dinner, Valour revealed the details of their expedition to the Untamed Land. His father wore a solemn expression while his mother, in shock, deemed it necessary to lower herself onto a chair. Allowing time to contemplate, Thorian excused himself and returned with a cherished elder.

Thorian introduced Lirion to the assembled party and explained that he had a greater understanding of the bee colony and that his knowledge would immensely benefit their imminent quest. Lirion bowed to the Princesses before taking his seat at the dinner table. He wore a rough woollen tunic and trousers embellished with patches and stitches. The kind man's weathered face bore the marks of time and of a well-lived existence. Despite his well-worn appearance, his eyes were deep and thoughtful, and he held a knowledge of secrets that seemed to illuminate his every expression.

Captivated, Lirion listened to the reason for their quest before recounting his perilous dions surrounding the hives in The Untamed Land. "My target was the flowers located nearest to the bee hives. These flowers, known as Golden Nectar Blossoms, are marked by their brilliant golden petals that shimmer in the sunlight, resembling tiny suns scattered across the landscape. Each flower stands tall on slender green stems, with delicate leaves cradling their base. The sap, extracted from the Golden Blossoms, is a thick, amber liquid that sparkles like liquid gold. Rich in antioxidants, vitamins, and minerals, this sap possesses extraordinary healing properties, making it an effective remedy for those suffering from various ailments.

What I'm about to describe is truly unimaginable." With a sweeping gesture, he held his hands apart to illustrate the immense size of the Queen's female workers. "Her guardians," he continued, "are twice as large." The hairs on Mia's arms stood on end, and her eyes widened. The description far surpassed anything Valour had foretold.

The pinnacle of fascination is the Queen, the only fertile female in the colony—a gigantic spectacle I witnessed just once. It occurred on a day when the rains descended, and an unprecedented deluge flooded the underground colony. The volume of rainfall was unlike anything I had ever experienced. The rising water level within the honeycomb had surged to the point of posing a threat of subsidence. I saw the Queen escorted to a nest on higher ground, one of many that stretch for as far as the eyes can see.

The cacophony of noise generated by the flapping wings of the swarm of guardians escorting the Queen built to a deafening crescendo as she made her way past the distance from here to the front gate," he emphasised. Max estimated the distance to be no more than a hundred steps. "The swarm showcased a breathtaking display, executed with precise, almost militaristic synchronisation. Discovered, I found myself frozen beside a tree encircled by a handful of workers. Their persistent hum reached an intensity, causing my ears to ache. Their communication mirrored telepathy of an undeniable connection, yet the intricacies behind it remain a mystery to me. The lead worker hovered just away from my face. I knew I had to maintain my composure and conceal any hint of panic. I fixed my gaze on them as they turned away, only to see a burst of amber radiance. It was an object carried by other workers following the Queen. This event remained a mystery until today when Thorian mentioned the amber crystal you seek."

Taking the initiative, Max disclosed the details gleaned from his grandfather's friend, Benjamin Hayes. Shedding light on the mystery that had eluded Lirion, he clarified that the connection observed among the bees was pheromones. "I read up on pheromones. It's a scent that conveys messages among mammals and insects alike. The aroma can serve as alerts for danger, locating a partner, markers for home or directions for locating food sources. The Queen gives off a unique scent known as the queen pheromone. This powerful scent commands every insect in her colony to protect her and the nest against intruders or predators."

"Your wisdom of knowledge is much appreciated," said Lirion.

"Lirion, how far do these things travel from their colony?" asked Isaiah.

"Their foraging activities cover a specific range. Regular visits to a blossoming realm of a nearby floral paradise supply the necessary nectar and pollen for sustaining the colony or individual survival. The entirety of their food supply is marked by no more than a glitchmark in flight; otherwise, it would expose the Queen to potential predators."

"Lirion, the Queen, and the amber light. Do you recall where she and the amber light relocated to? Also, is there a way for us to access a passage discreetly?" asked the Princess.

"Yes, to both questions, your Highness."

"Should you lead us there, a substantial reward awaits you." Believing that refusal would likely result in a command, Lirion reluctantly agreed, emphasising that they all must adhere strictly to his advice. "Max has explained several methods to divert the workers. Smoking the drones out of the Queen's nest would have a safer and more favourable outcome."

Lirion disagreed. "The smoke would be my last resort, your Highness."

"Your first choice, surely?"

"May I speak candidly?" The Princess nodded. "I would provoke a war to distract all the workers away from the queen."

"Incite a war?" Mia gasped.

"How can you manipulate them into battling one another?" queried Valour.

"It wouldn't be against each other. It would be against the wasps," Lirion clarified.

"Wasps!" Max exclaimed, taken aback by the unexpected revelation.

"Please allow Lirion to finish," the Princess ordered, her gaze firm and steady.

"Wasps exhibit a higher level of aggression and predatory behaviour than bees, often engaging in raids on their colonies to secure sustenance, primarily targeting their stored nectar and the developing brood. The brood can become appealing targets for wasps seeking nourishment. Their superior strength and aggression give them the ability to infiltrate and attack. Such behaviour can stem from a shortage of food resources, particularly during periods of limited natural food availability, which their region is currently experiencing. Territorial conflicts further exacerbate this behaviour; if a wasp nest is situated too near a bee colony, clashes between the two species arise, and I have witnessed such an event. It truly is a sight to behold and also quite terrifying."

"How would you incite such a war?" asked Isaiah, intrigued.

"With the most significant enticement: honey-infused sugar. Bees and wasps exhibit reduced activity during the night. They return to their hives/nests and cluster together for rest. You could carry sealed sacks filled with honey-infused sugar to the Queen's nest during this period. Sprinkle the bait around the circumference at the top ridge of the hive's mound. Sugar and honey are the most potent scents to provoke wasps into hunting mode, a pivotal development that will aid your undertaking to descend underground before the airborne conflict unfolds at first light."

"Once underground, the blue crystal will light our way through the honeycombs by guiding us to the queen's nest,"elucidated Valour, sharing the most effective method for finding the precious gem.

"That would indeed be a tremendous asset, but once you're in the chamber, you must separate the Queen from her protectors. To enter that space without a specific scent to ward off the bees would be lethal. The Mentha pulegium, with its minty essence, is a powerful deterrent." Lirion laid out his plan of utilising the mint in the Queen's chamber while Max wondered why Benjamin Hayes did not mention such a scent.

Thorian interrupted the silence. "I will gather the entire village's supply of sugar and honey."

"I will disperse the sugar around the nest," declared Valour, convinced that Lirion's idea was the best way to separate the Queen from her guardians.

"I will accompany Valour," said Isaiah, agreeing to the plan.

"I'm ready to assist," Max said, his expression resolute. "Why should you bear all the risk?"

"Max, your courageous words are commendable, but your unique skill in deciphering the sacred map prevents me from allowing you to take such a risk," said the Princess.

"I'd consider that a blessing," Mia remarked, appreciating the wisdom of the Princesses. "Are the wasps the same size as the bees?" Mia added, her expression serious.

"Smaller," Lirion clarified, "but in battle, bees can only sting once; that action ultimately leads to their end. Wasps can sting repeatedly without facing such a dire consequence." Agreeing to set out for the Untamed Land at noon, Lirion bid them goodnight and took his leave.

Mia and the Princess were the first to retire for the night. Arabella's eyes roamed around Seraphina's bedroom with a pleasant appreciation. Ornamental lamps emitted a soft, inviting glow, warming the quaint surroundings. The cozy pillows on the bed beckoned a night of peaceful rest. With a playful giggle, Mia couldn't help but remark, "My friends would never believe I'm having a sleepover with a princess!"

Arabella settled into the bed, the comfort setting her at ease as she initiated their first truly heartfelt conversation. "Being a princess doesn't mean I've missed out on the joys of my existence. I've always believed that we all share similar interests and experiences, whether royal or not. The title may come with its responsibilities, but it doesn't define who I am at my core. I cherish the simple pleasures just like anyone else." The Princess needed to discover the unique passions that shaped Mia's existence, hoping it would deepen their connection and friendship despite the differences in their worlds. "So, Mia, what do you enjoy most when you're back home in your world?"

Mia's eyes sparkled as she began to share her passions and hobbies, ranging from venturing into the hidden nooks of her new home to her enthusiasm for the wonders of technology. The Princess listened intently, occasionally offering her story that resonated with Mia's interests. The Princess's grace and openness set the stage for an interaction that felt as comfortable and intimate as a conversation with a close friend. Mia thought the bond would forever be a cherished memory of their extraordinary connection beyond titles and backgrounds.

Valour's mother tearfully said goodbye to the group as they set out on their dangerous quest. True to his word, Thorian fulfilled his promise by securing two sacks of sealed sugar infused with honey. These were securely fastened to a leather pannier and balanced on Valour's steed for maximum stability. Leading the procession on horseback were Lirion and Isaiah. Seraphina and her father could only look on helplessly as they prayed for their safe return.

Under Lirion's guidance, they embarked on paths that defied conventional understanding, trails not mined by zenizens but sculpted by the elements of time. The pathways were often narrow, winding precariously between towering trees and over babbling brooks. With every step, the apprehension of journeying into the untamed land became increasingly daunting. They came to a sudden halt at the base of an imposing mountain with no visible path upward or around. They looked to Lirion with uncertainty and confusion, and he disclosed the mountain's secret: a concealed passageway that bore through to the other side.

Dismounting, they continued on foot with Lirion leading with a solitary stick torch. Along the passageway's uneven walls, the air turned damp with the redolence of earth and stone. To Mia, walking through the claustrophobic passageways felt like an eternity. But it was just a matter of a short time until she felt the rush of fresh air emerging from the end of the darkened passageway into the encircling embrace of daylight. The magnificent view overhead was breathtaking. Eagles glided gracefully on the thermal air currents below the snow-capped mountains. Meandering streams carved winding paths through the descending terrain, cloaked in shadows, as the sun's golden glow highlighted the contours and crevices in brilliant detail.

They chose a secluded clearing for the night, resting securely under the protective canopy of ancient trees while a nearby stream bubbled over pebbles and rocks. Spirits refreshed at the first light of dawn, and they continued their journey to reach the bee colony before nightfall. Max marvelled at the surrounding plants, which towered well above his family's new farmhouse.

The colossal stems, releasing a sweet, intoxicating fragrance, bore fruit that glistened like jewels, their colours ranging from deep amethyst to fiery crimson. Lirion, displaying the agility of someone thirty years younger, unexpectedly yanked hard on his reins and urgently instructed everyone to dismount and seek refuge beneath a colossal flower that resembled a gigantic parasol. Lirion urged each rider to quiet their mounts as a distant rumbling became a deafening hum generated by the rapid fluttering of cyclonic wings. Overhead, swarms of diligent worker bees surged past, heading to their hives before dusk. Gradually, the noise receded, replaced by an eerie stillness that felt as vast as the sky above. They moved onward until they reached an expansive open area dotted with countless massive mounds made of soil, chewed wood, and saliva. Towering thirty feet high, they hid a network of burrows beneath the hives.

Their ascent up a hill covered in foliage provided them camouflage and a strategic position with a clear view of the foreboding landscape. Valour retrieved a spyglass from his saddle and handed it to Lirion, who focused on the hive housing the queen bee. Princess Arabella raised the blue crystal aloft, its brilliance intensifying as it pointed toward where Lirion directed the spyglass. It emitted a clear signal that the amber crystal lay concealed within.

Lirion turned his focus to the wasp nests in the far distance. Like the bees, the wasps made nests from layers of chewed wood fibres and saliva but exhibited an asymmetrical design, resembling giant globes rising from the earth. He shifted his gaze back toward the Queen's old abandoned hive, ravaged by the flood. The entrance had become overgrown with vegetation. It appeared accessible, and the question was why the worker bees hadn't secured or strengthened it. His only plausible answer was that the burrow would be too tight and challenging for an attack. Another concern was the hive's steep incline and the potential difficulties Valour and Isaiah could encounter while hauling sacks loaded with sugar-infused honey up the ascent. He watched as both analysed the incline and the surrounding terrain, taking note of the scattered boulders that could provide adequate cover if necessary.

Valour and Isaiah used the leather water skins to rinse away their scent as nightfall descended. Lirion coated their arms and legs with a distinctive paste of clay, silt, and sand, adding mint to mask their bodily scent after changing into lightweight, dark cotton clothing. Mia enveloped Valour and Isaiah in a heartfelt embrace while Max exchanged sturdy handshakes. Despite Princess Arabella's regal demeanour, her stomach churned with anxiety, praying for their safe return. Bolstered by encouragement, the duo balanced the sugar sacks on their shoulders and quietly slipped away, descending the hill under the cover of the cloud-covered moon.

They moved closer to their goal, leaving discreet markers along their path to ensure a trail for their return. Stealthily circling and bypassing numerous smaller hives, they reached the Queen's lair without encountering any obstacles. Evaluating the steep slope, they noticed what the spyglass failed to reveal: rugged, jagged protrusions perfect for gripping and supporting both hands and feet. The ascent up the hill still proved challenging, yet Valour emerged as the first to reach the summit. Swiftly discarding his sack, he leaned over to assist Isaiah in his climb. Slicing open the sealed sacks, they paced the manageable path around the top of the hive, allowing the sweetener to spread down the outer slope. Valour took a moment to look down into the abyss and saw nothing but a faint green shimmer emitted by fungi species thriving within the damp, shadowy recesses of the hive.

Not wanting to overstay their welcome, they descended the slope. Stable footholds proved more challenging to come down. Isaiah lost his grip and tumbled to the bottom of the crater, twisting his ankle. The noise provoked a rush of activity inside the hive. Limping, Isaiah urged Valour onward, reassuring him he'd catch up at his own pace. Ignoring the plea, Valour helped him seek shelter behind a boulder and cautiously peered out to witness two bees emerging from the crater's ridge. Watching and waiting was their only option as the colossal insects circled the perimeter, investigating the area.

The bees focused on the sugared slopes. Their confusion was evident, but would it escalate to the point of raising an alarm within the hive? His thoughts were interrupted by the loud flapping of their wings as they briefly hovered before descending back into the hive. Valour's focus shifted to Isaiah's ankle, tender to the touch and swollen to the size of an egg. Encouraging Isaiah to climb onto his back, he returned to the hill, mulling over Lirion's words about bees' vision being weaker in darkness. They relied on detecting ultraviolet light or rapid movements through their compound eyes of several minuscule lenses to compensate. Lirion attended to Isaiah's sprain. Breathless, Valour recounted the success of their mission. Isaiah's frustration grew as he found himself unable to continue. Bowing his head, he begrudgingly accepted that he was no longer an asset but a hindrance. Recognising the risk of pursuing the amber crystal alone, Valour highlighted the importance of their partnership.

Lirion spoke up. "I will come with you. Although I may be old, I am still strong enough to offer support. I will carry the torch and the blue crystal to guide us because you will need your weapon drawn for any danger we may face."

"Your courage is beyond words," said Valour, knowing his father's friend was right.

"Courage that will be rejoiced for dions to come," declared the Princess with gratitude.

Lirion half-smiled. He couldn't bear letting Valour, whom he had known since childhood, go alone. "We must prepare ourselves to leave now," he announced.

"Now?" exclaimed Mia in astonishment, considering Valour had just returned.

"Yes, we must enter the burrow before the sun awakes."

Princess Arabella raised a valid concern, "How will you know if the conflict has begun if you're underground?"

"The burrows will reverberate like an earthquake. The cacophony of noise will serve as a clear indicator as the bees emerge to confront the wasps. The aerial battle will etch into your memory as an unforgettable spectacle." He took a sealed pouch from his saddle and looked at Valour.

"Within this pouch is the mint that bees abhor most. I have condensed the mint into tiny spheres. I'll guide you on what to do once we're inside the Queen's chamber." Smearing himself with the unique mint, clay, silt, and sand, Lirion slung the pouch containing the mint over his shoulder and announced, "I am ready!"

Valour and Isaiah clasped each other's wrists in a parting gesture. Having forged a strong bond with the siblings, Valour offered them a comforting smile. He turned to face the Princess. "I command you to come back alive," she said tearfully. He nodded proudly in appreciation of her royal words and turned to help Lirion through the foliage and descend the hill. He felt their eyes track their every movement until they disappeared from view.

Quietly, they approached the entrance of the deserted burrow hidden beneath a web of gnarled roots, creeping vines, and withered tumbleweed. They feared the sharp snap of a twig would reveal their whereabouts as they navigated through the thicket. Painstakingly clearing a path, they cautiously delved into the depths of the underground burrow. Lirion ignited the torch, illuminating the dried sections of propolis—a sticky resin harvested from trees, offering extra wall strength and insulation, though vulnerable to floods.

Lirion tightly gripped the weighty blue crystal. Its cerulean glow guided them to take the correct turn at a fork in the path, which navigated them through sunken floors and weakened ceilings. With every pile of earth pushed aside, another danger proved more challenging. Fuelled by the pressing nature of their mission, they forged ahead. Their silent labour was accompanied by the rushing water of an underground stream that hadn't breached the burrow. The air carried a damp, earthy scent, and it felt like an eternity before they reached a tiny caveat that squeezed them inside the Queen's chamber.

Perched on a pedestal of beeswax, the amber crystal at the centre of the chamber radiated a glow, reminiscent of a gem in a royal crown. Valour gazed in wonder at the immense form of the sleeping Queen. Lirion was enveloped in a sense of exhaustion mixed with reverence, drawn from the powerful aura of both crystals.

Valour felt a strong urge to grab the amber crystal while the Queen's guardians stood watch outside the chamber, but he suppressed the impulse, knowing it would lead to a frantic chase through the tunnel. Instead, they patiently waited for the first light of dawn. In hushed whispers, they discussed how to leverage the despised mint to their benefit. Valour stood poised, keenly observing Lirion as he weighed their options, ready to move at the opportune moment.

Chapter 13

The Royal Palace
Valaria

Prince Golen dispatched his messengers to inform his sister of their father's passing and the funeral arrangements. Cloaked in garments bearing the royal insignia, the messengers raced across the kingdom. When the news of the king's death spread, artisans worked ceaselessly, creating banners and flags with the royal crest to adorn the streets of towns and villages, casting a dignified display of sorrow for their revered monarch, King Osred.

Organising the preparations was the responsibility of the king's most trusted advisor, Lord Elric, whose loyalty to the royal family spanned dions. He believed the solemn occasion should be more than just a reflection of the esteemed king; it was to symbolise the unity and strength of the realm in response to its profound loss.

The funeral would be held in the illustrious Royal Gardens, a sprawling haven of lawns, vibrant flowers, and a serene lake that had been a sanctuary for King Osred during his reign. The garden was converted into a tranquil space for the ceremony, decorated with floral displays of white roses, the kingdom's symbolic flower, and dazzling crystals that sparkled like stars in the night sky. Dominating the area was a vast, magnificent marquee erected to house the catafalque to support the gold-gilded coffin while the king lay in state. Adorning the marquee's entry, silken drapes in the royal colours of deep blue and gold swayed in the breeze.

Whispering Grass took advantage of this moment and planted the seed of resentment against the princess by revealing her connection with two mysterious humans who had arrived in Cyberia from a different reality. He explained her pivotal role in aiding the humans in navigating unfamiliar terrain and uncovering the majestic Crystals of Time that could rejuvenate the Great White Clock.

Golen's heart burned with a searing sense of betrayal as he learned that his father and his advisor, Lord Elric, had conspired to keep Princess Arabella's quest hidden from him. He felt a mix of humiliation, anger, and yet gratitude as Whispering Grass furnished him with the information. Despite his father's reputation for wisdom and foresight, keeping this matter secret in collaboration with Lord Elric suggested a concealed motive for their mistrust. Perturbed by the revelation, Prince Golen paced up and down, his steps echoing the turmoil in his mind.

When summoned, Lord Elric entered Golen's chamber. Advanced in age, with silver hair cascading down to his shoulders and a well-groomed beard, his sharp and calculating gaze betrayed a sign of wariness. He was grappling with disquieting thoughts concerning Whispering Grass, rumoured to possess the power of persuasion through his entrancing whispers. He shot a look of discontent at Whispering Grass, which didn't escape Golen's notice.

Golen's intense stare locked onto his father's advisor, and he spoke with a venom that sliced through the silence like a knife. His demand for answers reverberated in the room, striking like a bolt from the blue. "Lord Elric, I have learned of your collusion with my father in concealing my sister's quest. Explain yourself. Why was I left ignorant of such importance of the Crystals of Time?"

Lord Elric met the prince's gaze, his voice steady despite the weight of accusation.

"Your Highness, I assure you, there were valid reasons for the secrecy surrounding the princess's quest—reasons your father believed were in the kingdom's best interest. Perhaps it would be wise to discuss this in private."

Golen's jaw tightened as he processed Lord Elric's words. The weight of his indignation filled the room. "Whispering Grass will stay. I find it hard to accept that such secrecy benefits the kingdom. Enlighten me, Lord Elric, or face the repercussions of your silence."

"Sire, I remain unclear about your father's reasoning. The decision was entirely the king's. I acted in accordance with my duties."

"Lord Elric, I want you gone," Golen stated, his anger evident in the careful selection of his words, reflecting his deep-seated mistrust.

Lord Elric bowed and left the prince's chamber. The idea of Whispering Grass exercising influence over the kingdom and its zenizens gnawed at his conscience. Like the prince, he had encountered Whispering Grass during a visit to Arbitration Land, where he had attended a diplomatic conference with the late King Osred. He perceived him as possessing a captivating and deceitful aura and believed his whispers were like honeyed poison, dripping with sweet temptation and half-truths. He was troubled by the increasing sway of Whispering Grass, who had spent excessive time with the heir apparent. What were his intentions? He believed they were far from benevolent. Did he seek to disrupt the delicate balance of power within the kingdom? If so, why? One thing he was sure of was that Prince Golen had always openly disagreed with the advice he had offered the deceased king.

In Lord Elric's eyes, the prince had always shown signs of weakness and folly, a worrying departure from the traditions and wisdom that had guided the kingdom for generations. He feared for the kingdom's future and saw a potential weakness that external forces could exploit in Golen. With every fibre of his being, he resolved to find a way to free the prince from the beguiling clutches of Whispering Grass and guide him back onto the path of authentic leadership and wisdom.

As the sun descended beyond the horizon, the kingdom's elite assembled in the Royal Gardens to pay their respects to King Osred in his open casket. The scene was adorned with regal drapery and flickering candles that twinkled like stars, casting a gentle light on the late king's face. Clutched in his hands was a single white rose, symbolising purity and remembrance. Nobles, courtiers, and advisors entered the marquee, their faces etched with sorrow as they silently honoured the king. Among them stood Prince Golen, dressed in his finest garments, his thoughts lingering on his sister, Arabella, while Lord Elric's mind wandered to Whispering Grass.

Chapter 14

The Untamed Land
Valaria

The first light of dawn unfurled its warm tendrils over the bee colony, painting the landscape in a breathtaking display of vibrant orange and soft pink. Hidden behind the foliage at the top of the hill, Isaiah adjusted his spyglass, scanning the terrain for any signs of movement. His patience was rewarded as workers began to emerge from the queen's nest, buzzing with curiosity as they hovered around the edges of the sugar-rich feast. Similarly, scout wasps emerged from their nests, their antennae keenly attuned to the scent of pollen drifting on the wind. Instinctively, they ascended into the air, drawn to the alluring sweet scent of sugar. Identifying the source deep within enemy territory, they circled in unison above the hive of the bee queen.

The workers responded with a series of alarm signals to alert their colony of the impending threat, prompting them to prepare for defence. Isaiah looked on as countless bee's erupted from their hives, racing to intercept the danger looming above. Initially disheartened, he thought the threat had faded when the scouts retreated to their colony, unaware that they were transmitting the appetising information they had discovered.

Driven by the intelligence of their scouts, the wasps surged from their nests in a flurry of activity. Their flight was synchronised and intentional, the hum of their wings vibrating like the distant approach of a thunder-storm. Isaiah swung his spyglass back toward the hives, watching in awe as the bees made a comparable response before lowering the spyglass to shield his ears from the overpowering noise. Stunned, he looked on as both factions converged, their numbers evenly matched, circling in eager anticipation of the impending clash. The sky transformed into a breathtaking spectacle, an aerial ballet of twists and dives that mirrored the chaos of close-quarters combat, with their stingers brandished like drawn swords in a dramatic dance that embodied the essence of a one-on-one duel. The territorial dispute escalated as Lirion had predicted —a full-scale war.

The harrowing encounter revealed the formidable strength of nature's warriors. Max and Mia clamped their hands over their ears, overwhelmed by the cacophony of noise. Battling against their restraints, Isaiah hobbled over to the Princess to help calm the terrified steeds. Overhead, the casualties increased as injured insects spiralled downward, their once-mighty wings faltering in a descent that marked a mournful surrender. The ground trembled with the heavy thuds of their final moments while the fierce battle continued to rage above.

The survivors fought on, their desperate movements unfolding into a struggle for victory in an arena filled with pain and brutality. Wounded bees sought refuge in their hives, while fresh waves of defenders consistently surged into the battle, maintaining their unwavering defence. Mia was visibly disturbed by the horrifying scene, shutting her eyes in disbelief as venomous stingers struck their targets with chilling precision. It served as a sobering reminder that within the beauty of the natural world, a relentless struggle for survival was unfolding, with the sky itself witnessing both triumphs and tragedies. Confronted with such merciless behaviour, her only wish was that the Grand White Clock, a symbol of hope, would somehow justify the heartbreaking events she had witnessed.

Lirion realised that the critical moment had arrived as the underground chamber quaked from the impact of fallen warriors above. The once-peaceful space had morphed into a realm of unsettling tremors. The queen's bodyguards promptly took action, establishing a shield at the entrance of the honeycomb to thwart any efforts to breach her domain. Valour opened the sack containing the hand-sized minted orbs. Following Lirion's signal, he rolled each orb around the queen's resting place, leaving a clear route for her to exit.

Lirion was troubled by the possibility that the queen's guards might not allow her to leave her domain. He understood their commitment to protecting their leader from any threat, yet he held onto the hope that her royal command would be respected, enabling her to flee the chamber. When the queen caught a whiff of the pungent odour, she instinctively pulled back. In her distress, she flapped her wings, generating a rush of air that swept through the chamber. Valour covered his ears, steadying himself against the sudden backdraft. After the queen's forceful push, her guardians dismantled their barrier, giving her the opportunity to escape the oppressive scent.

Without hesitation, Valour raced forward and snatched the priceless gem from its pedestal; its warm brilliance coursing up his arm filling him with a wonderful sense of exhilaration. With no time to waste, he swiftly reunited with Lirion to escape the chamber with their hard-won treasure. Sensing the fading pulse of the amber crystal, the queen sent urgent, powerful vibrations to her guardians, urging them into to her chamber. They warily navigated past the strong smell and caught sight of the amber light flickering from the empty burrow. To safeguard the queen, only one scurried through the tight passageway in pursuit.

Through the labyrinth of burrows, the pair carefully sidestepped familiar pitfalls, but an unsettling sound came from behind, signalling that they were being followed. Valour had no choice but to have Lirion carry the two crystals while he held his sword in one hand and the fire stick in the other. He instructed Lirion to take the lead, his focus split between the dangerous path ahead and the approaching enemy behind. The crystals felt particularly weighty, but the radiant light of the new dawn illuminated the burrow's exit, inspiring Lirion to quicken his pace.

Valour urged Lirion into the light while igniting the fire stick against the dry and brittle vegetation that had obstructed their passage. The vegetation ignited swiftly, erupting into a smoke-filled blaze. With the fiery barrier as their only defence against any pursuers, Valour snatched the crystal back from Lirion to ease his burden and shouted for him to run.

Isaiah directed the spyglass towards the burrow's entrance and felt a surge of euphoria sweeping over him as he saw Lirion and Valour emerge unscathed. "They must have been followed!" he yelled, justifying

Valour's reason to ignite the bush. Looking up at the sky, he prayed that the chaos would draw attention away from their escape. Silently, the group urged their companions to safety as they weaved through the battlefield strewn with fallen warriors. The magnitude of their achievement washed over them as they scrambled breathlessly over the hills summit.

Disregarding her royal status, Princess Arabella embraced her fatigued guardian tightly. Lirion, panting, was struck by his own stamina, surprised at how nimble he still felt at his age. Without wasting a moment, Max attached the two crystals to his pannier. They mounted their steeds quickly and urged them forward, galloping away from the battlefield as it receded into the distance. Eventually, they slowed to a trot, allowing their steeds a moment to regain their strength.

Lirion recounted the dangers they had faced in the burrows and the queen's chamber. Valour remained silent, a broad smile on his face, allowing the village elder to bask in his moment of true bravery —a reward he had genuinely earned. Sensing his thoughts, the princess stole a sidelong glance at her guardian, feeling an unexpected flutter in her stomach and a surge of warmth that caught her off guard. Blushing, she quickly dismissed the idea that their bond was anything deeper than friendship.

Upon reaching Emberfall Village, Valour immediately felt the weight of sadness hanging over the community. The vibrant energy that once filled the air had transformed into an atmosphere of sorrow and unease, and the marketplace, usually bustling, now seemed quiet and subdued. While the villagers continued their daily routines, their spirits were dampened by the troubling news awaiting the princess. In a gesture of respect, the elders chose to refrain from donning the traditional black mourning attire until the princess had been informed.

Valour's father, weighed down by the responsibility of delivering the devastating news, waited until the princess had dismounted. With a heavy heart, he drew a deep breath before addressing her. "Your Highness," he said, his voice quivering with sorrow, "King Osred, your beloved father, has passed away. It is with great sadness that we share this truth. By decree of Prince Golen, a legion of royal messengers has been dispatched to spread this somber news throughout the realm."

"The king has passed!" Valour gasped in shock.

Always poised and regal, Princess Arabella gracefully carried the burden of her royal role. Yet, with the news of her father's passing, tears flowed freely as she struggled to find the right words or actions. Valour instinctively stepped closer, enveloping her in a warm embrace, as if cradling a soulmate in their darkest moment. 'My princess,' he said softly, 'there are no words that can lessen your pain. But I am here for you, now and always. This promise I hold dear in my heart.'"

"Valour," she choked, "my father is gone. He meant everything to me, to both of us."

Mia dismounted and approached the princess, who had become the sister she had always longed for. Tears glistened in her eyes as she spoke with heartfelt compassion, her words raw and sincere. "I can't imagine the depth of your pain, Arabella," she said, dropping the royal title. "I struggle to find the right words, but I want you to know that I'm here for you, no matter what."

"Me too," Max added, visibly moved, while Isaiah and Lirion bowed their heads in respect.

Thorian turned to his son, his expression solemn as he glanced at their steeds. "The funeral is in four lunar moons," he said gravely. "They may struggle to travel far without proper rest."

Valour nodded in agreement with his father's counsel. "I understand this is a difficult time for you, Your Highness," he said softly. "But we must prioritise the well-being of the steeds. We still have ample time to reach the palace." Arabella looked at the animals and recognised their exhaustion. She too felt drained and needed solitude to grieve. She thought Valour's sister's bedroom would be a fitting refuge.

Chapter 15

The Royal Palace
Valaria

Princess Arabella approached the palace gates with emotions about the haven she proudly called home. The guards acknowledged her presence with a nod of respect as she crossed the threshold into the courtyard with her companions trailing closely behind. Dismounting, she walked the cobblestone path leading to the inner residence. Each step echoed wearily as if the very stones were grieving for her father. The once-familiar sights and serene sounds now were a poignant reminder of her father's absence.

Valour felt the overwhelming silence as word of the Princess's return swiftly spread among the courtiers and servants. Their sympathetic nods and respectfully lowered gazes conveyed a deep reverence as she passed. The siblings and Isaiah gazed in wonder at the royal residence. Everywhere they looked, affluence displayed a picture of wealth that existed only in their dreams.

The Great Hall was the epicentre of the castle's social scene, encapsulating the spirit of castle life. Arabella thought about the joy that once echoed off its high walls and towering ceilings while hosting countless banquets. A rush of activity erupted from the far end of the hall as the large arched doors opened.

Prince Golen's followers hurried to keep pace with his stride as he rushed towards his sister, momentarily setting aside the simmering tension that had always lingered between them. The deep-seated discord had festered since their youth, rooted in a genuine or imagined perception that the Princess held higher esteem in King Osred's eyes. Whether it was her father's heartfelt praises or the court's adoration, it always felt the attention was always on Arabella. Consequently, Golen's attempt to tarnish her reputation became a twisted form of retaliation.

Golen welcomed her with open arms, a fleeting glimpse of sorrow shadowing his expression, revealing the emotions he had fought to suppress. Arabella lifted her hand and stepped back, rejecting the feigned gesture of welcome. A powerful urge for clarity surged within her, driving her to speak out about the circumstances surrounding their father's passing.

"Heart failure," her brother stated, pressing his hand against his chest to underscore the cause of his passing.

Lord Elric hurriedly approached, breathless as he expressed his sorrow. "Your Highness, it is with a heavy heart that I welcome you back in such sorrowful times."

The Princess immediately voiced her distress. "Lord Elric, I understand my father passed away from heart failure, but I find that hard to comprehend; he was always so robust and full of energy."

"Your Highness, that is the diagnosis given by the royal physician," Lord Elric stated. Isaiah sensed the heavy silence as the Princess weighed her response. It was not the reaction he had anticipated.

"Lord Elric," she said, her voice calm yet firm, "please see to it that my guests and Zenturion Valour are accommodated in the finest suites within the palace." Golen's expression fell back into the familiar downtrodden look he often wore around his sister.

"Valour? Zenturions have their own quarters," he remarked, a trace of disapproval evident in his tone.

The Princess met his gaze. "Valour is my bodyguard, and I require his constant presence. Do you have any objections, dear brother?" Without waiting for Golen's reply, she proceeded to introduce her guests. Golen glared uncomfortably at the humans, envious of his sister's knowledge about how they had arrived in Cyberia.

"I'll see to your guests' rooms personally," Lord Elric assured, sensing the Princess's unease regarding her father's passing. He planned a private discussion with her before dinner to confront their mutual doubts about his demise.

Captivated by the extravagance of their chambers, adorned with sumptuous furnishings and rich fabrics, Mia bounced on her brother's bed. Mid-jump, she noticed Lord Elric passing by the open door. Instantly, she stopped, realising that her playful antics were ill-timed. Intrigued, she leaned cautiously out to watch. She wondered why Lord Elric was eyeing the corridor with a wary expression before gently knocking on the Princess's door.

Arabella was surprised to see Lord Elric, although she had often observed him entering her father's chambers. "Your Highness, I must apologise for this unexpected intrusion," he said, his tone sincere. "May I request a moment to discuss a matter that requires utmost confidentiality?"

Arabella glanced up at the man who had guided her in court etiquette since childhood. He had stood by her father's side when he tasked her with assisting the humans. Looking back, she questioned why her father had chosen her over Golen for this task. Choosing to hold her questions for now, she waited for Lord Elric to reveal the purpose of his visit. "The trust and confidentiality between my father and yourself were exceptional. As his daughter, I aspire to uphold this tradition."

"I sincerely appreciate your kind words, Your Highness. I want you to know that my concerns come from a heart of genuine care, not envy. On the night before your father's passing, I was troubled by the presence of a certain individual constantly by your brother's side. I believe this is a matter that warrants discussion." His words were crafted to enlighten suspicions and read that the Princess had picked up on it, and a sense of pride filled him at her keen perception; his teachings had not been in vain.

"What is the name of this individual, and what title does he hold?"

"He is a commoner without noble lineage, known as Whispering Grass. His background remains enigmatic, yet he has amassed significant influence within the palace. Like a sorcerer, his words and actions have planted doubt and uncertainty in your brother's mind, which I find difficult to comprehend. I first met him in Arbitration Land alongside your father, where it was indicated that he had the trust of Malice Malware. In essence, he walks a precarious ethical line."

The Princess's expression conveyed her shock. "Malice Malware! Is my brother aware of this?" she exclaimed.

"Yes, Your Highness. I broached the subject with him as gently as I could. Regrettably, for reasons I cannot fathom, he dismissed my advice while giving weight to the words of Whispering Grass."

With her concern mounting, the Princess chose to voice her question. "Lord Elric, why did my father select me instead of my brother to aid the humans?"

Lord Elric let out a sigh. "Your Highness, it was because you were the chosen one. That's all your father shared when I expressed my concerns for your safety. It was the only secret he ever kept from me," he lowered his voice, "but not from General Titanous. The king held him in as high esteem as I held your father."

"It seems nothing escapes the general's attention. My human friends have encountered him twice in such a short span—one more time than I've had in my entire existence. Is Whispering Grass joining us for dinner tonight?" she asked, her tone echoing her father's.

"Indeed, it was at your brother's request. It would allow you to evaluate the situation yourself, Your Highness."

"Very well, I will be mindful of my words," she replied. "However, there is a more explosive question on my mind. I will keep it to myself, cautious of your response. I look forward to dinner, Lord Elric."

Lord Elric gently closed the door behind him, sensing the unasked question that hung in the air. Had her father been assassinated? He found himself increasingly questioning the royal physician's diagnosis. The late king's death did indeed seem ill-matched with the robust and energetic spirit he had always exhibited.

Unlike the grand banqueting hall, the Epicurus dining room exuded a more intimate charm. The cream walls, adorned with intricate floral designs, radiated a natural elegance. The rich wooden panelling enhanced the rustic atmosphere, creating a cosy retreat that felt inviting and timeless. Polished square oak tables were arranged in a rectangular formation, seating up to 14 guests. An elaborate crystal chandelier cast a warm, comfortable light despite the underlying tension in the room.

Prince Golen had not invited Valour to join the table, prompting Isaiah to decline. Max and Mia took their places on either side of the Princess while other diners engaged in quiet conversations. Lord Elric noticed that the broad-shouldered Whispering Grass had undergone a significant wardrobe change. The wide-brimmed hat and cloak were gone; instead, he had copied his fashion sense ruthlessly, allowing him to blend in as a courtier. To Lord Elric's annoyance, his rival was seated beside Golen, whispering closely in the prince's ear.

Arabella's heart went to Lord Elric as she noticed his evident embarrassment. "Tell me, Whispering Grass, what brings you to Valaria, and from which province do you come?" she inquired.

With quiet confidence and a voice barely above a whisper, he responded, "I've come to Valaria for a personal matter with the esteemed prince. My father's heritage traces back to the far-off province of Volcanis, while I bear the red code inherited from my Valarian mother. Think of me as a self-proclaimed nomad, having journeyed through every province, sharing meals and conversations with the most influential leaders in each region."

The Princess sensed a flame of self-importance in his words, with a barely concealed conceit that stirred a subtle discomfort within her. She couldn't help but wonder if his traveller's tales were as extraordinary as he claimed or merely a facade to impress his unsuspecting audience. Most of all, Arabella wondered about his business interest with her brother. She felt the urge to inquire, but probing into such matters would lead her too deeply into scrutinising the business affairs of the future monarch.

"Pray tell, humans," antagonised Whispering Grass, "may I inquire how you arrived in the land of Cyberia?"

Maintaining a steady voice, the Princess responded, "To avoid misunderstanding, I introduced my friends by their true names. Furthermore, such information is known to a select few."

His sister's response agitated her brother, prompting him to speak. "Indeed, the privileged ones who hold this knowledge are you and

General Titanous," he declared, his voice tinged with irritation and jealousy.

Whispering Grass pressed further, "Whispers reached my ears suggesting that you all crossed paths in Glimmerhavan, within the heart of the Never Ending Forest."

"Your whispers were quite accurate," the Princess affirmed. "But did they also mention that we encountered Admiral Malice Malware that day? If so, I'd be curious to learn how he knew about our visit."

"Have you ever had the misfortune of meeting him?" Mia innocently inquired. The Princess felt a surge of gratitude. While she had subtly steered the conversation in that direction, Mia had innocently and effortlessly done so herself.

Whispering Grass smiled. "I'm a staunch believer in defending the misunderstood."

Avoiding a direct answer to Mia's question, the Princess persisted. "I find myself perplexed; was that a yes or a no?"

"I've had the pleasure of dining at most of the top tables in Cyberia." Arabella had gathered sufficient information; she now had the answer. "That is something I never misconstrued," she interjected, dismissing his evasive explanation. Unaware of the reasons behind the growing discord, Max felt the tension in the air thicken as dinner unfolded. The Princess found comfort in the news that King Kronos of Drakonia would not be present at the funeral, opting instead to send a regent to represent him. The conversation drifted from the kings funeral to Prince Golen's unexpected rise to the throne.

After dinner, Mia followed Max to his chambers, eager to study the sacred map that would guide them on their upcoming journey. In light of the king's recent passing, they had postponed their quest to give the princess the time she needed until after the funeral. As they examined the map, the amber and blue crystals shone brightly toward the south-east. Tracing the markings, Max concluded that the Crystal was located in the province of Verdantis. Not unexpected, a riddle emerged before them.

"I'm a gem that's not green but bright. In a crown or a ring, I shine bright. What colour am I?"

Mia looked at a small stone on a ring on her finger. "Emerald!" she said confidently. The wording on the map changed and Max recited the riddle to his sister.

"I dwell in the realm where shadows linger, finding refuge in the corners of your mind—a phantom, elusive and sly. I quietly spy. Seek me not in the light; I am the emerald crystal of power guiding you through your flight. What am I that haunts your thoughts every night?

Do you think a bad dream might be the solution to the riddle of the Emerald Crystal?" Max questioned uncertainty in his tone.

Mia nodded in agreement. "I think it's worth exploring, Max. Let's see what Valour says; his room is just down the hall."

Valour welcomed them into his chamber with a friendly smile. After listening to the riddle, a sudden flash of inspiration hit him, and he encouraged them to follow him. He led them through a twisting maze of hallways until they reached the door of an elderly chambermaid, who responded to his soft knock. With her silver hair neatly styled in a bun, Ophelia's eyes shone with wisdom and kindness. The deep lines on her face spoke of an existence of hard labour. She smiled wide as Valour looked fondly at the elderly figure who had been a nurturing presence during his quest to become a zenturion.

Valour, momentarily breaking from his usual calm demeanour, offered a heartfelt apology. "I'm sorry to interrupt you, Ophelia," he said earnestly, "but we must speak."

Bemused, Ophelia welcomed them into her small yet inviting chamber. The room radiated a warm charm, filled with antique trinkets and well-worn furniture that whispered stories of days gone by. The soft glow of candlelight created an inviting atmosphere of comfort and familiarity. Valour, fully aware of Ophelia's esteemed reputation for her extraordinary skill with riddles, stood before her with eager anticipation. His eyes reflected a blend of respect and curiosity, recognising that she held the key to uncovering the Emerald Crystal. Clearing his throat, he began, "Ophelia, your legendary wisdom in deciphering riddles is well-known. We present to you a riddle of great importance, and I seek your insight to unveil its hidden meaning.'"

A faint smile tugged at the corners of Ophelia's lips, her curiosity piqued by the significance of their visit. Her respect for the young zenturion led her to agree without a second thought. As Max recited the riddle, the old chambermaid sank into an armchair, quietly humming it to herself.

I dwell in the realm where shadows linger, finding refuge in the corners of your mind—a phantom, elusive and sly. I quietly spy. Seek me not in the light; I am the emerald crystal of power guiding you through your flight. What am I, that haunts your every night?

Ophelia halted and regarded Valour with a chilling stare. "DreamStealer is your answer," she murmured, her brow furrowing with deep concern as she shifted uncomfortably in her chair. Her frail hands clutched a steaming cup of herbal elixir, and her voice trembled with urgency and fear as she began her tale. 'Listen closely, dear Valour,' she rasped, 'for I have witnessed the horrors wrought by the DreamStealer, and its evil is beyond compare." Her gaze turned distant, as if she were delving into the depths of her memories. "The DreamStealer is no ordinary spectre; it is a creature of pure wickedness, born from the darkest recesses of the mind. When you close your eyes and surrender to sleep, this abomination creeps into your thoughts, its presence concealed within your subconscious. It is a shapeshifter, a master of disguise, feeding on your deepest fears and insecurities. I watched my beloved uncle transform into an unrecognisable and grotesque figure—an incoherent, wide-eyed fool whose convulsions contorted his once-familiar form into a nightmarish shape."

Silence enveloped the room as Ophelia immersed herself in an authentic ancient legend, dispelling the whispers of myths. Her voice wove a tale of a malevolent entity lurking in the shadowy corners of the dream world. As she spoke, the flickering candle on the table cast unsettling shadows on the walls, amplifying the ominous atmosphere; Mia gasped, entranced by her narrative. "When the DreamStealer invades your dreams, it can assume many forms. It might appear as a loved one, a friend, or a treasured memory. It preys on your vulnerabilities, exploiting your trust, and once it has gained that trust, it distorts the very fabric of your dreams with pure malice." A chilling sensation swept through the room, as if an evil presence had settled among them, causing Ophelia to shudder. The weight of her warnings was not lost on either of them.

"Is there any way to protect ourselves from this evil creature?" Valour finally asked, breaking the silence.

Ophelia's eyes, filled with wisdom, bore into him. "First and foremost, you must cultivate a strong sense of self-awareness. Know your fears and insecurities, for the DreamStealer preys on them. By confronting your inner demons, you can weaken its hold on your mind." She paused, her gaze sweeping over the room. "Somehow, you must recognise the signs if you allow its presence in your dreams. You must wake yourself, for it may be the DreamStealer at work, for it thrives in the darkness of isolation."

"Do you know where this evil dwells?" Valour asked.

"In the land of the Twin Peak Hills, in Verdantis," she affirmed, echoing Max's thoughts. "A place feared by travellers. Cherish your dreams, for they are your most valuable treasures. Protect them fiercely, as they embody the essence of your spirit." Her words carried a weight of foreboding, yet also conveyed a profound message of resilience and hope. The chamber appeared to lighten, and the oppressive atmosphere began to lift.

Valour expressed his gratitude to Ophelia and quietly closed the chamber door behind him, leading them back to their rooms in silence. He was the first to break the heavy silence that hung over them. "I think it would be wise not to mention any of this to the Princess until after tomorrow's funeral," he suggested.

"Where will you be tomorrow?" Mia asked.

"I won't be joining my fellow Zenturions in the guard of honour. Instead, I'll be standing beside my Princess," he replied softly as he slipped into his room.

To lighten the mood, Max turned to his sister with a gentle smile. "Pleasant dreams," he said, hoping to ease the tension.

"Max! That kind of humour isn't funny," she shot back, shutting her door with a decisive slam.

Chapter 16

The Royal Gardens
Valaria

Inside the huge marquee, eight royal Zenturions, facing away from the casket, assumed a solemn parade rest with their heads bowed in reverence. Their long periods of standing in uniform formation demonstrated their commitment to honouring the monarch's legacy. Max rose to find the sky shrouded in grey, a reflection of the day's somber mood. The wall clock chimed with a mournful sound, heralding the sad events to come. After dressing in dark, borrowed clothing, he gazed out his window at the funeral procession that was unfolding. It was graced by royalty and dignitaries from surrounding realms. The palace staff and a large assembly of mourners had gathered to pay tribute to the late King. Black banners adorned every tree, and the scent of fresh flowers blended with the sorrowful atmosphere.

Mia entered the chamber, wearing a borrowed black dress. She exchanged a sorrowful glance with her brother, acknowledging this day of profound mourning and uncertainty. Together, they left the chamber and joined Isaiah, who displayed no trace of a limp. Once brimming with vibrant colours and laughter, the royal gardens now exuded a sombre and muted atmosphere. They walked towards the family mausoleum where the King would rest.

Onlookers watched in solemn silence as a procession of Zenturion guards, resplendent in ceremonial attire, carried the King's casket from the grand marquee to the mausoleum. Their synchronised steps and stoic expressions added to the gravity of the moment. The mournful notes of a violin echoed through the gardens with a haunting melody.

Standing at attention, royal guards lowered their flags in a final salute to their leader as the coffin passed. Mia saw Valour standing by the

Princess, his sorrowful expression tugging at her heartstrings. As her eyes roamed, she noticed the prominent figure of Elder MossFoot, the mayor of Glimmerhavan. Her eyes widened at the regent sent by King Kronos. He stood as tall and formidable as General Titanous, with a muscular build hidden beneath a black armour cape. His face held an animalistic fierceness, accentuated by a cascade of jet-black hair flowing longer than hers.

Soft tolls of mourning bells echoed as the King's casket, adorned in the royal colours of the kingdom, was laid upon a marble pedestal before its final descent into the vault of eternal rest. From the silent crowd, a wave of disturbance grew steadily louder. The gathered mourners began to disperse, forming a pathway for an unexpected and extraordinary visitor whose name was murmured in hushed tones by those who recognised him. The Princess turned, and her bouquet of lilies slipped from her trembling fingers. Max and Mia mirrored her shocked expression as collective gasps reverberated around the domed structure.

Murmurs faded into silence as the titanic figure of General Titanous strode through the open passage. His silent brooding left an indelible impression, and his presence added an extra layer of intrigue to the already sombre proceedings. The General's steel-blue eyes shot Whispering Grass a look that sent shivers down his spine. It was as though the General understood he carried the weight of a dark secret, which implicated him in the tragic loss of the King. Yet, such a thought seemed impossible. The General's presence was a harbinger of impending trouble that whispered danger on the winds, a figurehead known to appear when least expected and vanish when unexpected.

Disregarding Prince Golen, the General halted and gazed down at the Princess. No words were necessary; she could see the sorrow in his eyes. With deliberate steps, he turned and walked towards the vault. Kneeling on one knee, he placed his spear beside him and bowed. Princess Arabella swelled with pride, witnessing the significant tribute the General paid to her father. Lord Elric kept a close watch on the heir apparent. He observed the fleeting expressions that crossed Golen's face at being rebuffed: the initial flash of surprise, quickly followed by a restrained blaze of anger. What struck him most was that beneath the veneer of regal composure lay a tempest of deep-seated emotions threatening to engulf him.

Lord Elric was in a precarious position, torn between his duty to the crown and a moral imperative to stand resolute for the kingdom. He wondered if General Titanous's decision to rebuff the prince was an attempt to recalibrate the court's intricate dynamics. He was still determining whether inciting such a reaction had been prudent or perilous.

General Titanous returned to Princess Arabella's side, where they conversed privately. Whispering Grass strained to eavesdrop on the elusive exchange, so hushed that even the breeze dared not carry their words. With a purposeful nod of admiration to her vigilant bodyguard, the General strode toward Max, Mia, and Isaiah. The assembly's collective gaze fixated on his every step. The General spoke briefly; again, the substance of his words remained concealed. It was undeniably clear that his act of ignoring Prince Golen held profound significance. With a final pivot on his heels, he strode away from the royal gardens, his departure resonating through the gathering like the tolling of a great gong.

In the aftermath of the pivotal encounter, a deafening silence enveloped the onlookers. Prince Golen grappled with the sting of rejection while Lord Elric found himself in a state of uncertainty. He couldn't shake the fear that the General's dramatic snub would alter the course of the realm's fate for generations to come.

Summoned later into the seclusion of Prince Golen's chambers, Whispering Grass listened intently as the prince recounted the unsettling rebuttal from the General. "Your Highness," he began soothingly, "this unexpected turn of events could be an opportunity to understand the undercurrents in the court more clearly."

Golen stared at Whispering Grass with a blend of curiosity and frustration. "What do you mean?"

"Sire, why not confront Princess Arabella and inquire about what transpired with the General? You can find peace of mind only by uncovering the true reason behind his blatant disrespect."

Golen, grappling with his wounded pride, responded, "And what if she refuses to divulge the information?"

"If she does, Your Highness," Whispering Grass warned, "it may suggest that a deep-rooted conspiracy is at work."

Recognising the wise and measured words of his new counsellor, Golen arrived at a decision that would reshape the trajectory of their relationship and cast an indelible shadow on his sister's destiny. "Very well, I will summon Arabella and confront her directly. If she withholds the truth, I will not hesitate to safeguard the crown and the kingdom."

Whispering Grass acknowledged his decision with a subtle bow. In the intricate dance of power, gold, and intrigue that defined the royal court, he was prepared to navigate treacherous waters, no matter the cost.

Chapter 17

In the Princess's chambers, the General's ominous words at the funeral added an extra layer of gravity, casting a shadow over the group's deliberations. Leading the conversation, the Princess expressed her concern: "The General warned that I was enveloped in treachery and urged me to leave the palace. He insisted that I continue our quest until fulfilled; only then will I find solace in my grief." Her voice trembled as she spoke, the weight of her responsibilities pressing heavily upon her shoulders, the flickering candlelight revealing determination, not fear. "I cannot ignore his warning," she continued, her eyes narrowing. "There are those within these walls who conspire against me. The General's words hold truth, but we must tread carefully. Trust is a fragile thing in times like these. We cannot act rashly, or we risk playing into the hands of our enemies."

"Treachery! From which quarters, Your Highness?" Valour inquired, his brow furrowed with concern. The Princess felt the weight of his gaze upon her, urging her to share her thoughts.

"I have a suspicion," she replied, her voice steady yet laced with unease. "The General spoke of shadows lurking in the corners of the court, whispers of discontent. They believe they can manipulate my father's passing to their advantage, sowing discord. The General feared that they might even attempt to turn my allies against me, painting me unfit to be a royal. I cannot allow them to succeed. I need to know who among my court is loyal and who is not. We must root out this treachery before it festers. But tell me, what did the General say to you, Max?"

"He commended our efforts in securing two of the five crystals," Max remarked. "I told him we now knew of the third's whereabouts," he inadvertently revealed.

Arabella's face tightened with annoyance at the revelation. "Why was this kept from me until now?" she questioned, her tone sharp.

Valour's words were measured and thoughtful. "We chose not to burden you until you had time to reflect on your loss, Your Highness." Their discussion was interrupted by a gentle yet persistent tap on the door.

Following the Princess's directive, a maid entered the chamber, her face revealing surprise at the assembly in the room. "The Prince wishes for you to join him in his chamber," she conveyed, bowing as she exited.

Arabella and Valour exchanged a concerned glance. The sudden summons and the ominous warnings of betrayal cast a chilling pall between them. "I sense a brewing storm," Arabella remarked, anxiety etched across her face. "Please remain here until I return. I need to understand what you know about the third crystal."

Moving through the corridors toward her brother's chamber, a disquieting premonition of the impending betrayal continued to unnerve Arabella. Could Whispering Grass be the clandestine source of such betrayal? The kingdom's fate now rested as an almost overwhelming burden upon her shoulders, casting a weight on her every stride. Arabella couldn't shake the nagging feeling about her brother's self-proclaimed counsellor. She pondered the depths of deception by Whispering Grass. Yet, she acknowledged in her heart that she already held the answer. Entering Golen's chamber, she was glad her brother was alone, but the air felt charged with unresolved tension. Golen's face was etched with an intensity she had never before encountered.

Arabella, keeping her composure, met her brother's gaze. "Golen," she replied, her voice laced with defiance, "I cannot explain why the General chose to disregard you, but I will not reveal the details of my conversation with him. Any private discussion is built on trust and confidentiality."

Golen's anger surged as his sister denied his request. He had foolishly counted on her to prioritise family loyalty over everything else. Through gritted teeth, he declared, "Arabella, your loyalty should be to me and the kingdom, not to others, like the humans you brought to dine at my table."

"My loyalty is indeed to the kingdom but also to the principles of trust and honesty. I cannot betray the confidence of those who confide in me, even for you, brother!" The confrontation had reached its boiling point, pushing Golen to the edge of his patience and flooding him with a torrent of frustration. In this tumultuous moment, he made a decision that would profoundly alter the trajectory of their relationship and cast an indelible shadow on his sister's destiny.

"Arabella," he declared, his voice carrying the weight of finality, "should you persist in collaborating with others to jeopardise the welfare of your brother or the kingdom, you leave me with no choice but to declare your exile from Valaria."

An oppressive silence descended upon the room as Arabella's eyes widened in shock. Banishment, an irreversible punishment, had never been invoked in the kingdom. It was a decree that tore at the very fabric of their unity. Tears welled in her eyes, but she refused to let them fall. Always a believer in honour and trust, she could not compromise them, not even for family. With a heavy heart and a regal dignity that remained unshaken, she turned and left the chamber, her banishment sealed by her refusal to betray her principles.

Golen's anger lingered like smouldering embers. His sister's expulsion was a drastic measure. In that fleeting moment, he comprehended the genuine price of power and the sacrifices it required.

The banishment weighed on Arabella like an unyielding force, pulling at the very core of her being. She carried a heavy heart as she steeled herself to disclose the news to her friends. She anticipated the shock mirrored in their eyes when she revealed her brother's decision. "I have been banished," she whispered, her voice carrying profound sadness and resignation. Mia gasped as she elaborated on the reasons behind her exile, unable to hide her dismay. Tears welled in her eyes, reflecting even more despair on the Princess's face.

Despite his disbelief, Valour channelled his aggression into persistence. "I shall resign from my position as a Zenturion forthwith. Your Highness, my loyalty is devoted to you and our noble cause!" he declared.

"Thank you, Valour," she replied with admiration but poignant regret. "I feel embarrassed admitting that I wish my brother had a fraction of your integrity." Questions and uncertainties flooded her mind. Accustomed to a life of privilege and nobility, the possibility of exile left her feeling vulnerable and adrift. Her voice tinged with concern. "Where would I go after our task is complete?"

Isaiah offered a glimmer of optimism. "I am certain Chief Elder will offer sanctuary if needed," he assured, attempting to provide solace. "He, like us, will not abandon you in this unjust moment of need."

"Your comforting words mean a great deal, Isaiah," the Princess expressed, clasping a cherished family heirloom. "I have enough jewellery to sustain me for now. However, beyond that, the path of my existence is uncertain. I'll summon Lord Elric for his wise counsel but away from prying eyes. Perhaps he can navigate me through this dark period. But first, enlighten me about all you know regarding the next crystal."

Arabella listened, her attention rapt as Valour shared the information they had gleaned from the chambermaid. Her unease intensified as Valour delved into the entity known as the DreamStealer in the province of Volcanis. The Princess absorbed each detail of this thing's ability to drain cherished memories and desires, leaving an eerie void filled with emptiness. The sheer horror of such power made her shudder with dread.

In the stillness of the night, the Princess moved warily through the gardens to her clandestine meeting with Lord Elric. She approached the bench where her brother and Whispering Grass had forged their pact for gold. Seated against the cool stone, she peered into the darkness, her mind awash with thoughts, yet amid the tangible unease, her composure endured. An imposing figure drew near, his silhouette cutting a striking presence against the fading light. Lord Elric approached the bench, and a flicker of hope ignited. He settled beside her, and their eyes met, hers brimming with deep respect. With a heavy sigh that hinted at unspoken burdens, he began the conversation that would alter their fates.

"Your Highness, I deeply regret the prince's decision to ostracise you from Valaria. Such a drastic action will have consequences that extend far beyond our realm." Taking a moment to collect his thoughts, Lord Elric knew it was time to disclose the troubling information his spies had unearthed. Leaning in closer, he lowered his voice to a conspiratorial whisper. "Princess, my spies have uncovered a conspiracy driven by dark forces that your brother has chosen to ignore."

"Does this connection extend beyond Whispering Grass?" she asked, suspicion dawning that the crystals she sought were at the heart of the conspiracy.

Lord Elric nodded. "Yes, it involves other untrustworthy figures: Admiral Malice Malware and King Kronos of Drakonia," he replied. "King Kronos has always been considered a threat. If your brother aligns with Kronos and Malware, it will create an unbeatable alliance poised to engage and triumph in war."

Arabella's eyes widened with horror. She had known that her quest would bring challenges, but the revelation of war pierced the core of her royal responsibilities. "Please continue," she said sadly.

"The attack orchestrated by Malice Malware on the Great White Clock and its ecosystem acted as a strategic decoy, diverting attention from a more critical reality. Embedded within Drakonia, my spies have put themselves at significant risk to deliver intelligence on the escalation of weaponry and troop deployments. A war that we all knew would come, but not so soon. Our only hope is to delay the inevitable. In the Land of Arbitration, the Drakonians have won so many concessions—due to this fear. King Kronos and Malice Malware believed you would fail in your quest. Given the ecological disasters affecting the provinces, they asserted that they could confidently advance across the borders with minimal opposition."

"I don't understand," she said, her brow furrowed in confusion. "How could they possibly hope to exist, let alone thrive, if the ecological system collapses?"

"That's an excellent question," he replied, his voice tinged with frustration. "It has baffled me and my spies alike. Yet, I assure you, King Kronos and Malice Malware are far from foolish. They possess a cunning that defies our understanding, and their plans may be more intricate than we imagine. Whispering Grass has undoubtedly informed them of your accomplishments thus far. Hence, I must warn you to be wary of assassins lurking in the shadows. I'm afraid your mission has now taken on an even greater danger and responsibility."

The Princess sighed heavily, the news of assassins settling over her like a dark cloud. Fear and anger churned within her, mingling with a sense of betrayal. The idea of such treachery lurking so close to home filled her with a sense of dread making it hard to trust even those she once considered allies. Yet, amidst the turmoil, a spark of determination ignited. She would not be a victim. With resolve in her eyes, she posed a direct question, ready to face the threat head-on. "Do you believe Whispering Grass played a role in my father's passing?"

"Yes, I do," he replied frankly, a deep sadness in his tone. "But how eludes me. No one would be foolish enough to admit to regicide."

Arabella dropped her gaze and vowed, "Should I find this to be true, I will seek justice and vengeance for my father using no other hand but my own."

Lord Elric consoled her by patting her leg. "I didn't intend to mislead you when you asked about your father's passing upon your arrival. I was concerned solely for your safety."

The Princess placed her hand on top of the sturdy man's hand. "Thank you for being you, Lord Elric."

"No, Your Highness, it is for me to express my gratitude. I truly believe you've shown remarkable courage in the face of adversity, undertaking a quest that few could fathom at such a young age," he replied with genuine humility.

Arabella planted a tender kiss on his cheek before rising from her seat. "Tomorrow at first light, we embark on our journey to secure the third crystal," she stated with a newfound purpose. Lord Elric's farewell smile bore sorrow as he watched her retreating figure disappear into the darkness. He nurtured the hope that their conversation had laid the groundwork for potentially influencing the destiny of their kingdom in the dire times ahead.

Whispering Grass awoke to the news that Princess Arabella and her companions had departed the palace before dawn. Taking care to check his surroundings, he followed his regular routine and headed toward the edge of the city centre. In a shadowy alley, he knocked on the side entrance of an inconspicuous shop owned by the spy known in Malice Malware's circles as the candlestick maker.

With sharp, observant eyes that missed nothing, the slender figure answered. The candlestick maker exuded a fierce determination in his two professions. He crafted candles of remarkable design and quality, which decorated the homes of both the nobility and everyday zenizens. These deliveries provided an ideal disguise, granting him access to the residences of the city's elite, where he could quietly eavesdrop on conversations of interest. With a brisk nod, the candlestick maker recognised Whispering Grass's unexpected presence and silently ushered him inside. He looked through a kaleidoscope peephole that provided a view of the front entrance to his workshop and the alleyway outside, ensuring he wasn't being followed. He guided Whispering Grass through the rear rooms to the birdcage in the backyard.

The WhisperWing Couriers, crucial for discreet communications, emitted a subtle, high-frequency sound that helped them create a mental map of their environment. They accurately assessed wind speed and direction, identified object locations, and detected potential threats, such as archers preparing to launch their arrows. Their instincts allowed them to adjust their speed and trajectory, enabling them to avoid incoming projectiles with unparalleled skill.

Whispering Grass reviewed the response to his earlier communication with Malice Malware, having learned that the Princess and her companions had obtained two of the five Crystals of Time. The admiral's order was clear: eliminate the humans. He felt relieved that this message had arrived after their departure, as carrying out the directive would have posed considerable challenges. He composed a reply and watched as the candle stick maker attached the small, sealed cylinder to the courier's leg. A smile graced his lips as he observed it taking flight. Exiting the shop, his large feet glided over the cobblestones on his return to the palace. He rehearsed the message he had sent.

Princess Arabella, exiled from Valaria, departed at first light with the humans. No other royal province should offer her refuge. Banishment would mark her relinquishment of royal status.

Whispering Grass smiled. He understood precisely how Malice Malware would interpret the message 'relinquishment of royal status' and his actions upon receiving it.

Chapter 18

Twin Peak Hills
Verdantis

Upon leaving the Valarian palace, they travelled through vast stretches of farmland and undulating hills that seemed to go on forever, lacking any notable natural wonders or obstacles. The sun hung low in the sky, casting a golden hue over the fields, but the beauty of the landscape did little to ease the tension in their hearts. As they entered Verdantis, Valour hoped the Twin Peak Hills would be nearby, sparing them a long journey.

Though the Crystals of Time pointed the way to the DreamStealer, a deeper understanding of where this elusive entity might strike relied on the knowledge of a villager, who could potentially reveal other secrets about the DreamStealer and guide them through the treacherous path ahead. With renewed determination, they quickened their pace, eager to uncover the hidden truths of Verdantis.

At night, they pitched their camp on the fringe of a dense forest; its verdant canopy provided a natural shield against unforeseen downpours. Despite Valour and Isaiah's proposal to set up camp earlier, the princess insisted on pressing ahead. The reasoning behind her insistence on pushing the group to their limits soon came to light. Gathered around the crackling campfire, she exposed the truth regarding the escalating peril they faced. Valour's grasp tightened on the hilt of his sword as he processed the conspiracy ensnaring his beloved king, the looming threat of war and assassins.

The dancing flames of the fire cast shifting shadows across their faces as they absorbed the gravity of their situation and the emotional strain it would impose if they failed. Isaiah felt profound respect and admiration for the princess, given the immense pressure she handled in such a short space of time. In her eyes, he didn't just see a courageous young princess; he witnessed the makings of a queen. Her determination and indomitable spirit in the face of such adversity painted a portrait of leadership and resilience that stirred his heart. It was as though destiny had chosen her to navigate Cyberia through the darkest times.

"How King Kronos and Malice Malware possess the extraordinary ability to heal the shattered ecosystem is of yet, no consequence. Our mission continues unchanged," Arabella remarked. "Our victories have taken Malice Malware and King Kronos by surprise. Complete success would compel them to push back their war plans for at least a Dion or more."

Mia voiced her concern. "I recognise the threat from Malice Malware, but Max and I know nothing about King Kronos, let alone horrible assassins." The princess invited Valour to continue, confident that he could explain in more detail about Drakonia, their king, and the assassins.

Valour's words heightened the mounting tension. "King Kronos is a towering figure whose imposing presence reflects in his physical appearance. His skin is as tough as dragon scales, a trait inherited from his Drakonian lineage. His eyes, the colour of molten gold, gleam with an intensity that can strike fear into the hearts of even the bravest warriors. His flowing hair is as black as coal, cascading down his broad shoulders like a waterfall of darkness. His words are laced with disdain for those he deems inferior, and he rarely bends his will to the desires of others. This arrogance stems from a long line of rulers who have never known defeat.

His standing army, beasts of a hybrid race, combines the features of Kronos and other creatures. They stand shy of their leader's height, boasting impressive robustness and heavily sculpted muscles. Each possesses distinctive characteristics, bearing their lineage. Some have raging bull horns, while others boast the wings of fearsome dragons. Their skin is covered in various scales, feathers, or fur, depending on their ancestral connection. Despite their diverse appearances, they share a commonality in loyalty to King Kronos. Their allegiance to their ruler is unbreakable, and they follow his orders without question. They are an army of relentless warriors ready to defend their realm at any cost."

Valour's words gripped Max and Mia, their focus entirely ensnared. The sudden crackle of a burning twig ejecting itself from the fire startled them both. "I must add," Valour said, "everything I recounted I learned at a Zenturion academy."

"Judging by how effortlessly you recited it all," Isaiah said, "I'd venture to say you were at the top of your class."

Valour smiled. "I should have said 'ingrained,' by order of my late King Osred."

Isaiah looked at the princess and reflected. "A wise and thought-provoking father and king who undoubtedly gazed into the face of the future." Aware of the formidable power of the Drakonians, Isaiah's focus remained firmly anchored in the present, and he steered the conversation back to what needed to be addressed. "Assassins! If you were to put yourself in either King Kronos or Malice Malware's position, what do you believe their next move would be?"

"The assassins will track us over great distances, but I doubt they would be of Drakonian lineage. The distinctive appearance of a Drakonian would be in our favour. They will likely select other operatives highly skilled in their respective fields. Therefore, we must exercise caution to avoid attracting unwanted attention."

Isaiah nodded in agreement, recognising the wisdom in Valour's words. Each of had a sharp awareness of their circumstances, and their insights would be vital for the challenges ahead. "May I offer a thought?" he asked.

"Please do, Isaiah. Your input is valued," the princess replied, her tone inviting.

"Valour mentioned discretion. We must shy away from villages or towns. The WhiteTails would give us away to our pursuers. The duty of collecting provisions and acquiring information about the elusive DreamStealer from villagers must fall upon me. Who would take notice of a solitary traveller and a horse?"

"Isaiah is correct, Your Highness," Valour said.

"I concur with my wise counsel," she replied with a knowing smile. She then turned her attention to the siblings. "You have been rather quiet. Do you have any thoughts to share?"

"I do," said Max. "If we encounter unknown company, we shouldn't address you as 'Your Highness' or 'Princess,' We could opt for a shorter version of your name, like Bella. It's similar and easy to remember. Only if the need arises," he assured.

The princess's eyes sparkled with enthusiasm. "Bella! I quite like it," she exclaimed, breaking into laughter. Considering the immense pressure she had been under, it had been quite some time since Valour had seen her laugh so freely. Witnessing it once more filled his heart with a comforting warmth.

Isaiah fixed his gaze on the flickering flames. "Together, we will grow stronger," he asserted. "We're a team, and with that unity, we can overcome any obstacle or foe!"

The WhiteTails surged with renewed energy as they set out early in the morning. By late afternoon, having covered a significant distance, they emerged from an olive grove. The grassy slopes, adorned with vibrant wildflowers, painted a deceptively serene picture. Yet beneath this picturesque facade lay an uneven and treacherous terrain, concealing hidden pitfalls that could easily trap the unwary. Once again, they dismounted, wary of the ground threatening their footing. With ample provisions, including fruits foraged from the land, they reached Verdantis within the timeframe Valour had predicted. As they skirted around villages and towns, they understood that their success now depended on Isaiah's ability to gather vital information at the next settlement they encountered.

Chapter 19

The Royal Palace
Valaria

Cloaked in the shadows of night, Whispering Grass seized the opportunity to enter Princess Arabella's chambers while the guards made their rounds. He lit a pocket candle, its flickering light illuminating the space. His attention was drawn to her wardrobe as he listened intently for any sounds outside the door. With a careful touch, he explored her footwear collection, his heart racing as he found the shoes she had worn the night they first met. Crafted from the finest cobalt-blue silk and embellished with silver embroidery, they sparkled like moonlight on a still lake.

Whispering Grass tucked the precious shoes beneath his cloak, his heart racing as he pressed his ear against the door. Muffled footsteps echoed in the silence, then faded as the guards continued their patrol. Timing his escape perfectly, he waited for the last sounds to dissipate before turning the handle and slipping back into the corridor. His movements were as quiet as the night itself, gliding stealthily away from the guards, each step bringing him closer to the safety of his chamber.

His first opportunity to leave the palace came when the sun peaked. The candlestick maker unlocked the alley door, checked the spy hole, and guided him down a dimly lit spiral staircase leading to the cellar. Four shadowy figures, cloaked in dark attire, stood bathed in candlelight. They seemed to come from a realm steeped in darkness and mystery. An air of sinister danger clung to them, but their unsettling, piercing gazes disturbed Whispering Grass the most. It felt as if they could peer into the depths of his soul, exposing his secrets for all to see.

The giant assassin, towering over the others, dominated the scene with a formidable presence. His muscular, imposing physique radiated immense physical power. Clad in dark, unassuming clothing, his broad shoulders and robust frame exuded an unmistakable air of authority. In stark contrast, the trio of average-height assassins kept their faces hidden beneath hoods, blending seamlessly into the shadows to conceal their identities yet appearing equally dangerous.

The figures suggested a well-coordinated team. Like shards of cold steel, their eyes glittered in the dim candlelight, emanating an unsettling intensity. An imposing companion was resting alongside one of the assassins—an elegant fawn-coloured SablePaw hound. With its sleek coat and amber eyes, the hound possessed attributes for detecting the faintest scents, earning its reputation as the most potent detector in all of Cyberia. The hound's sensitive nose twitched as it breathed in the presence of Whispering Grass.

The atmosphere in the cellar grew tense as the four assassins and the SablePaw watched him with unwavering intensity. Whispering Grass unfurled his cloak, revealing a sealed bag. The hound's nostrils flared as he opened the bag, its amber eyes narrowing in sharp focus on the princess's shoes. A deep growl vibrated in its throat as it detected the scent needed to pinpoint Princess Arabella's location. Now, Whispering Grass understood why his last message instructed him to retrieve an item of Princess Arabella's clothing. He sealed the bag and handed it to the leader of the four assassins. As the fearsome figures departed, he stood back, exhilarated by the imminent danger awaiting the princess and the humans. Whether it was just his perception, he couldn't shake the feeling that the hound seemed hungry and mistreated.

Whispering Grass was taken aback by the swift barrage of messages as the candlestick maker passed him another note from Malice Malware. It revealed two individuals from the admiral's inner circle were planning to visit the palace. The message emphasised the need for him to adhere closely to their instructions. As he returned to the palace, his mind was preoccupied with the cryptic message that lingered long into the night. In the early morning light, a gentle knock on his door roused him from sleep. After being informed of visitors, he hurriedly dressed, to meet the expected callers outside in the royal gardens, where they could avoid unwanted attention.

Slade and Scarlet, the Siren of Deception, stood poised for their encounter near Swan Island. The stunning cobalt-blue lake stretched before them, its surface a perfect mirror reflecting the swans that glided effortlessly across the water. Their snowy feathers sparkled in the sunlight, and their graceful necks swayed with the gentle breeze. Greeting and listening, Whispering Grass absorbed the unfolding narrative along the peaceful shores—a war was on the horizon. If Scarlet could charm Prince Golen before his coronation, her persuasive powers would be essential in uniting him with Malice Malware and King Kronos of Drakonia.

Whispering Grass pioneered his innermost thoughts to Scarlet, weaving webs of logic and intrigue to help convince Golen of war. He assured that power, ambition, and potential greatness were ideals appealing to Golen's aspirations. Scarlet's challenge was to artfully depict Lord Elric as a figure motivated by personal gain, self-interest, and a deep undercurrent of allegiance with Princess Arabella.

With an informal dinner planned for that evening, Prince Golen showed little interest in extending invitations to other guests. However, after hearing Whispering Grass's portrayal of Scarlet's beauty, his perspective changed significantly, leading him to reconsider and extend invitations.

Golen and his distinguished guests gathered for dinner, bathed in the soft glow of twilight. As Slade and Scarlet made their entrance, Whispering Grass stepped forward to introduce them. With a voice as smooth as a gentle evening breeze, he bowed gracefully to Scarlet and presented Slade as her loyal guardian. Scarlet's hair, flowing like spun gold with hints of silver and platinum, was elegantly arranged in a regal bun. Her eyes, reminiscent of the deepest ocean gems, sparkled with an enchanting allure. Clad in a gown that exuded grace and charm, she performed a graceful curtsy to Golen, instantly captivating the room and becoming the undeniable highlight of the evening.

Captivated by her presence, Golen found it impossible to avert his gaze from Scarlet, seated directly across the table. Each time their eyes connected, she showed him a smile that left him breathless and others envious. Whispering Grass observed keenly, realising that this was the moment he had patiently awaited—a chance to manipulate the threads of fate for his gain, filling him with subtle, empathic satisfaction. With a heart as calculating as his greed, he had already contemplated his next move to orchestrate a clandestine meeting involving Scarlet and Golen.

The future monarch required more than just infatuation with her beauty; he needed to be utterly captivated by her wisdom and persuasive arguments. Having captured Golen's interest, he purposefully chose his moment: "Your Highness, if my eyes do not deceive me, it seems your presence completely entrances Scarlet. If I may be bold, I could help organise a private meeting, perhaps a leisurely walk or an encounter under a tree's shade on Swan Island." He left the temptation lingering, cautious not to overexert too much of himself. Subtlety was critical in the delicate choreography of romance.

Smitten, Golen beamed with an eager smile of approval. A satisfied grin lingered on his lips as he watched the prince's quick and enthusiastic agreement. Whispering Grass proposed a romantic boating trip to Swan Island, where he could further influence the unfolding events as a chaperone. His amusement grew as Golen, eyes shining with anticipation, requested a hamper filled with the finest delicacies and exquisite wines for their journey. Little did the prince realise that Whispering Grass had already foreseen and arranged for such desires.

Chapter 20

Swan Island

Piloting the slender rowboat through tranquil waters with his two passengers, Whispering Grass marvelled at the moment he thought would never come. The glistening lake mirrored the azure sky, setting the stage for a romantic escapade to the idyllic Island. Scarlet's hand dangled in the water, allowing the ripples to dance around her fingers. Her eyes, sparkling like stars, led her to exclaim, "Your Highness, you are indeed fortunate to witness such mesmerising beauty, not only within the peaceful walls of your palace but also in the wonders of the royal gardens."

Inspired and bewitched by her words, Golen spoke with a soft smile. "Indeed," he began, his voice filled with genuine warmth, "it is your beauty that enriches the brilliance of everything I see, sparking a sweet energy within my heart." This heartfelt remark, delivered so early into their outing, was music to the ears of Whispering Grass. As the boat glided toward the Island, it became clear that the journey had crafted a faux romance, where the natural beauty of the surroundings perfectly mirrored the overflowing affection from the prince for Scarlet the Deceitful.

Indulging in a sumptuous feast and savouring the finest wines, Whispering Grass expressed his desire to explore the charming confines of the Island. "Your company has been a delight, but the allure of this Island deeply moves me. It beckons for exploration, or it will forever remain a lasting regret. Would you permit me to depart for a while to explore these peaceful surroundings?" he proposed, offering a respectful bow, which Golen eagerly accepted. Allowing them this privacy, Whispering Grass wandered the winding pathways, discreetly observing from a distance. Delight engulfed him as they seemed to exchange significant moments.

Scarlet spoke with heartless empathy and feigned sincerity as she addressed the prince amidst his grief. "Your Highness, please accept my deepest condolences. Words fail to convey the depth of sorrow I feel for the loss of your father. His absence leaves a profound void, echoing throughout your kingdom and Cyberia. May his soul find eternal peace in the dimensions beyond." Pausing briefly to select her words, she continued, "I understand if now may not be the most opportune moment to discuss such matters, and forgive me if my request seems presumptuous, but it would be an incredible honour if you would allow me to witness your anointment as king. To be present for such a significant occasion would be an unmatched privilege. Your leadership is a beacon of hope in these uncertain times." Her gaze fixed earnestly upon him as she awaited the answer.

Scarlet's words elicited a blend of gratitude in Golen's voice. "Lady Scarlet, your words are soothing to my wounded heart. I am profoundly grateful for your kindness and condolences during this challenging period. Your presence would not be perceived as presumptuous but rather as a heartfelt and warmly welcomed gesture of support during this pivotal transition." A warm smile graced his lips as he concluded, "I would be deeply honoured to have you near my side on this momentous occasion. Your wisdom and counsel will prove invaluable as I enter this new role. Your presence alone has already evoked a much-needed smile," he remarked.

Scarlet deftly guided the conversation toward Arbitration land. With subtle finesse, she skillfully directed the discourse to a point where the prince, captivated by her insights, listened to her opinion on governance matters. Falling into her cleverly laid trap and seizing the moment, she articulated her perspective, describing the arbitrators as dictators who utilised that authority to confront and challenge those who held sway, like Valaria—all in the pursuit of self-protection.

Scarlet exuded an air of strategic brilliance as she framed the act of 'bullying the powerful for the sake of the weak' as an unjust means of achieving an equitable rule. Her words carried a weight of intellect and cunning, leaving the unsuspecting Golen impressed with her manipulative prowess. With a growing sense of intrigue, the prince felt compelled to delve further into Scarlet's distinctive and thought-provoking vision of reshaping the flawed dynamics in Arbitration Land. His curiosity drew him deeper into the unfolding drama.

Whispering Grass returned from his solitary stroll along the tranquil island shores. Scarlet's welcoming smile held the subtlety of their successful scheme. With the prince potentially trapped, they had time to persuade him to join forces with King Kronos and Malice Malware. Their shared vision for Valaria was tantalisingly close and set for the delicate and strategic negotiations that would ultimately mould the destiny of Cyberia as the final act of their manipulation drew near.

Chapter 21

Twin Peak Hills
Verdantis

Isaiah retraced his steps to the village they had passed. It marked his third visit to a village where he was trying to gather information about the DreamStealer. Bathed in stretched shadows and clusters of small trees, the inhabitants of Briarfield village observed the stranger with cautious interest as Isaiah rode into their midst. Seeking refuge in an inn characterised by wooden beams and low ceilings, the vibrant atmosphere of patrons chatting and mugs clinking quieted as he found himself at a table and waited for serving. Overcoming their initial reluctance, the villagers soon shared insights into the village's history and unique customs with the intriguing-looking visitor.

Isaiah sparked a discussion about legends and myths. His curiosity was piqued by tales of an elderly outcast purportedly ensnared by the DreamStealer dwelling on the outskirts of the neighbouring village. Over sips of frothy ale, the villagers shared fragments of information, as Isaiah unearthed the recluse's name—Corbin Aldhelm—and his eccentric way of life, frequently wandering into the woods in search of herbs and peculiar trinkets. Grateful for the information, Isaiah returned to their overnight campsite.

The evening stars glittered like countless diamonds against the darkness as Isaiah dismounted to join the group around the campfire. His expression bore a mixture of reward and concern. "I've learned of an elderly zenizen who goes by the name Corbin Aldhelm, residing in a rural area in the neighbouring village," he relayed, stooping to coax the dwindling flames with a stick. He is known as the one who has endured the loss of his family to the DreamStealer. He lives in solitude, carrying the burden of his sorrow. This was the only information

I could gather. I believe it wise to uncover more about Corbin Aldhelm ," he added. "We should reach his region when the sun reaches its zenith. .

"Thank you, Isaiah," acknowledged the Princess with gratitude. "The mention of Corbin Aldhelm offers a glimmer of hope amidst the uncertainty."

Setting out on their journey at first light, they forged ahead until, at last, luck was on their side; they stumbled upon the cottage of Corbin Aldhelm—an old dwelling in the thick underbrush. Max thought the dilapidated building presented a pitfall scene, its thatched roof drooping under the weight of vines draped in moss and ivy. Dark and grimy windows hinted at a life in solitude. The garden, a tangled maze of weeds and overgrown bushes, added to the overall sight of neglect.

The front door creaked on its hinges as Valour pushed it open, revealing a sad figure slumped in a rocking chair. Seeing nothing untoward, he beckoned the others to join him inside. Corbin Aldhelm's eyes held a distant expression as he observed the strangers, treating them like unwelcome ghosts passing through. His sorrowful appearance cast a sombre mood. Princess Arabella revealed the purpose of their visit, carefully explaining their quest for the crystal they sought, and gently pressed him for any insights he might have regarding the DreamStealer and its whereabouts.

Corbin Aldhelm slowly understood that the figures before him were not apparitions, and stammered as he spoke, his words a disjointed jumble of thoughts. Long estranged from society and haunted by his demons, it was clear that he struggled to communicate. Earning his trust, the Princess gently clasped his hand, a sensation of comfort he had thought long lost, and tears welled in his eyes. After some tender coaxing, he took a swig from a frosted-coloured bottle, its contents helping to steady his speech pattern. His words gradually became meaningful as he began to share his story, piecing together the fragments of his life and the secrets he held.

"You… mentioned an emerald crystal," he began. "I can vividly recall a spectrum of colours, ranging from a vibrant, almost translucent green to a delicate hint of blue. This memory is embodied in my mind. When I emerged from the depths of my unsettling nightmare—a tale I shan't recount—the light emanated from the hollow of a tree, casting a glow unlike any other. Its colossal trunk displayed a fusion of mossy greens and earthy browns, forming an almost camouflage-like pattern against the forest backdrop. Its twisted branches bore leaves that shimmered with an inner luminosity. From its roots to its tip, it appeared to bathe in the glow of this emerald light, a place where secrets you seek might unfold."

Princess Arabella questioned, "We've heard tales of the DreamStealer, but Corbin, you hold a first-hand account. While I respect your hesitation to share, we've come to confront this demon. Your assistance is crucial. Please help us shed light on the challenges we're about to face." Amid his soul-searching, the Princess's eyes, reflecting genuine honesty, caused Corbin Aldhelm to experience a change of heart to his misfortune. He took another swig from his bottle.

"The DreamStealer is a creature shrouded in darkness and mysteries, an ethereal entity whose presence defies the confines of our realm. I believe it exists solely to feed on the most priceless treasures—the hopes and dreams of those who dare to sleep in its vicinity. I lived a quiet life with my wife, Eliza, and our grown son, Tarrant. On this fateful evening, we decided to venture for a night's camp at the Twin Peaks. We had heard of the legend surrounding the DreamStealer, but I foolishly called it what I believed it was—a falsehood. We made a campsite, and the stars above gleamed unnaturally. While we slept, the DreamStealer emerged from its depths, irresistibly drawn to my family's dreams like a moth to a flame. It stealthily pilfered fragments of our souls. We were leaving in its wake a haunting sense of emptiness and despair.

At sunrise, I awoke to find Eliza and Tarrant transformed, their spirits broken. Once full of love and laughter, my wife was now an empty shell, her eyes hollow and distant. Tarrant had aged far beyond his 30 dions. His hair had turned white and he was haunted by different nightmares that perpetually disturbed his sleep. The anguish that overtook Eliza was heart-wrenching. She wept endlessly, her words a lament for the good dreams she could no longer recall. She spoke of forgotten ambitions and lost desires, and as the glitchmarks turned into splintrills, her existence became a fading echo. Despite my attempts to find answers and cure our affliction, the surrounding villages remained silent. It was as if they had become complicit in the DreamStealer's wickedness, afraid to speak its name or acknowledge its existence.

Unable to bear the torment any longer, Eliza vanished, leaving only an empty bed and my shattered heart in her wake. I searched high and low, but to no avail. Left alone to care for my son, I watched as he descended into a heart-wrenching figure. Driven by desperation, Tarrant sought refuge in wine, finding temporary relief from the horrors that plagued him. In the end, however, it was the very drink that led to his early demise.

"I'm truly sorry," said the Princess, "I cannot imagine the pain and anguish you endured."

"Your eyes radiate a compassion surpassing that of any villager," he replied sadly.

"Did you ever see or catch sight of this horrendous being?" she asked.

Corbin shuddered as he nodded. "It emerged as a shadowy mist, gradually morphing into the horrifying form of a ghoul that wore a grotesque, eerie grin as if savouring the fear it instilled. Its face is a mask of terror adorned with razor-sharp, needle-like teeth. Its eyes emitted a crimson glow akin to smouldering embers in the abyss. Its long, bony fingers extended, adorned with gnarled, claw-like nails, poised to snatch. Inexplicable dread would wash over anyone unfortunate enough to encounter this entity."

"Why did it affect your family so much more than you?" asked Max.

"It was my resilience to find a cure. The focus required to unearth a remedy while battling this demon in my mind was unparalleled."

"Cure?" asked Mia.

"I am an herbalist who has mastered crafting remedies for many afflictions. This tradition has been passed down through my family for generations. The intensity of focus required to discover a cure while grappling with the inner demon that plagued my mind was a plague beyond compare." He raised the bottled potion from which he had drank. “Regrettably, when I eventually crafted a potion that momentarily alleviates the affliction, it had reached a point where it could no longer save my son.”

“Is there a weakness we could exploit to rid us of this thing?” Valour asked.

Corbin Aldhelm sucked in a long intake of breath before answering. “While taking the potion to combat my dreams, I envisioned mirrors capable of reflecting the attack onto the ghoul.” He rose unsteadily from his chair. “Join me.”

Opening the door to his bedroom, he revealed an assortment of mirrors of various shapes and sizes surrounding his bed. “I believe these can offer protection, but I haven’t the courage to return to the tree and try, fearing it will completely consume my soul. I urge you to take everything. I could never defeat the DreamStealer by myself. Perhaps you can restore the smile I haven’t held in Dions and return the joy I’ve lost. That will be a clear sign of my freedom. You’ll need the potion, but only to be used if someone falls prey to the ghoul.”

“Anything else?” asked Valour.

“If you have no axe, take mine. You will need it to open the hollow to climb inside the tree to remove the crystal.”

“Why can’t we open the hollow while we’re wide awake to take the crystal?” asked Max.

“Because the DreamStealer would remain undefeated and pursue those who possessed the crystal,” he replied firmly.

“How far is this tree from here?” Isaiah asked.

“You can reach the peaks before nightfall. I’ll guide you along the quickest route as far as I dare possible.”

A particular mirror caught Max’s eye. Etched onto the glass was a unique cross, emitting an aura of profound significance that softly shimmered in the room’s dim light. Its design radiated a sense of protection and fortitude. He felt an unexplainable connection to it and claimed the cross-etched mirror as his own. Valour opted for a rectangular mirror with a robust wooden handle, effortlessly slinging it over his shoulder.

Isaiah shrugged and remarked about an old carriage he spotted outside. "If it holds together, I'll harness your carriage to my horse to carry the two larger mirrors."

Sharing the saddle, Corbin clung to Isaiah's as his horse surged forward. The two crystals continued to act as guiding beacons. Both aligned seamlessly with Corbin's direction. Their journey was short and uneventful as they arrived at their destination: the foot of Twin Peaks. Corbin Aldhelm dismounted, weariness evident in his eyes as he extended his best wishes to the group before he began his long trek back home.

Soon, a colossal tree came into view, exactly as Corbin had described. Its branches stretched like eerie, dark limbs, almost seeming to lure unwary travellers from the flat land around it. Elongated shadows cloaked the tree's surroundings as the sun descended below the horizon. What truly added to its sinister aura was the hollow at its centre—the entrance to the realm of the DreamStealer. With intense wariness, they dismounted to set up camp before nightfall.

Isaiah lit a campfire as dusk fell into darkness—a pulsating emerald glow emitted from the hollow within the tree. Isaiah and Valour exchanged a meaningful glance as if the lurking entity was keenly aware of their presence. Mia and the Princess sat anxiously beside each other while Max positioned himself between Valour and Isaiah. In stark contrast to their purpose, they engaged in conversation to stave away sleep. Exhaustion gradually eclipsed their fears as tiredness began to wage its impending battle.

Surprisingly, Isaiah's eyelids grew heavy first, eventually closing as he succumbed to the relentless pull of sleep. Isaiah's dream materialized —a haunting image of his childhood shrouded in darkness.

A profound sense of unease consumed him as he neared his parents' tent, a painful recollection he had buried deep in the recesses of his mind. The haunting repercussions of his parents' arguments replayed incessantly; shouts, screams, and accusations echoed without respite. Viewing the scene through a child's eyes, he cautiously lifted the tent flap. It was a vivid recollection of his father's murderous act, extinguishing his mother's life before ending his own. The clamour of arguments abruptly ceased as he saw their bodies crumpled on the floor.

The dream deceitfully teased that his mother still existed, placing the burden of her salvation on him alone. Hovering above, the red-coded knife, wielded by his father, darted toward him like a javelin, piercing Isaiah's heart, and he cried out in agonising pain.

Valour tried to awaken him, but Isaiah remained unresponsive. Max hurried to retrieve Corbin's healing potion from his pack. Valour struggled to get Isaiah to drink the magical herbs, grappling fiercely with him. Undeterred, he held Isaiah's head steady, determined to persist until the potion finally made him choke. Isaiah's eyes flew open, blazing with a fiery yellow intensity that caused Valour to instinctively draw back from the hatred emanating from his friend. The mist Corbin Aldhelm spoke of from the tree's hollow began to emerge, its swirling anger evident of its broken spell. A tormenting vortex of grief twisted in a spiralling motion, echoing the cries of a thousand trapped souls as they joined together in a unified scream for freedom. Every plea was a heart-wrenching testimony of being ensnared in an unfathomable anguish. It was a tangible reminder of the depths of their torment that would leave an indelible mark on those who bore witness.

Max rushed for the mirror as the DreamStealer advanced menacingly toward his sister while morphing into a horrifying form. Summoning courage he didn't know he possessed, he clutched the cross-etched mirror tightly in his trembling hands to face his enemy. Max took a hesitant step forward, the mirror held before him like a sacred shield against the darkness. His heart raced, and his palms were slick with fear, but strong willpower surged within him as he walked toward the ominous figure.

Mia stood frozen. The DreamStealer ceased its eerie hovering, but its hollow eyes radiated evil, burning with a sinister hunger. Rows of serrated, red-coded, stained teeth leered from a mouth oozing decay, emitting a foul stench that curdled in its soul. Jagged, razor-sharp claws twitched with sadistic anticipation, poised to rend flesh and bone. A spine-chilling howl rendered the silence, promising eternal agony.

Fortified by the insights he had gained from spiritualists on TV who had driven away evil spirits, Max stood his ground. His voice boomed as he recited strong words, urging the entity to depart for good. The authority in his warning echoed through the unsettling quiet. The DreamStealer let out a chilling wail, a haunting sound that took all by surprise. It resonated with a deep sense of despair. Ominously, it thrashed back and forth as if battling against an invisible force in a desperate attempt to break free from the etched mirror.

Max escalated the confrontation, a surge of intensity propelling his words. "If you ever dare to return, know this: your reflection will be eternally enslaved within this mirror." His declaration rang out like a powerful promise, born from deep fear but strong will. The image of Corbin Aldhelm flashed in his mind, inspiring Max to take his vow a step further. He raised the mirror high, the threat of destruction palpable. "If you do not release the souls of the dreams you've stolen, I will break this mirror into a million pieces, ending your existence once and for all."

The DreamStealer had long been familiar with the cacophony of sounds, scents, and vibrations that defined the night's drama. Yet, the being reflecting its captured image was unlike any it had encountered. It felt like the darkness was transforming into a foreboding cloak of radiant light, signalling imminent danger if it chose to remain. A jarring wail erupted, mingling with the jubilant cries of tormented souls trapped within its nightmarish grasp. Having endured unimaginable suffering, these spirits burst forth into the night sky like shooting stars, their cries of liberation a bittersweet echo of their torment. The DreamStealer began to dissolve in a haunting shimmer, its form fragmenting and leaving a lingering sense of unease and relief.

Overwhelmed, Max sank to his knees, his strength fading, breathless and drained. He pondered why he hadn't given in to paralysing fear when faced with the most terrifying creature he could ever imagine. Arabella hurried to kneel beside him, her eyes brimming with admiration and gratitude. She touched his shoulder and softly said, "There are acts of bravery that earn the highest respect from a princess. What you just did would earn the admiration of a king. You should never doubt your bravery again—be proud of yourself." Helping him up, she kissed him on both cheeks. "That was from Bella," she whispered in his ear.

Witnessing such courage, Mia was filled with profound pride, clutching her brother with renewed strength. Valour's voice resonated with admiration, praising Max's bravery and declaring him a true hero. Isaiah, his eyes now clear of fear and his stance unwavering, stepped forward to express his sincere gratitude for being saved from his harrowing ordeal. Choosing to wait until the morning light to recover the crystal from inside the tree, Max watched the others slowly drifting off to sleep. The image of a smile on Corbin Aldhelm's face was the final comforting thought before he slipped into a peaceful dream.

Max was roused from his slumber by the sound of wood splintering. He rubbed his eyes and saw Isaiah using the axe to enlarge the opening in the tree trunk. Despite his fatigue, he noticed that the space was large enough for him to volunteer to crawl inside.

Suspended by a sturdy vine, Max was lowered towards the crystal's guiding light. Each snatch of being lowered was filled with apprehension from being inside the DreamStealer's former haunt. He was drawn to the emerald crystal encircled by twisted roots. Lifting the weighty object, he planted a grateful kiss on its surface, only to release a scream of terror.

Valour's urgent shout reverberated through the narrow passage. "Max! Are you all right?"

"Quickly! Pull me up!" he yelled, passing the heavy crystal to the Princess as Isaiah and Valour hoisted him out. "Spiders!" he recounted, "there were hundreds of them."

Mia couldn't contain her laughter. "He likely meant one or two. He really, really hates spiders," she remarked. Valour and Isaiah exchanged a glance before joining in her laughter, finding it amusing that someone as brave as Max had a fear of spiders.

The Princess firmly held the emerald crystal, turning until a beam of light stretched towards the west. "That guides us to the province of DragonForge," Valour declared.

Mia's voice faltered. "Please, don't tell me we must face dragons next."

"Every province holds its legends, and some are said to have several," the Princess remarked.

Max focused on the map. The hieroglyphs changed into a legible riddle:

"Beneath the pale and haunting light, Deep within the forest's shroud, I lay low. With long, hairy legs and threads so fine, A venomous kiss awaits within my intricately twined design. What am I, in night's embrace, A spinner of secrets, a keeper of space?

Mysterious and cunning, yet often unseen, Untangle my riddle if you're keen."

"With long, hairy legs and threads so fine, a venomous kiss. It has to be a specific breed of spider!" Valour exclaimed.

Max's complexion turned ashen. Now liberated from the anguish of such terror, Isaiah gave him a comforting pat on his shoulder. "Valour saved my existence, and you saved my sanity. If it is indeed a spider, I will deal with it."

"The teamwork we've displayed is heartening," the Princess remarked. "However, with Max's crucial role in deciphering the map and Mia's task of placing the crystals in the Great White Tree, we need to be more cautious in safeguarding them from unnecessary risks."

"That's strange, it usually gives the riddle of the crystals colour first?" Max stated. New words emerged on the parchment, seemingly responding to his question. Max cringed. "Spiderweb Obsidian."

"What kind of colour is that?" Mia queried, looking perplexed.

The Princess fondly recalled, "My mother used to wear a crystal necklace crafted from Spiderweb Obsidian. It featured a black base adorned with distinct silver and grey veins, creating a pattern reminiscent of an intricate web. The contrast between the dark base and the web-like design made the crystal visually striking and a unique piece within the spider family."

“Maybe that’s why no riddle was given for its colour?” Mia suggested. Max appeared unimpressed with the mention of the Spiderweb Obsidian, while Valour and Isaiah began mapping out their route to DragonForge, opting to take all the mirrors on Corbin Aldhelm’s worn-out old carriage.

Chapter 22

The Four Assassins

Stepping out from Corbin Aldhelm's dilapidated cottage and edging closer to their elusive quarry, the old hermit's haunted face reflected the terror of his last breaths. They had obtained the crucial information they sought—a grim reminder of the ruthless reputation of The Four Assassins and the hound without a name.

The Assassins glided swiftly through the forest, their names spoken only in hushed tones. Leading them was Mortis CryptCrawler, bearing war scars and tattoos. His weapon of choice, a colossal battle axe, symbolised his brute strength and unrelenting cruelty. RavenShadow, whose noiseless strides left no trace behind, epitomised the art of stealth and deception. Armed with a blow dart tipped with curare vine toxins, his eyes gleamed with the predatory chill of a hunter. SerpentStrike, a sinewy figure, donned a cloak adorned with serpent-like scales and bore a lethal arsenal of poisoned daggers. His agility and cunning were unparalleled, making him a deadly adversary. SilentWraith, enveloped in an ethereal grey robe, melded seamlessly with the shadows, sending shivers down even the bravest souls. His existence seemed ghostly, haunting those who dared to joust against his lethal sword.

Bounding along the same route as its prey, the hound advanced. Its muscles were tense, and its senses were sharp. It followed the scent-filled path, driven by an instinct to narrow the gap between hunter and prey. Detecting its target close by, a soft whimper escaped as it glanced meaningfully back at its handlers. The seasoned assassins, energised by the hound's actions, exchanged understanding nods. They advanced with deliberate, quiet movements, ensuring minimal noise to avoid detection. Reaching a ridge hidden by foliage, they crouched behind the concealing leaves and observed the area below. Beside the stream, their mark rested—a party consisting of Princess Arabella, the humans, and two companions who had established a camp for the night, their silhouettes illuminated by the flickering flames of the campfire.

The SablePaw stood watchful, its senses keen as it surveyed the campsite. Its handlers, equally alert, exchanged silent, knowing glances, their anticipation of impending action clear. With patience as their ally, they bided their time, waiting for the perfect moment to set their plan in motion and unleash chaos upon their unsuspecting targets.

Arabella's WhiteTail betrayed a sense of unease. Valour and Isaiah, noting her anxiety, exchanged an urgent look of acknowledgement. They readied their weapons, their actions calculated and purposeful as they braced for the unseen danger lurking in the shadows.

Mortis CryptCrawler watched as the two companions unsheathed their weapons. Ignoring caution in the presence of what appeared to be easy targets, he surprised his comrades with his sudden move. The tranquil night was abruptly interrupted by Valour's urgent warning, which startled the Princess, Max, and his sister. Mia's terrified scream pierced the darkness, her grip on her brother tightening in panic as they faced a looming figure charging toward them with an axe raised high, followed closely by others.

Valour's quick reflexes engaged as he stood toe-to-toe with Mortis CryptCrawler. He managed to dodge a lethal axe swing, but a powerful scissor kick knocked him down, leaving him winded and struggling to catch his breath. In the flickering firelight, the CryptCrawler's tattoos seemed to writhe and pulse as he lifted the axe above his head. The menacing blade loomed ominously, and in a desperate bid, Max grabbed a fallen log, aimed it at the assassin's back, and swung with all his might. But the impact was futile; the log bounced off the CryptCrawler's shoulders like a toy. With the axe still raised, the CryptCrawler slowly turned to confront him, a murderous glint in his eyes.

The opening was too tempting for Valour to ignore. With the agility of a seasoned Zenturion, he rolled forward, his blade finding its target. The sword cut through the assassin's Achilles tendon, sending a jolt of searing pain through his foe. The CryptCrawler howled in agony, collapsing to the ground and thrashing in torment.

Isaiah, demonstrating remarkable swordsmanship, confronted the dual menace of RavenShadow and SilentWraith. Their battle erupted into a cacophony of clashing steel, each blow ringing out with brutal intensity. Amid the fray, SerpentStrike, the knife thrower, focused intently on his target—the princess—preparing to hurl a deadly poison that could seal her fate. Without hesitation, Valour hurled his sword, striking him in the heart. He wrenched his blade free from the fallen assassin, ready to aid Isaiah in confronting the relentless threat that loomed before them.

Isaiah's agile manoeuvres caught RavenShadow off guard. The CryptCrawler's petulant impatience was evident, leaving him unprepared and unable to utilise his blow darts. Isaiah's strikes methodically chipped away at RavenShadow's defences, rendering him incapable of mounting a successful counterattack. He delivered a decisive thrust directly to RavenShadow's lung in a pivotal moment, incapacitating him as the battlefield echoed with the fierce clash between Valour and SilentWraith.

The CryptCrawler managed to rise, dagger poised to strike Valour from behind, but Isaiah's lightning-fast reaction flared. He materialised before the CryptCrawler in an instant, pressing his blade against the assassin's throat. With a fierce intensity in his gaze, he ended his enemy's existence, then forcefully shoved him back to the ground.

Despite his considerable expertise, SilentWraith become overpowered by the Zenturion's breathtaking swordsmanship. Valour's movements flowed with precision, foreseeing every one of his enemy's thrusts. Each clash of their swords highlighted Valour's talent. As the duel reached its zenith, he unleashed a stunning display of technique. With a rapid succession of strikes, he disarmed SilentWraith and, showing no quarter, delivered a fatal blow. Valour and Isaiah gripped each other's hands in a powerful handshake, their chests heaving with deep breaths. Together, they represented a formidable partnership, pledged to confront whatever trials lay ahead. Mia, her hands covering her face in fear for her friends' safety, found it unbearable to watch the battle unfold to the end.

Before letting the horses roam until discovered, Valour found a pair of the princess's shoes tucked away in a saddlebag. They cleansed themselves and their weapons in a nearby stream, washing away the red code of battle. Isaiah returned to the campfire, attempting to ease his companions' frayed nerves with a sense of calm in the aftermath of the chaos.

The princess remarked, "Lord Elric and the General were right. This betrayal has the unmistakable signature of King Kronos and Malice Malware. It indicates they are disturbed by our progress and its implications. But how did they manage to find us?" Just as she asked, a visibly shaken SablePaw hound entered their camp.

"There lies your answer," Valour exclaimed, returning to the group and emphasising the hound's exceptional tracking abilities. "I found this shoe in one of the assassin's pouches, Your Highness."

"This shoe belongs in my palace wardrobe, she gasped. "likely taken by a spy—or Whispering Grass," she declared.

Mia couldn't ignore the hound's evident distress. The sight of bones protruding beneath the skin of its skeletal frame caught her breath. On bent knees, she softly encouraged it to approach. The hound perked its ears and widened its eyes. A puzzled yet endearing look crossed its face as it cocked its head, displaying a blend of curiosity and innocence. Gradually, with its head drooping low, it tentatively approached.

Mia wanted to persuade the others to let the dog accompany them on their journey. With conviction and honesty, she highlighted the dog's worth, portraying a convincing image of its possible contributions and appealing to their compassion. Arabella promptly understood why Mia had been recognised as 'the one with the purest heart' and warmly approved.

When faced with the challenge of giving the dog a name, Mia quickly settled on the name Oscar, a choice she had in mind for a potential pet she hoped her parents would consider. Gently, she whispered his name, offering Oscar food scraps to help his gradual recovery.

Feeling secure against the imminent threat of another assassin attack, the princess acknowledged with Valour and Isaiah that this setback would deal a significant blow to their enemies. Unaware of their whereabouts, she agreed that the optimal location to lay another trap would be their final destination, the Great White Clock in Glimmerhavan. "Until that time arises, we must set aside this concern. Securing the fourth Crystal of Time is our priority, just as GlimmerHavan holds importance for our enemy," she responded, observing weariness enveloping Mia and the hound nestling side by side.

Chapter 23

The Fortress
Malware Island

Preparations unfolded for the arrival of King Kronos, his seasoned strategist and entourage. The atmosphere brimmed with grandeur, heralding a gathering that would be both significant and unforgettable. The courtyard walls displayed stunning tapestries, each illustrating the illustrious history of Drakonia and its legendary heroes. Torches and braziers lined the pathway, their warm amber glow merging with the encroaching twilight. At the centre of the courtyard, a grand oak table gleamed with a polished finish, surrounded by robust chairs crafted from the same timber. Each backrest was carved with motifs of mythical creatures, adding an air of mystery.

Malice Malware scrutinised the assortment of maps, scrolls, and documents meticulously arranged on the table, each one a crucial piece of the strategy to come. Gold goblets stood ready to be filled with the finest wines, while platters with roasted meats were arranged to satisfy his royal guest's appetite. Malware anticipated that the most challenging and incisive questions would come from the Grand Strategist, known for his sharp military insight. From the battlements, he peered through his spyglass, spotting the commanding figure of King Kronos as he disembarked from his battleship, the Infector, stepping onto the island's shores for the first time.

The King's imposing frame emanated an aura of power, a testament to the beastly code that flowed through his veins. His eyes, molten gold in colour, scanned the surroundings as his heavy boots sunk into the volcanic sand. The island's eerie, surreal landscape, with its jagged cliffs and ominous fissures, made an indelible impression. The optimism of conquest consumed the King's thoughts. He envisioned the five provinces, each rich with coveted resources and strategic significance, firmly under his control. The key to his success lay with the diminished Crystals of Time.

Without Princess Arabella finding the last remaining gems of their kind, any resistance would crumble like sandcastles against an approaching tide. The urgency of the Princess securing them weighed heavily on his mind. He was prepared to wield every resource, strategise tirelessly, and confront the challenges of anyone to ensure the fulfilment of his ambition – the subjugation of the five provinces and the unbridled power it promised.

Striding alongside him was Tarries Gorgarim, the hybrid known throughout Drakoria as the Grand Strategist. His physical form was a fusion of monstrous qualities. The upper body appeared zenizen. From the waist down, a bestial amalgamation. His lower limbs featured sinewy, scaled, and taloned appendages resembling those of a fearsome dragon, evoking a sense of fear and reverence in those who met him. Tarries Gorgarim's fiery red eyes gleamed with an eerie intensity, while the intricate tattoos on his face mirrored the swirling chaos of a thunderstorm. In his grasp, he held a carved baton etched with cryptic runes symbolising his authority, marking him as a master of strategic brilliance.

Malice Malware and King Kronos engaged in a firm handshake, their hands locked in a grip that highlighted the importance of their meeting. Malware motioned for King Kronos to take the seat next to him at the table, deliberately arranged to signify their equal status. Both leaders opted to postpone the main topics of their discussion until after the meal, allowing the moment to resonate with unspoken tension. It was only at this point that the genuine negotiations commenced.

Malware signalled his staff to withdraw, leaving behind only a select few who had earned his most profound trust. The atmosphere shifted into one of confidentiality and strategic intent. Former adversaries now united, a clash of minds unfolded in the evolving saga of power and deception. Tension mounted as they observed the Grand Strategist engage in a crucial matter. Though outwardly composed, a trace of unease shadowed his expression. “Admiral Malware, our primary concern lies in the princess and humans’ quest for the Crystals of Time.”

A murmur of concern rippled from King Kronos, an anticipation Malware had foreseen, and spoke with a heavy heart of regret. “The banishment of Princess Arabella brought me significant satisfaction, but under her guidance, it pains me to inform you that the princess and humans have retrieved two of the five crystals. I’ve dispatched four assassins, each a master in their field, to intercept any further attempt. I await news of their success.” A charged silence enveloped them, the weight of potential failure overshadowing the intricate strategy they had painstakingly developed.

Unflinching, Malware stood resolute. “A SablePaw hound has been deployed to aid the assassins in tracking and neutralising the target. As you are undoubtedly aware, their hunting skills are unparalleled throughout Cyberia. A garment taken from Princess Arabella’s wardrobe detects the undetectable.” He became heartened by the slight shift in their perspective, but Tarries Gorgarim contemplated the gravity of the situation.

“Regardless of the assassins involved, and having meticulously considered different possibilities, we must remain prepared to adapt our strategy,” Tarries Gorgarim asserted. “If the Princess is successful, my primary focus remains on preventing the insertion of the crystals into the Grand White Clock in Glimmerhaven. The King has agreed to deploying 600 skilled warriors to establish a formidable perimeter around the White Clock until the threat is neutralised. Once the ecosystem has collapsed, I have devised a contingency plan for the safe retreat of the 600 from the airless domain. A domain that will eliminate the existence of the Princess and the humans. The next stage of the ecosystem restoration is safeguarded by the certainty that only you, the King, and I understand how it will be initiated.”

King Kronos’s rare smile signalled a shift in their talks. “What measures have you taken to persuade Golen to forge a military alliance with us?” he inquired.

Malice Malware’s response was immediate and calculated. “Golen’s fixation on gold has been deftly manipulated by an agent known as

Whispering Grass," he disclosed. "This operative has now replaced the royal advisor, Lord Elric. He has since provided counsel on all matters concerning Valaria. In tandem, I dispatched Scarlet, the Siren of Deception, to Valaria." He smirked and elaborated on the story of Golen's infatuation.

King Kronos's discerning eyes absorbed the manipulation of deceit, a sign that their intricate plans were nearing fruition. Though not complacent, he leaned back in his chair with an air of satisfaction. He contemplated the demise of King Osred, regarding Malware with an expression that suggested he possessed the answer, yet he recognised it was a truth best left unspoken.

"After Golen's coronation," Malware continued, "I intend to visit him in Valaria, a decision I consider prudent to secure an agreement of our pact."

Tarries Gorgarim spread the scrolls across the table, his fingers delicately tracing the borders of various provinces. Each line he followed and pointed to was a roadmap defining their impending invasions. His keen eyes, as sharp as daggers, dissected each target's terrain, resource potential, and vulnerabilities with a laser-like focus. He tapped on critical points, like grand prizes on a chessboard.

Knowing that the outcome of their operations relied on his strategist's plans, King Kronos questioned the absence of General Titanous in their discussion. Malice Malware anticipated the inevitable question. "As you are aware, the most recent sighting of General Titanous was at King Osred's funeral. He alone would be no match to war against myself and the combined force of two armies," he declared with conviction.

Caught between interpreting this as a positive or negative development, the King couldn't disregard the validity of Malware's reasoning. Energised by the unfolding meeting, Malware dismissed any remaining doubts regarding the Princess and the humans, projecting a sense of assurance that their fates were either already sealed or imminent. However, his thoughts circled back to General Titanous's mysterious absence. Quietly, Tarries Gorgarim harboured identical thoughts.

Chapter 24

The Royal Palace
Valaria

Lord Elric was keenly aware that Valaria had enjoyed lasting peace and prosperity under the fair and charitable reign of King Osred. Yet, with the unsettling emergence of the Whispering Grass, it seemed as though a shroud of darkness had descended upon the land. Alone in his chamber, he reflected on how swiftly Whispering Grass had spread his influence throughout the palace. His beguiling exterior attracted many, presenting an illusion of tranquillity and warmth. Yet, beneath this charming mask resided deceitful ambitions, sowing the seeds of discord and division among those he ensnared. His thoughts turned to Scarlet, whose captivating charisma equalled her beauty.

Like Whispering Grass, she appeared out of nowhere and entranced the thoughts of Prince Golen after winning his heart. Even the council orchestrating the coronation was influenced by her ever-increasing participation. She had become the central figure. Decisions made appeared tailored to enhance her status and authority over the event. It had become unmistakably clear that both had been recruited to further Golen's relentless pursuit of power, acting as instruments in a war orchestrated by King Kronos and Malice Malware.

Lord Elric had witnessed the horrors of war firsthand and comprehended the devastation it could unleash. Thus, the notion of the prince being manipulated on such a dangerous course weighed heavily on his conscience. What further weighed on him was the painful recognition of his fading loyalty to the prince. He dispatched a discreet message to the GranMother in Arbitration Land, believing she could negotiate a solution to the impending crisis. As he had anticipated, the Whisper-Wing couriers' messages quickened as the topic of war emerged.

Lord Elric recognised that sending these messages constituted an act of treason against the heir apparent. Yet, his loyalty had shifted; it was no longer to the prince but to the kingdom's well-being.

The GranMother's planned journey to Valaria for the coronation marked a pivotal moment. He hoped she could discreetly mediate his mounting worries. Treading a fragile path, he recognised the harsh reality that, amid an impending disaster, he had to make this painful decision. His only solace was in the possibility that Thalassa Starling's involvement would result in the peace and harmony he ardently sought.

In his thoughts of Princess Arabella, he felt an ominous danger that threatened the safety of all. He mused over the mysterious forces that King Kronos and Malice Malware could wield to revive the ecosystem after its collapse, questioning whether Prince Golen was privy to their plans for its restoration. If so, it implied one thing – Golen had aligned himself with their cause, and the very thought sent a chill down his spine.

Chapter 25

AmberLeaf
DragonForge

Their journey took them to a cargo ship headed for Port Wyrmbane in DragonForge. Isaiah negotiated with the ship's captain, using his silver tongue and persuasive skills to ensure their passage. The well-established trade routes allowed them to rest and revitalise during the voyage.

Alongside the families on board, a diverse array of travellers filled the ship: merchants laden with valuable goods, scholars seeking knowledge, and a troupe of performers who infused the journey with their vibrant energy. The children, especially, were captivated as they watched the graceful WhiteTails being guided into the hold while Oscar whined at being separated from Bilko, their growing bond becoming increasingly evident. Dockers removed the ropes from the robust wooden dolphin piles in the riverbed. The wooden hull creaked as it drifted away from its mooring.

On deck, the crew hurried to secure the lines and unfurl the sails. The brilliant white fabric expanded, straining against the rigging, fluttering and billowing to harness the boundless energy of the wind. With the boat picking up speed, shoals of fish shot up from the depths, their silver scales glimmering under the warm sunlight. Mia peered over the edge, mesmerised by their vibrant colours as they swam alongside the vessel or glided just beneath the water's surface. The dazzling hues of turquoise, emerald, and gold danced in the light, forming a breathtaking spectacle.

Valour and Isaiah conversed with the other passengers, intent on uncovering any nuggets of valuable information. Although each traveller had tales, none were relevant to their journey until a young woodchopper named Kael began to weave a legend from his village.

Kael's rugged frame mirrored his outdoor way of life. With his tousled chestnut hair and a wiry beard, his eyes gleamed with intensity as he spoke of a colossal spider called Arachnida, which whispered to lurk in the depths of the ancient forests beyond his village. "This tale has been passed on by my uncle Johan. He maintains that this creature possesses a unique ability to craft colossal webs of exceptional strength and beauty. The threads of its webs can trap the light of the moon and stars, creating a spectacle of crystal-clear clarity." The young woodchopper shared accounts of brave souls who dared to witness the wonder of the spun webs. "My uncle asserted that some had seen the elusive Arachnida herself, while others vanished without a trace."

Understanding that Kael's village, AmberLeaf, signified the next phase of their journey, they took the opportunity to accompany him after disembarking. The radiant sparkle of the Crystals of Time validated their travel direction.

Cradled in the tranquil heart of a valley, the village of AmberLeaf reminded them of Valour's hometown. The villagers greeted them with genuine hospitality. They accepted the offer of a stable and lean-to, providing a restful refuge for themselves and their steeds. Catering to their needs, Kael ensured their comfort with food and drink before searching for his uncle, whose knowledge about the elusive spider was too valuable to ignore.

Exuding an air of authority, Johan stood tall and steadfast. His streaked grey hair and well-groomed beard added a touch of wisdom to his demeanour. Dressed in a worn dark coat and a wide-brimmed hat, he tapped his fingers thoughtfully on the brim during moments of reflection; under the shelter of the lean-to, Johan and his nephew perched on two empty oak barrels. His deeply set eyes mirrored the profound depth of his knowledge as he spoke.

"Kael has told me why you are here." His brow knitted with worry as their intentions matched the ominous rumours circulating about the province's endangered ecosystem. Before the strangers came, he had dismissed such thoughts, struggling to fathom the reality of such a catastrophe. Now, he recognised that neither he nor the villagers had an alternative refuge if the rumours were true. "I am willing to share all the information I possess," he declared, "but I expect the same regarding the challenges my village might face." \

With no alternatives left, the princess disclosed her royal lineage and fervently expressed her belief in the spider's existence, compelled by a profound responsibility to defend the five endangered provinces. The uncle and his nephew stood up, their discomfort evident as they faced both royalty and the stark honesty of the confession. Johan promptly offered the hospitality of his humble home, but Arabella graciously declined, asking them both to sit back down.

"Your Highness, I can only share what I learned from an elderly villager who has sadly passed away," said Johan.

"Please, enlighten us," Arabella urged.

"Canood maintained a constant and respectful presence, never once speaking an untruth. When under the influence of his favourite wine, the old sage would allude to Arachnida, painting a vivid yet chilling image of a creature residing in the depths of a mine known as Nebula Ore. This mine was said to have contained rich veins of ore capable of illuminating even the darkest cavern. Following the mysterious arrival of Arachnida, the Nebula Ore became abandoned." Johan leaned in, his eyes shining with both reverence and apprehension. "Canood described the creature as monstrous, with a body three times the size of your steeds. Its eight powerful legs, covered in sharp barbed hair, act as lethal weapons, capturing prey with grim precision. Draped in a foreboding black shade akin to the abyss, it merged with the forest shadows, rendering it nigh invisible. Canood highlighted that its venomous fangs, as long as a forearm, could pierce through the most resilient armour to inject its poison."

"So, Nebula Ore is its lair?" asked Max. The shallow candlelight cast shadows across his face, enhancing his dread.

Johan nodded. "Canood described the mine as having interconnecting shafts. The otherworldly light it emits," he warned, "is a trap to entice, ensnaring the mind into a web of lethal intrigue. It could appear and vanish in a heartbeat—a speed beyond comprehension." Johan's eyes took on a distant look, broken by the spit of the dwindling candle. "The most disturbing element was not its shape but its objective.

An objective that you have clarified. But why would the spider safeguard the mystical crystal you seek, and why in DragonForge specifically?"

"That is an unsettling enigma between this province and others," came Arabella's honest reply.

"Does Arachnida have a vulnerability?" inquired Isaiah.

Johan shrugged. "All I can do is share what my friend thought about stabilising it," he stated.

"Please, continue!" implored the princess. "So much depends on us completing this quest."

"Canood's idea was indeed logical yet fraught with peril. Beyond the mine lay a clearing encircled by sturdy trees. His plan involved crafting lassos from vines in the clearing to trap the spider's legs, with the other ends anchored to the trees, ready to be pulled. If eight lassos could capture just three or four of Arachnida's legs, it should immobilise the creature. The real challenge is to lure Arachnida toward the lassos while remaining hidden behind the trees, poised to tighten the grip of the vines at the right moment."

"Tightening the grip via a slip knot" infused Isaiah.

"Yes, but deciding how to attract its attention to that particular spot is a challenge for you all to consider," he admitted.

"Once we've surveyed the clearing, we'll come up with a distraction," Valour announced, offering Johan a grateful pat on the shoulder for suggesting a practical plan they might not have even considered.

"Is there any other valuable advice you can provide?" the princess asked.

"Spiders are less active during sunlit periods. They tend to hide in dark corners or retreat to their sanctuary. Nocturnal creatures prefer to hunt and conduct their activities at night."

"How far is the mine from the village?" she asked.

"Your Highness, I am willing to lead you to the mine. We should reach our destination before nightfall if we depart at first light. This serves as my acknowledgement of your candidness. The province of DragonForge and others owe you all a significant debt for your noble mission," Johan added.

The princess felt pride in the face of such a heartfelt compliment. "Thank you. Your words and kind offer are greatly appreciated. It seems that bravery knows no bounds in each province we have ventured into. However, I urge you both to keep my identity and our quest hidden from the village to avoid causing alarm and because there are adversaries who would try to thwart us by any means necessary."

"You have our word, your Highness. I'll set off to ensure we have an abundant vine supply," he concluded.

Isaiah briefly disappeared, only to return with a long, slender vine. He divided it into five equal sections, eliciting curious glances from the group. Max and Mia examined the vine, noting its distinct characteristics compared to traditional materials like hemp, cotton, or synthetic fibres used in rope-making. Isaiah clarified that the vine was sourced from forest trees and soaked in water to improve flexibility and minimise the chance of breaking under strain. "This vine is smaller in girth than the vines we will be using, but how quickly you secure the knot could determine your existence, be it yours or mine."

They observed as he wove the knot slowly, demonstrating how to loop the vine together to create a double-slip knot. "Pull the working end to close the loop but leave a loose bite; this end will act as a double trigger that tightens when tugging to ensure the knot doesn't slip."

Max completed his knot in seconds. "I used to be a Boy Scout in my hometown," he bragged.

Visibly frustrated, Mia struggled with a skill that came naturally to her brother. She quipped, "You're quite the show-off, right?" Beside her, Oscar watched as Mia persisted until she finally succeeded, after which she retired for the night.

As the morning mist lifted, the shapes of cottages and trees emerged, gradually revealing the entire village in the sunlight. Johan prepared a breakfast featuring freshly baked bread and golden crust pastries—a woven basket overflowing with fruits in exotic colours served alongside steaming cups of herbal brew.

Mia placed Oscar's care in Kael's hands, confident in his capability to look after her newfound companion. After securing their saddles and loading their supplies and vines onto the carriage, the group prepared to leave. The rhythmic sound of the steeds' hooves offered a comforting undertone to their thoughts and discussions as they journeyed from the village.

Chapter 26

Nebula Ore
DragonForge

The sun cast long shadows over the hills where wildflowers swayed with the melodies of chirping birds. They pressed on steadily, the approach of dusk marking their journey toward Nebula Ore. Eventually, the terrain surrounding the abandoned mineshaft looked rugged and uneven but characterised by a clearing of vegetation.

The hill opposite the mineshaft rose at a lesser angle, its slopes dotted with tufts of grass and clusters of wildflowers. The winding trail that snaked upward was a narrow path carved by time. It meandered through the underbrush, occasionally revealing glimpses of the valley below, where remnants of mining equipment lay rusting in the sun. Sturdy shrubs flanked the trail and the occasional tree, providing a sense of enclosure for those who dared to ascend. At the summit, the terrain opened into a broad expanse, offering a view of the surrounding area and a moment of tranquillity amidst the remnants of a once-bustling mining operation opposite.

Max took charge of the steeds as they grazed while Valour peered through the spyglass, scanning the mineshaft that loomed across the open terrain, now shrouded in the fading light. At the foot of the mountain, weathered timbers framed the entrance to the shaft, a testament to years of neglect. As Johan had described, a cluster of sturdy trees encircled the outer clearing surrounding the mine, their gnarled branches reaching out like sentries guarding the forgotten site.

Mia's voice sliced through Valour's thoughts, pulling him back to the moment with a jolt. "I've been thinking about a plan since we left the village," she said, her eyes gleaming with a hint of courage. "What if we set up Corbin Aldhelm's mirrors in the clearing? If we arrange them beside the stick torches, the reflections could create an illusion that disorients the spider, potentially slowing it down or halting its glide over the vines. A brief pause could give us the opening we need to capture it. We could hide behind the trees and bang our pots and pans to create a loud noise that draws it in. The sound would echo through the clearing, a call that lures it into our trap. If we time it perfectly, we could catch it off guard."

Valour smiled, recognising the brilliance of Mia's idea. "You would make an excellent Zenturion," he remarked before sharing the plan with the group.

The princess was the first to grasp that the best moment to position the vines and mirrors would be when the sun reached its zenith, ensuring the nocturnal creature remained asleep. "We will rest until the sun returns with no campfire," she said, gesturing toward a spot on the opposite side of the hill. "Our conversations must remain whispers. We wouldn't want to alert the creature to our presence," she concluded sternly.

As darkness descended, Max turned to Arabella, speaking softly to unveil the source of his deep-seated fear of spiders. "I learned about their strange feeding habits during biology class at school, a chilling reality that still haunts my thoughts. These predators possess a venomous bite, a deadly injection that paralyses their prey, leaving it helpless and at their mercy. But the horror doesn't end there. They ensnare their victims in a silken shroud, suffocating any chance of escape. As if that weren't enough, they unleash potent enzymes, a grotesque cocktail that dissolves flesh and bone, transforming their catch into a gruesome liquid meal. That was the moment my phobia of spiders took root—Mealtime!" Arabella shivered at the thought.

With the sun at its zenith, Valour and Isaiah, Valour and Isaiah stealthily made their way to the clearing, and the group of trees. They strategically coiled the vines around the trunks, making sure they were aligned, and concealed the lassos with leaves scattered across the ground. After several trips to gather materials, they completed their setup by arranging the mirrors and firesticks with care. Once their work was done, they made their way to the hilltop, waiting patiently for the night to envelop the area. Each moment dragged in tense silence. The plan's success depended on everyone's involvement, except for Johan, assigned to watch the steeds for a swift retreat. Valour and Isaiah would create a protective barrier if things went wrong, allowing the others to escape.

As the time to enter the clearing drew near, Max's anxiety grew, his heart pounding like an unyielding hammer. Valour and Isaiah ignited the torches, casting a flickering light upon the staked mirrors. They took their positions alongside the rest of the group, concealed behind the thick trunks of the trees. The princess signalled to Max and Mia, urging them to clatter their camping utensils together, hoping to draw the spider out from the depths of the mine.

The strategy quickly proved effective as the massive black spider burst forth from the mine's entrance in the blink of an eye. Max peered cautiously from behind his tree, his eyes widening in shock as Arachnida skittered back and forth with erratic, unpredictable movements, its extraordinary agility both mesmerising and terrifying. A cold sweat trickled down his brow as he turned to meet his sister's gaze. In that moment, he faced a daunting choice: succumb to the clutches of fear or rise to the challenge of protecting Mia. In that critical moment, her safety took precedence, pushing aside the inner conflict that had plagued him.

Arachnida possessed an extraordinary vision that granted it unparalleled clarity in the abyssal darkness. With eyes gleaming like molten moons, she hastened towards the circle of mirrors. Confusion gripped, it's illuminated reflection created the illusion of another spider in its midst. Its numerous eyes flickered with uncertainty as she came to a standstill. Valour ordered the vines to be pulled. Arachnida detected the vibrations of sound through its legs and body, unsure whether the noise indicated prey or danger, and readied itself to strike. As the vines were yanked, leaves swirled into the air. Four vines slipped away from the spider's feet, while one coiled around the tarsus of its hind leg. Valour, Isaiah, and the princess raced toward the last three vines.

Noticing the creature's middle leg in position, Valour quickly seized the opportunity and captured another leg, while Isaiah and the princess failed to hit their marks. The Arachnida thrashed against the two vines, trying to escape, but its struggles only tightened their hold. Valour and Isaiah stepped boldly before Arachnida, blades drawn and ready. Their mission was twofold: to serve as a distraction and to thwart the spider's efforts to bite through the vines with its formidable chelicerae, designed for seizing and piercing prey.

As they locked eyes with the creature's fiery gaze, they felt her surge of defiance. To their horror, Arachnida shifted her focus to the very thing they feared. Valour snatched a fire stick, waving it back and forth in a desperate attempt to deter her from severing the vines. "We don't have much time!" he shouted, urgency lacing his voice.

Fuelled by adrenaline, Arabella and Mia hurried toward the ominous mineshaft, each gripping a fire stick to illuminate their path. The loose boards creaked and groaned inside the shaft, echoing the eerie sounds of miners' long-gone footsteps. Scampering rats darted in all directions, causing Mia to scream. Despite the unsettling atmosphere, they pressed on until they finally glimpsed the pulsating light radiating from the Spiderweb Obsidian Crystal. They came to an abrupt halt, their breaths catching in their throats.

Before them lay an aperture in the shaft, cradling the crystal behind an ultra-thick layer of cobwebs that glimmered like silver in the torch-light, pulsating with an unsettling essence of its own. With a hard glint in her eyes, the princess stepped forward, fire stick raised high. She ignited the web, flames licking hungrily at the silken strands. The air filled with the acrid scent of burning as the web crackled and hissed, slowly consuming the barrier between them and the crystal.

Mia felt a surge of determination that overshadowed any fear as she reached out to grasp the crystal. The warmth emanating from it was powerful, but the exhilaration of holding it surpassed that sensation. They quickly backtracked through the twisting tunnels of the mine. A rush of exhilaration filled them as they stepped into the cool night air. Ringing with excitement, shouts of triumph erupted from their lips. They sprinted up the hillside, their legs moving as fast as they could carry them, with Max bounding in close pursuit.

Arachnida succeeded in severing one of the vines, a motion that sent a shiver through Valour and Isaiah. They exchanged a knowing glance.

Without hesitation, Valour dropped his fire stick and sprinted up the hill with Isaiah at his side. Halfway up, the chilling sound of the last vine snapping echoed behind them. Released from its restraints, the spider lunged forward with a sudden, sharp movement, its legs propelling it swiftly toward the hill as the severed vines cracked like whips in its wake. Arachnida scrambled up the hill with frantic urgency, its long, spindly legs moving in a blur as it ascended the uneven terrain. Each powerful push sent her surging forward, the ground beneath it crumbling slightly with the force of its ascent. Its many eyes glinted, scanning the movement of its prey.

Poised on his saddle, Johan held Valour and Isaiah steeds in check at the precipice. With haste, both vaulted onto their mounts as Arachnida began to edge unbearably close to the summit. The resounding thunder of hooves striking the earth echoed like drums, provoking the spider as it cascaded over the ridge to give chase. Leaving the rickety carriage of Corbin Aldhelm behind, their hearts beating in synchrony with their trusty steeds, the trio raced down the slope to catch up with the others.

Gaining momentum, the mining mountain, once a looming threat, diminished in the distance. Valour resisted the urge to glance back, focusing intently on the horizon. Arachnida gradually faded away, its imposing shape dissolving into the darkness.

Chapter 27

AmberLeaf Village

A wave of exhilaration swept over Johan's nephew as he spotted his uncle returning safely. Oscar raced toward Mia, his excitement radiating as he bounded and twirled around Bilko's hooves, his tail wagging furiously in delight at their reappearance. Inside the lean-to, Kael listened intently, hanging on every word as Johan recounted the heroic feats he had witnessed during their quest to protect their province. As twilight settled over the landscape, they gradually withdrew, recognising their saviour's need for rest after the trial they had faced.

As the mist finally lifted long after dawn had broken, the enticing aroma of freshly prepared food wafted through the air, rousing them from their slumber. Once again, Johan had crafted a hearty breakfast, fuelling them for their final adventure ahead. Yawning and stretching, they gathered around the makeshift table, grateful for the warmth and generosity of two remarkable villagers—Johan and Kael.

Max sought a quiet moment in the stable to study the sacred map, craving solitude and freedom from distractions. He felt a growing certainty about the direction of the bearing, leading him to believe that Volcanis rather than Drakonia was their final destination. Memories of the dinner at the Valarian palace flooded back, where Whispering Grass had unveiled Volcanis as the distant origin of his lineage. In that fleeting moment, he couldn't help but ponder whether their paths would ever cross again. He laid the map out on the ground, the gentle sounds of the steeds shifting in their stalls creating a serene atmosphere. Sitting on a bale of hay, the thought of victory and the magical amulets infused him with renewed energy as he examined the riddle, each word drawing him deeper into the mystery that awaited.

In a rainbow, I'm one of seven: Vibrant and bold, not just a leaven, What am I, in this colourful arc? A hue that warns, a fiery spark.

Max reasoned that the term 'fiery' indicated the colour red or crimson; the only rainbow spectrum that matched the description. He was interrupted by Mia, with the princess by her side. "We were wondering where you disappeared too," his sister remarked.

"The final crystal we are searching for is red or crimson," he stated, as the riddle had transformed into a new puzzle, challenging them to discover the location of the last Crystal of Time.

"This riddle is rather lengthy," he read aloud.

"On the lone, untouched summit, within nature's fiery forge, the earth's heart beats. Its mystery encircles a gem of fiery crimson, a rare and brilliant prize, yet it stands apart, hidden from seismic eyes. Amidst chaos and quakes, in silence it gleams , emitting a light like a beacon on a mountain's peak. This mighty place of power, answer the riddle's call. Dare to face its volatile might, or risk losing it all."

"Or risk losing it all," repeated Mia. "We've certainly come too far for that to happen."

"Absolutely," said the princess, and it confirmed the colour as crimson, "yet, we appear to be jousting from one nightmarish encounter straight into another. Volcanis is a province of unexplored potential but subject to earthquakes, hence the cryptic wording and seismic amidst chaos and quakes. The fiery crimson gem marks our final mission. Conquering this unpredictable task could be our ultimate challenge," she stated solemnly.

When Valour and Isaiah learned of the riddle, they wisely chose to confide in Johan who shared information about a family from the far-off lands of Volcanis living on the outskirts of the village. He was certain that the family's elder held significant knowledge about his ancestral homeland and with Valour's permission discreetly informed the elder of the princess's presence, believing it might persuade him to help their quest.

Kristian Elowen bore the marks of time on his face, with wiry strands of silvery grey hair framing his features. Though his frail physique suggested vulnerability, there was a quiet strength within him, shaped by a life filled with both triumphs and setbacks. Yet, despite the weight of his experiences, his eyes still sparkled with curiosity and warmth.

Standing in the presence of royalty, Kristian Elowen felt a flutter of unease. having been taken by surprise with no warning of the questions to come. He focused on the specifics of their quest and the riddle given by Max. The riddle instantly struck a chord.

"The location you mention is called the 'Pinnacle of Hope, a mountain situated on a volcanic island, separated from the mainland by the widest river imaginable.A fitting analogy would be to imagine a fortress encircled by an expansive moat. The name' Pinnacle of Hope' was not bestowed due to its desolate landscape, where neither livestock nor vegetation could thrive. Instead, it's a testament to the collective hope that it remains dormant, averting potential devastation on the mainland if it were to erupt.The mountain peak emits a beacon that resembles molten magma; despite the mountain lacking any volcanic activity for countless Dions. The locals refer to the phenomenon as the Optical Illusion of Light. I scoffed at such nonsense until I witnessed such a beacon with my eyes.

Even though the volcanic mountain remains inactive, local seafarers avoid venturing past the boundary known as the exclusion zone. Odd as it may sound, the Pinnacle of Hope starts to stir if the exclusion zone is breached. Should you succeed in locating a seafarer willing to transport you across the great expanse, be ready to compensate generously."

"Are there any underwater threats lurking beneath the river that encircles this island?" Valour asked.

Appreciating the thoughtful question, Max, convinced that something would reveal itself, added, "Perhaps a giant octopus or shark?"Kristian Elowen, taken aback by the strange remark, showed it in his expression. "To my knowledge, only fish are caught by the locals from their riverside. If anything lurks beyond the exclusion zone, I have not heard of such a tale."

Isaiah asked, "How long does it take to make a return journey?"

Kristian Elowen considered the question. "A round trip by rowboat usually takes around three chronos." Max calculated that to be roughly three hours in Earth time.

Worried about the impending snow season, Valour asked how long it would take to reach their destination. "Travelling by horseback, you should arrive at the Pinnacle of Hope in 9 to 10 lunar cycles." Despite Kristian Elowen plotting the fastest route, Mia sighed in disappointment at the lengthy duration the elderly man had provided.

As they left the village of AmberLeaf, the princess thanked Johan for his generous donation of provisions for their journey. Riding next to Valour, she shared her growing unease about a troubling thought. "The more I think about it, the more I fear that King Kronos and Malice Malware might attack before we arrive at Glimmerhavan—perhaps even sooner than expected."

Hearing the last part of the conversation, Max interjected, "How could they possibly know our destination is Volcanis when we've only just discovered it ourselves?"

"You raise a valid point, Max," the princess responded. "However, I may have been too presumptuous and failed to consider that greed lurk's in every shadow, with zenizens ready to trade their honour for the promise of gold. Their information can spread faster than the speed of the quickest arrow. We must all remain vigilant. By now, our enemies are likely aware of the assassin's failure."

They journeyed across an endless stretch of desolate land, a vast expanse of cracked earth and scattered stones that seemed to go on forever. The unyielding sun blazed overhead, its oppressive heat forcing them to shield their faces beneath hoods that offered scant relief. As their gruelling trek neared its end, the sun dipped low on the horizon, painting the barren landscape in vibrant shades of fiery orange and soft pink. In that fleeting moment, the stark surroundings transformed into a stunning twilight masterpiece, a brief beauty that concealed the harshness of their reality. When night fell, the temperature dropped dramatically, and the warm glow of the flickering campfire became a welcome comfort against the biting cold. The crackling flames danced in front of them, illuminating the fatigue etched into their weary faces. Yet, beneath the exhaustion, the princess sensed a strong resolve among her companions. She understood that the Pinnacle of Hope was not merely a destination; it was a guiding light, a beacon urging them onward toward their final trial.

With the new dawn, the sun rose slowly, its golden rays spilling over the horizon like a promise fulfilled as it revealed an unexpected miracle in the distance. Something emerged from the mist, standing tall and majestic. The sight filled the princess with renewed determination, igniting a spark of hope within her heart. She felt an undeniable urge to share this moment with her companions. With a gentle nudge, she roused them from their dreams, her voice soft yet filled with excitement. As they blinked away the remnants of sleep, she pointed toward the horizon. As the light spread, it revealed an unexpected miracle in the distance: the Pinnacle of Hope emerged, its peak seemingly reaching for the moons above—a testament to their perseverance and the journey that lay ahead.

"Gaze upon the Pinnacle of Hope," the Princess declared, her heart swelling with pride and joy. "For here we stand, at the centre of our ultimate quest." Draped in their blankets, they stood side by side, staring in a wordless sense of wonder.

Breaking camp they ventured onward until they came across the grand river Kristian Elowen had described. Like a mystical barrier, the river encircled the mountain. Dismounting on the shore, it signalled that their arduous journey was nearing its end.

Chapter 28

Valaria Palace
The Coronation

Lord Elric's heart brimmed with anticipation for GranMother Starling's impending arrival at the palace. Her imminent presence carried an undercurrent of unease, marking a pivotal juncture where the provinces teetered on the edge of conflict, and the delicate ecosystem they both treasured hung precariously in the balance. Upon the arrival of her coach in the courtyard, Lord Elric greeted Thalassa Starling, her eyes radiating both reverence and a sense of reassurance. After a warm embrace, they slipped away to a secluded chamber where their conversation could unfold without the threat of eavesdroppers.

With urgency lacing his voice, Lord Elric began to reveal the critical information he had painstakingly gathered from his network of spies. "My intelligence sources reveal that Drakonia is mobilising brigades of their armed forces near our borders, all under the pretence of military manoeuvres. We must confront the unsettling truth: the spectre of War draws nearer. I commend the courage of the princess and her allies for their noble quest to rejuvenate the ecosystem. However, even if they succeed, they can only postpone the inevitable; the onset of conflict cannot be avoided, merely delayed."

"I confess, your message about the alliance between Malice Malware and King Kronos is deeply troubling. The fact that Prince Golen has been swayed to strengthen this alliance is a great miscarriage of trust. Such a development would never have transpired under King Osred's leadership. However, your observation carries weight; the untimely passing of the late King Osred seems far from coincidental. Although speculation, the participation of Whispering Grass in this nefarious plot is unnerving, considering his mastery of persuasion. If so, one wonders what motivated him to become an assassin. I wish to express no disrespect towards your prince, but I feel compelled to inquire whether he possesses a sound state of mind, immaturity, or both?"

"If you consider Scarlet the deceitful, his hormones suggest all three. I will speak plainly; this beguiling witch and the weasel of an assassin have their lips pressed to Golen's ears. I am given nothing but a blank stare."

"Have your spies uncovered any supplementary details regarding their backup measures for the ecosystem rejuvenation in the event of the princess and humans' failure?"

"No. It is very much a guarded secret."

"Could this crucial information be found on the sacred map?"

"The text can only be unravelled by the human called Max. I would wager my very existence that the princess would have forewarned me of such a miraculous discovery. At the king's private dinner tonight, both Scarlet and Whispering Grass will have their sharp senses poised to grasp your words. Tread carefully."

"I will request a private audience with the prince in the presence of the insidious pair. I will broach matters of Arbitration Land, a topic only to be discussed with the future head of state. During our one-to-one meeting, I will stress that my information originates from my homeland, where even spies have their spies." Her eyes narrowing with concern, she added, "War is a destructive force that not only shatters the existence of our zenizens but also disrupts the intricate balance of nature that we have safeguarded for generations. Our forests, rivers, and creatures all depend on our maintained peace."

Lord Elric sighed. "Your words breathe hope, yet the desire for battle grows ever stronger. Time is not on our side with the coming of snow."

Prince Golen sat in his father's chair at the head of the dining table. Whispering Grass sat to his left, lending a sense of gravity to the gathering. On Golen's right, Scarlet positioned herself, her observant gaze carefully studying Thalassa Starling. Next to her, Slade, who had purposefully remained in the shadows until now, assumed his position.

Thalassa Starling leaned forward slightly as she addressed Prince Golen. Her voice was measured and respectful yet carried an undercurrent of urgency and importance. "Your Highness, I am grateful for your invitation to dine on the eve of your coronation. I apologise for the timing, but a matter of great importance requires your immediate attention. It pertains not only to the governance of your realm but also to the significant responsibilities you are about to assume, encompassing the welfare of your kingdom and its territories. I respectfully request a private audience to discuss these pressing issues." Her words were deliberate and measured, and her demeanour reflected the seriousness of the topic. The room fell silent, and all eyes turned to Prince Golen.

To her astonishment, Golen showed no hesitation in declining a private meeting. "Anything you wish to convey, GranMother," he declared, "can be shared with all present. My father concealed information that proved harmful to his inner circle. My rule shall commence with transparency. Please feel free to discuss this significant matter or any other concerns."

"Your Highness," she replied, undeterred, "I strongly advise that the matter in question should be addressed in private. Its potential consequences could be harmful if it were to circulate unnecessarily." Lord Elric raised his eyebrows. The implication she drew carried a double-edged significance. He recognised that Scarlet and Whispering Grass understood she was alluding to them.

Golen tilted his head, listening as Whispering Grass murmured into his ear. "My Liege, it is incumbent upon me to caution you about covert schemes to undermine your authority. Just before this gathering, I received intelligence indicating that whispers are gaining traction among nobles from five provinces to seize control from your grasp. Ignoring this peril will cast a shadow over your rule and reputation. King Kronos, a trusted confidant, echoes this information. These revelations of growing discord should compel us to scrutinise the loyalty of even those whom you once held in the highest regard, most notably Lord Elric. May I suggest you fight for time? It will give me time to gather more irrefutable evidence."

Thalassa Starling struggled to conceal her irritation in response to the presumptuous meddling of Whispering Grass. Lord Elric's assessment appeared accurate, which she had now personally observed.

"Your words have not gone unheard. Nevertheless, there shall be no private meeting in the immediate future. There are other more important issues that warrant my time. My decision is final," said Golen, raising the palm of his hand to amplify his point. Thalassa Starling caught sight of the sly grin that played on Golen's face. At that moment, she realised that Golen, as Lord Elric had forewarned, had been irreversibly corrupted. Her heart sank with despair.

Scarlet, poised like a patient hawk, deftly guided the conversation towards the topic of the coronation by gently clasping Golen's hand. "Your Highness," she spoke with infectious excitement, "I simply cannot contain my enthusiasm for your crowning tomorrow. I doubt if I will be able to sleep. What say you, Lord Elric?"

Lord Elric concurred with diplomatic grace, his thoughts illuminated by the heir apparent's embarrassing response to the GranMother. It was now clear to him that the fate of their cause rested solely with Princess Arabella.

Whispering Grass summoned Slade and Scarlet to his chambers that evening for a critical discussion about the GranMother. The idea of assassination was dismissed as reckless, especially so soon after King Osred's death. Their main concern was the uncertain nature of her message; the true danger lay in her ability to articulate her thoughts with both skill and persuasion—whether concerning his father's demise, the humans, or the impending War. The trio devised a plan for Scarlet to remain close to Golen, acting as a protective barrier to ensure the GranMother wouldn't have the chance for private discussions on such sensitive matters.

The sun shone brightly, casting golden rays over the royal gardens, where the coronation of the heir apparent was about to begin. A quiet anticipation filled the air as nobles and commoners gathered to witness this crucial moment in Valaria's history. Prince Golen stood proudly on the grand dais, resplendent in deep sapphire robes and a striking crimson velvet cape. Flanked by a retinue of distinguished courtiers and

Zenturions, he embodied the occasion's significance. The crown, a stunning creation of gold adorned with sparkling sapphires, gleamed in the light, poised to be placed on the new king's head.

Scarlet concealed her genuine emotions, shedding feigned tears of happiness. She had executed her role flawlessly, orchestrating Golen's ascent to power, but understood that her work was far from complete. With King Golen as a pliable puppet, she planned to manipulate the course of his reign with cunning and subtlety.

A solemn hush enveloped the crowd as the magnificent crown, a timeless symbol of kingship, was passed with reverence to the High Eparch, the regional governor tasked with anointing the young monarch. Clad in ceremonial robes, he approached Golen with an elegance matching the moment's gravity. Silence fell like a shroud over the assembly. Golen knelt before the Eparch, his heart racing in the stillness. With hands trembling under the weight of history and the importance of his role, the Eparch lifted the crown high. The crowd held its breath, anticipation swelling as the crown descended with regal grace, finally settling upon the head of the new ruler.

At that moment, the onlookers erupted in jubilation, their cheers resounding throughout the royal gardens. The joyous sound echoed beyond the castle's stone walls, reaching those who could not attend the celebration. The kingdom welcomed a new king and a future filled with both hope and uncertainty. King Golen rose to his feet, his eyes glistening with steeled purpose. Scarlet set her eyes on the GranMother and Lord Elric for the reaction to the king's unexpected speech that she helped orchestrate.

"Today, I stand before you as your king. I pledge to uphold the responsibilities of this crown with unwavering dedication. I make every decision with a profound awareness of the immense responsibility this crown places upon my brow. I do so for the well-being of all Valarians. However, I intend to lead with a different approach than my father, prioritising the prospects of Valaria above all else. Our province deserves a ruler who places our interests at the forefront, fostering prosperity and unity within our borders. As your king, I am committed to working tirelessly for the betterment of Valaria, ensuring that our great land continues to flourish and that the dreams of all Valarians are realised. Together, we shall chart a new but bright future for Valaria."

Both the GranMother and Lord Elric felt anguished over Golen's deliberate use of double meanings in his choice of words— "I intend to lead with a different approach than my father, prioritising the prospects of Valaria above all else." Thalassa Starling turned to Lord Elric, her hand shielding her lips to keep her words private. "The battle for Golen's loyalty is lost. Relying solely on the princess and humans is too precarious to risk. General Titanous lingers in the shadows, and now, more than ever, we need his assistance." Elric nodded approvingly. The pivotal inclusion of the general was a welcome approach that lit up his face.

Their discreet exchange piqued Scarlet's curiosity, causing her to flash a winning smile in response. The smile intensified Thalassa Starling's determination to locate the elusive but all-knowing general. She requested Lord Elric to dispatch a Whispering Courier to the central region of Lumina—DataDome City, aiming for it to reach the general's notice.

After composing the message together, she felt anxious for Lord Elric's safety and urged, "I implore you to come with me."

"No, GranMother, I belong here, yet, I vow to tread carefully through this ominous dark of menacing gloom."

"Had I been in your position, I would have echoed your sentiments. How I wish for a farewell under happier circumstances, Lord Elric," she shook his hand and unexpectedly kissed his cheek, wondering if this would be their final encounter. She left his company without a backward glance.

Within the seclusion of his estate, Lord Elric huddled inside the bird coop. Constructed with wire mesh walls for ventilation and protection, he navigated past perches and nesting boxes to find the Whispering Courier that had flown the path to the Province of Lumania. Attaching a tiny canister to its leg, he cradled the bird outside the coop, releasing it with a silent prayer. Returning to the palace, he repeated the urgent message in his thoughts.

I am en route from the Valarian Palace to DataDome City on a matter of urgency. In seeking your assistance, five provinces hold their collective breath, filled with hope that you will receive this message. Signed, Thalassa Starling.

In the company of Whispering Grass, Scarlet made her way toward Golen in the royal gardens, her face a mask of feigned sorrow and concern. "Your Majesty," she said, her voice trembling. "I must express regret in informing you that the GranMother has left the palace without expressing her gratitude for your generous hospitality or offering a farewell."

"Indeed, Your Highness, to my knowledge, I have never known the GranMother to engage in such arrogance towards royalty," Whispering Grass declared."

"I approached Lord Elric with the utmost courtesy and inquired about the reason for her sudden departure," Scarlet recounted, her tone laced with frustration. "Yet, my inquiry was met with resounding silence. He merely turned away, leaving the answer unspoken—a barrier of silence and indifference."

"It seems Lord Elric's favouritism toward the general and the GranMother is as evident as it is with my sister," Golen stated, raising an eyebrow.

"May I propose a solution?"

"By all means, Scarlet. I'm eager to hear your thoughts," he encouraged.

"Allow Slade to maintain a vigilant watch over Lord Elric. Slade's loyalty and impartiality can reveal the truth, whether it proves to be genuine or unfounded. Unlike some other courtiers, I recommend Slade because he has no particular allegiance to Lord Elric."

"An exceptional idea," Golen mused with an appreciative smile, his mind already contemplating the potential advantages of her suggestion.

Whispering Grass felt a wave of astonishment at the announcement of the GranMother's unexpected departure. It was a welcome relief; her absence lifted the burden of concern about her sneaking around to speak to the king. He had long admired her boldness, but curiosity tugged at him. Where could she be? What was she planning? Was she in pursuit of allies? Regardless of her intentions, he feared she might come back even more formidable than before.

Chapter 29

Thalassa Starling's horse-drawn coach rolled along the winding roads, the wheels rattling in a steady rhythm that mirrored her thoughts. The journey to Lumina was more than just a physical trek; it was a test of her faith. Outside, the view was a monotonous stretch of thick undergrowth and dense forest, a stark reminder of the isolation she now felt. The weight of her mission pressed heavily on her shoulders, and each stop to rest the weary horses felt like a moment stolen from time. The carriage pressed on into the unknown as the sun sank below the horizon, casting a pall over her thoughts. A persistent worry gnawed at her: had the general received her message? His whereabouts were perpetually shrouded in secrecy, and his talent for stealth only deepened her frustration.

Suddenly, the carriage came to a jarring halt. The horses reared up, their metal shoes clattering against the stony ground. An eerie noise echoed through the air, reminiscent of colliding thunderstorms. Like a mirage, the path ahead rippled and distorted until a large sphere, crackling with electrical charge, materialised. The unexpected sight left Gran-Mother and her companions in awe. They gazed, wide-eyed, at the portal, its swirling, iridescent colours casting a mesmerising glow that illuminated their faces. The sphere seemed to defy reason as the restless horses whinnied, becoming increasingly difficult to control, unsettled by the strange presence blocking their path.

With a bold and assured stride, General Titanous stepped from the portal in a brilliant flash of swirling energy, moving with the elegance of someone who had journeyed across countless dimensions. His confident gaze took in the scene around him, and in that instant, Thalassa Starling realised that the sphere was the very mechanism that had transported the humans from their world to Cyberia. A whirlwind of questions filled her mind, but she was momentarily too astonished to speak.

The general looked reassuringly at the coach drivers while steadying the team of horses. As he helped GranMother out of the coach, he explained the extraordinary phenomenon that had left her speechless. He disclosed that the force behind the portal's emergence was a gift from the Pathfinder himself.

Taking a moment to compose herself, the general listened attentively before replying, his voice heavy with duty and responsibility. "GranMother, your concerns are warranted. Though the threat of war lingers, the princess and the humans embody hope, even in the bleakest times. Their journey has brought them to the earthquake-affected region of Volcanis," he explained. "This is a crucial step for them to become the genuine heroes Cyberia longs for. Teeming with unseen dangers, they must face their destinies, revealing their true strength as they strive to complete their ultimate mission of obtaining the last Crystal."

"What if they falter?" she asked.

The general's fist tightened in frustration. "I wish to assist, protect, and guide them. Yet, my oath to the Pathfinder compels me to listen instead of take action. We must trust in the chosen few as we face the imminent threats of Malware, King Kronos, and Golen."

Thalassa Starling nodded gravely. "I stand by your decision, general. The hopes of every inhabitant and our splendid creatures rest on this. They must and will emerge victorious," she reassured herself.

The general placed a reassuring hand on her shoulder. "I possess a contingency plan that I cannot reveal. My responsibility is to remain vigilant, wait patiently, and uphold faith in the Pathfinder's vision." As he said his farewells, he stepped back into the portal. Thalassa Starling couldn't help but contemplate the nature of this plan as the magnificent machine faded and disappeared.

Chapter 30

Valarian Palace

King Kronos capitulated to Golen that treachery was afoot from the five provinces against their kingdoms. He spun a tale of political unrest, fuelled by his disdain for Arbitration Land and his collusion with Admiral Malice Malware, whose ties with Drakonia were due to the unrest. Golen listened attentively, his brow furrowing as the weight of the situation became increasingly apparent.

The GranMother's unexpected exit from the palace only heightened the suspicion directed at the five provinces. What struck him most was the revelation that Lord Elric's spies, albeit under torture, had confessed their loyalty to the Princess and Arbitration Land. The tangled web of this dark misinformation left Golen speechless and embarrassed.

Whispering Grass invited himself to speak. "Your Highness, the expedience of King Kronos's visit, like the impending arrival of Admiral Malware, was to consolidate, as promised, the news of such treachery. With three of the most powerful figures in Cyberia whose thoughts align, it's only fitting that you should be seated together to plan the next step for self-proclaimed dominance."

"Our liberation from Arbitration Land can only be achieved by depleting the ecosystem," said Kronos. "It is frustrating that your sister and these individuals relentlessly pursue these last five Crystals of Time, an endeavour that, as I understand, had been hidden from you." He found satisfaction in observing Golen squirm in his chair but then shifted tactics to ease his embarrassment and align him to their cause. "I believe they gravely underestimated you. I witness a distinguished king, relentless in his pursuit of elevating his reign to a new pinnacle of power."

"There is no higher praise that anyone could bestow upon me," replied Golen, gratified by the comment. "I eagerly await Admiral Malware's arrival to advance our common ideologies," he stated. Whispering Grass also derived satisfaction from the comment. Since he arrived in Valaria, he has fulfilled every task assigned to him.

In the vast expanse of the Royal Garden, all eyes were drawn to the horizon as the battleship Infector descended, its landing gear gently touching the green lawn at the garden's edge. King Golen awaited the Admiral in splendid attire, exuding regal elegance. Beside him stood King Kronos, clad in gleaming armour, ready for conflict as if the battle had already commenced. Golen extended a welcoming hand, his voice rich with authority. "Admiral Malware, the kingdom of Valaria is deeply honoured to receive you in these turbulent times."

The Admiral grasped his hand firmly, a mischievous smile playing on his lips as he cast a knowing glance at King Kronos, fully aware that the fate of five provinces now teetered on a knife's edge. He bellowed an order, and a contingent of the ship's crew emerged, carrying a chest overflowing with gleaming gold coins: the promised treasure glimmered enticingly, a seductive lure. With a gracious nod, King Golen accepted the offering, his discerning gaze revealing a blend of power and ambition. He recognised the treasure's potential, not solely for the kingdom's prosperity, but as a means to fulfil his grand ambitions.

They advanced toward the palace's most impenetrable chamber—the formidable war room. The three dominant figures took their seats around the imposing round table, which showcased an array of documents and strategic artefacts telling tales of Valaria's ancient battles. Whispering Grass meticulously arranged markers, scrolls, and planning tools on its surface, each item serving a purpose in its strategic discussions.

Speaking to his counterparts, King Kronos revealed the dire warning sent to Arbitration for the five provinces: they must relinquish weapons and allow access to their forces or face the threat of extinction. Golen couldn't contain his excitement upon discovering the intricate details of the ecosystem's rejuvenation shared by Malice Malware. The closely guarded information brought a smile to the fledgling king's face, and Whispering Grass shared that smile upon hearing it for the first time.

Golen inquired, "And what of my sister and the humans?" Malice Malice signalled his consent with a nod, granting permission for Whispering Grass to unveil his knowledge.

"Your Majesty," through an extensive network of spies, I have received information that they are actively searching for the final crystal in the province of Volcanis. An attempt to apprehend them failed. They eluded their trackers' grasp. The specific orders to avoid harm to Princess Arabella or any royal proved to be the setback," he lied.

"My sister has waived royal protection by banishment with her unprecedented treachery with these humans," he declared. "Let this be widely known." Whispering Grass nodded in understanding, his carefully chosen words effectively clearing any lingering suspicion Golen may have harboured regarding his father's demise.

King Kronos acknowledged Golen's words with an approving clap and grunt, expressing that he would have reached the same decision. "I remain unperturbed by the outcome of their quest for the final crystal. I have dispatched a battalion of warriors to seize control of Glimmerhavan in the heart of the Never-Ending Forest. Their objective is to establish a protective perimeter around the Great White Clock, thwarting any attempt to replenish the Crystals of Time. The battalion of warriors has been dispatched primarily as a precautionary measure. Even if our adversaries were to obtain the final crystal, the sheer enormity of traversing various provinces is a lost race against time. An unattainable feat before the ecosystem deteriorates."

"I agree with your judgement," said Malware. He gave a curt nod for Whispering Grass to finalise before they prepared to pore over the charts outlining their invasion strategy and agree on reallocating captured lands.

"The precise whereabouts of Princess Arabella and others lie at the 'Pinnacle of Hope, a volcanic island in Volcanis. Here, they have solicited aid in crossing the river encircling the pinnacle, seeking passage by boat. The source of this information derives from a trusted spy, one in whom I have the utmost confidence. I have charged this operative with the vital task of obstructing their acquisition of the ultimate crystal, a mission that promises substantial wealth in return. Beyond the imminent depletion of their time and the arrival of King Kronos' warriors at Glimmerhaven, this spy stands in their way – my beloved nephew, who goes by the name Argent.

Chapter 31

The Pinnacle of Hope
Volcanis

Overlooking the expansive shoreline, seagulls circled overhead, their screeching cries echoing above the sprawling village that commanded the bay. The salty breeze, mingling with the rhythmic sound of the choppy waves below, felt like a serene ending to their final quest. Riding into the village, Valour couldn't help but admire its proud stature as a bastion of maritime existence. Crafted from new and weathered wood, its collection of thatched buildings and taverns stood as a testament to generations of naval tradition. In the distance, Max watched seafarers sift through a tangled web of nets pulled from the depths, repairing any weakness or damage with agile fingers and robust twine.

The strangers on majestic WhiteTails quickly attracted a crowd as they halted outside the Welcoming Tavern in the heart of the village. Recognising this as their best chance, the Princess rose high in her stirrups, beckoning for attention. The crowd was amazed to hear how the newcomers wanted to hire a boat and await their return from the Pinnacle of Hope.

With grumbles of concern and rising hostility, the seafarers insisted on knowing why they wanted to land on the island, having already pointed out the threatening volcanic rumblings to all who neared. Arabella decided it was wiser not to reveal their true intentions and concocted a tale about a mystical plant called Luminaflora. "Legend has it that those who consume its petals will be blessed with unmatched courage and true wisdom." The crowd erupted in laughter at the absurdity of the myth.

One seafarer seized the moment like a ripe fruit ready to be plucked. He stepped forward, his heart pumping with excitement. The crowd's murmurs faded into the background as he concentrated on the task, his thoughts swirling with dreams of financial reward. With a voice piercing the chatter, he boldly declared his willingness to take on the challenge. The crowd responded with scoffs and derisive laughter as they began to disperse. In that instant, he shifted from a mere observer to a key player in the unfolding drama, invigorated by the thrill of uncertainty. The group dismounted, fastened their steeds to a rail, and stepped inside the tavern to negotiate a fee. The lounge offered an inviting rustic charm, with its wooden beams and a hearth that crackled with warmth. Dimly lit, it emitted a sense of history, furnished with aged, cracked oil paintings of bygone maritime adventurers on its walls. The landlord merged two tables, fostering the space for his patrons to gather, chat, and place their orders for food and beverages.

Taken aback by the exorbitant sum he demanded, Arabella was pleased that Isaiah brokered a deal with the seafarer named Argent that was mutually beneficial to both parties. Argent's undeniable good looks contrasted with his uncle, Whispering Grass. His sun-kissed, windswept, fair hair flowed over his broad shoulders, adding to his rugged appeal. Shaped by the hand of fortune, his well-defined jawline and striking sapphire-blue eyes captivated the female residents of the area. What truly distinguished him was his fashion sense. While the seafarers dressed in worn, ragged clothing, Argent had a taste for style that turned heads. He favoured rich, deep colours that sharply contrasted with the muted tones of his peers.

Argent leaned forward, his voice steady as he explained his reasoning for volunteering but hesitating to proceed with the treacherous journey until dawn. "The villagers are afraid of even their shadows," he said, his tone firm. "I've ventured into the forbidden zone many times," he lied, "yet here I stand, ready to recount my experiences. But if we're to traverse a storm of deadly projectiles, I'd much rather do so under the sun's illuminating light. In the darkness, it's all too easy to lose one's way, and in such difficult waters, I'd prefer to see the threats we face rather than navigate blindly."

Although Argent spoke with a blend of wisdom and caution for their safety, Valour instantly disliked him. Was it the way he leered with flirting eyes at the Princess? Nevertheless, he dismissed such jealousy and recognised that this was a moment for the group to reflect on the importance of safely navigating the waters ahead. Unaware of Valour's feelings, Mia had reservations about Argent. She observed the intensity in Oscar's gaze, his sharp eyes fixed with a critical focus. The SablePaw's posture radiated disapproval, clearly indicating his lack of trust and unease towards the villager. But the group's thoughts swiftly transformed into frustration when Argent announced, "We set sail in two glitchmarks." The news washed over them like a cold wave, leaving them stunned. Argent's unforeseen commitments felt like a betrayal, plunging them into disappointment and a sense of helplessness. They reluctantly agreed to meet on the proposed date and parted ways with no other option.

The Princess was glad that Isaiah had managed to secure accommodation at the tavern and arrange a stable for their steeds until they returned from the island. The two bedrooms were cramped and sparsely furnished, but they appreciated the simple comfort of having a roof over their heads and a comfortable bed. As they settled into their quarters, with Oscar nestled beside her, Mia listened closely as the Princess shared her concerns about the urgency of reaching Glimmerhavan, knowing that hidden challenges still awaited them. She felt relief that information about the ecosystem had not yet reached Wyvern Bay, safeguarding her true identity. Argent's warning about the villagers' fear of shadows only strengthened her resolve to keep the truth hidden, preventing unnecessary panic.

Across the village, Argent lay in his bed, astonished by his good fortune as he watched unfamiliar riders arrive on strange steeds. He pondered the extent of his uncle's coded messages to various regions. The description of the riders, their strange steeds, and the directive he had given was unmistakable: stop them by any means necessary. Reflecting on his message to his uncle through a whispering courier, he marvelled at the incredible reward that awaited him. Yet, despite his careful planning, sleep eluded him.

With the gentle light of dawn illuminating the sky, the five adventurers, led by Argent, approached the white timber-frame boat.

They assembled on the beach around the modest vessel, their faces reflecting a blend of eagerness and anticipation as the snow season drew ever closer. Having left Oscar in the care of the stable hand, Mia's expression showed both hope and concern. Together, they pulled the boat away from the sandy shore, with Argent boarding last after guiding it into deeper water. The vessel swayed gently as the Princess and Mia settled into their seats at the back, while the others took up their oars, rowing through the calm, windless waters. Rowing with his back turned to the Pinnacle of Hope, Max kept his gaze fixed on the village of Wyvern Bay, which slowly disappeared from sight.

Upon reaching the opposite shoreline, Argent's plan was clear: he intended to abandon them on the desolate island, stripped of any flourishing vegetation. With no resources for sustenance or escape routes, their chances of survival were slim to none in the river's dangerous currents. As they crossed the exclusion zone, the one fear he had dreaded failed to materialise. Without any volcanic rumblings, the gold promised by his uncle was now tantalisingly within reach, and he had the added benefit of receiving his payment upfront for their boat passage.

They took short breaks from rowing as the Pinnacle of Hope grew more extensive in the distance. Its striking silhouette dominated the horizon, showcasing a rugged peak and vast slopes in a blend of earthy browns and greys. Jagged rock formations jutted out from the base, creating bold shadows that contrasted sharply with the sunlight, enhancing the mountain's awe-inspiring presence. The entire view conveyed a feeling of solitude, sparking a distinct sense of danger in all who dared to explore its sacred ground. From the eerie stillness, a deep rumbling began to rise like the growl of a slumbering giant, followed by a ferocious gust of wind that whistled with a ferocity Argent had never before encountered. The boat rocked wildly, lurching from side to side as it fought to stay upright against the onslaught of the sudden bluster. Without warning, the river's surface transformed into a chaotic dance of churning water, leaving Argent with a tight knot of anxiety coiling in his stomach to the surprising fury of untamed nature.

Concerned for their safety, the Princess attempted to voice her worries, desperation etched on her face. However, the rumbling intensified, swelling into a deafening roar that eclipsed her voice, swallowing her words in the pandemonium. The mountain's peak suddenly erupted in a chaotic burst of debris, akin to a fireworks display gone awry. Rocks fell from above, and they could only gaze in horror as countless fragments descended toward them, crashing into the water with a resounding boom. Each impact sent enormous splashes into the air, rocking their boat as the rocks hissed beneath the surface.

There was an eerie silence before several bone-shaking blasts erupted, its noise more deafening than they could have imagined. The river convulsed, its surface churning and frothing, sending waves pounding against the hull. A colossal eruption turned the boat into a target for a barrage of flying granite spears, sporadically slicing through the air with a sharp hiss as they struck the water's surface. Heavy boulders followed, crashing down with a thunderous crack, sending shockwaves across the water. Each impact unleashed a deluge of water, drenching everyone on board and heightening the sense of it capsizing.

Arabella's voice rose in urgency as she implored the rowers to turn the boat and flee back to the village, desperate to escape the relentless rain of projectiles. Drenched and gripped by fear, she and Mia scrambled to find anything they could use to bail out the water rapidly filling the boat. Mia's gaze shot skyward, her breath catching as she spotted a gigantic boulder hurtling toward them. The immense rock soared overhead, its thunderous crash drowning out her terrified scream as it struck the water. It sent a massive wave crashing toward them, rendering their frantic rowing futile as it lifted them high upon its crest. The boat descended with a jolt as if recoiling from the relentless assault, yet it teetered precariously in the choppy swell.

The eruptions subsided, leaving an eerie stillness in their wake. Max leaned heavily over his oar, gasping for breath and trembling from exertion. Recognising his bravery and effort, Valour offered a reassuring pat on the back. A strange sound suddenly pierced the air, causing the water to shudder as if the mountain was taking a deep, quaking breath, a harbinger of the disaster to come. Massive crevices split the rugged volcanic peaks, releasing ominous plumes of dust and smoke that spiralled into the sky. They watched in horror as the mountain summit began to implode, resembling a mammoth sinkhole collapsing. The eruption was nothing short of apocalyptic, a roar that reverberated through the air, sending shockwaves creating a monumental vacuum, yanking the boat backwards as if caught in the grip of an unseen force."

Max watched the heated exchange between Valour and Argent, quickly realising that they were now facing the imminent threat of a mini tsunami. The ominous water swell seemed to gather strength, echoing a looming catastrophe on the horizon. As the river surged, the boat pitched wildly beneath them. Valour's voice rose above the chaos, cutting through the turmoil as he shouted commands, urgency threading through every word. "Brace yourselves! Lie as flat as you can and grab onto something sturdy!"

Max and Mia huddled tightly between the rowing seats, their bodies pressed together for support. Max clutched one of the thwarts, his grip fierce, while Mia held onto her brother, both bracing for the tsunami's imminent surge. The distant rumble intensified, resonating like a freight train barreling toward them. Mia's grip on Max tightened, her fear mounting. Valour's last command to hunker down echoed in their ears just before the boat thrust skyward, soaring like a surfboard riding a monstrous wave, leaving them suspended in a moment of sheer terror.

Above and below the water's surface, a dynamic interplay of light and shadow unfolded, creating a mesmerising spectacle. Sunlight streamed through the waves, casting vibrant rainbow patterns that shimmered like liquid prisms. Marine life swirled up from the riverbed, their movements adding an extraordinary element to the underwater scene as they struggled to navigate the turbulent waters. Valour closed his eyes, surrendering to the moment and hoping for the best possible outcome. As the boat surged toward the rapidly approaching village shoreline, the tide collided with a dense thicket of trees, forming a natural barrier that significantly diminished the wave's force. Overhanging branches lashed out mercilessly, striking the vessel as its hull scraped against the rough bark of the obstructive trunks. The boat plunged downward, the water churning noisily around it. Just as it reached the final line of trees guarding the village, the vessel succumbed to the chaos and capsized, sending its passengers tumbling into the turbulent waters.

Submerged beneath the churning water, Max fought desperately to keep hold of his sister. With one hand gripping a sturdy branch, he struggled to maintain balance as the water's pull rapidly receded. Both gasped for air, sputtering as they expelled water from their lungs, their wide eyes scanning the bedlam scene around them.

Valour broke the surface, one arm wrapped protectively around the Princess while the other clutched a branch for stability. Nearby, Isaiah, thrown a considerable distance, clung tenaciously to a tree trunk, showing no signs of releasing his grip.

With Argent missing, their anxiety escalated, leaving them in a disorienting predicament. They were consumed by uncertainty, questioning his fate and grappling with deep confusion as they struggled to make sense of the bedlam around them.

The villagers ascended to higher ground, preparing for the anticipated tsunami following the implosion of the Pinnacle of Hope. Fortunately, the village had emerged largely unscathed, allowing them to descend and offer their assistance cautiously. Despite their fatigue, Valour and Isaiah summoned their remaining strength to join the arduous search for Argent. His absence cast a shadow of uncertainty over their determined efforts, infusing their mission with a poignant sense of loss as they pressed on through the debris, driven by hope and desperation.

Weary and bedraggled, the group sat on the shoreline, gazing at the horizon. Their dishevelled appearance mirrored the exhaustion etched across their faces. The Pinnacle of Hope, once majestic, now lay in ruins before them. The final crystal they sought looked buried beneath the colossal weight of flattened rock.

The Princess wrestled with an immense sense of responsibility, weighed down by the shattered dreams of her friends sitting broken-hearted at her feet. The elusive key to the final crystal eluded her grasp, and the burden of her failure felt unbearable. The journey's conclusion left Max with a face marked by disbelief and frustration. Mia struggled to conceal her profound sorrow. Throughout their trials, she had been the beacon of hope, but even her indomitable spirit had dimmed by the weight of their failure. Her customary radiant smile had now given way to a tearful gaze. Valour, the steady and composed group anchor, felt a hollow defeat he had never known. Isaiah struggled with the harsh reality and shared a profound responsibility for the failure that had befallen them.

The unsettling calm was shattered by a deep, resonant rumble reverberating through the air. The ground quaked beneath their feet, fear etched on their faces. The group braced themselves for yet another earthquake. Instead, a tremendous wave of energy surged through the atmosphere, heralding the arrival of something otherworldly. A swirling vortex materialized, radiating a blinding light and a cacophony of thunderous sound. The air crackled with electricity as the portal ripped through the very fabric of reality. Villagers along the shoreline scattered in every direction, their instincts driving them to flee from the terrifying spectacle.

The siblings stood frozen, their hearts heavy as they faced the portal that had once been a gateway to wonder and adventure. Now, it loomed before them like a dark spectre, a stark reminder of their failures and the impending return to Earth. The vibrant colours that had once danced around the portal now seemed muted, casting an eerie glow that mirrored the whirlwind of emotions swirling within them. Disappointment, sorrow, and a haunting fear of the unknown gripped their hearts as they wrestled with the reality of what lay ahead for Cyberia.

Mia broke the silence, her voice trembling with uncertainty. "I don't know what any of this means. Will I ever see you, Bilko, or Oscar again? I don't know." Her words hung heavy with the weight of her fears.

Max felt Cyberia had become more than just a fantastical realm; it had transformed into a second home, where they had forged bonds and created memories that would last a lifetime. The thought of leaving it all behind was unbearable. His expression turned to despair as he looked at the portal, its once inviting glow now a stark reminder of their impending departure, overshadowed by the uncertainty of their future.

They had faced challenges that tested their courage and resilience and emerged stronger for it. Yet, the thought of returning to Earth, a place that felt increasingly foreign, filled them with dread. Would they adjust to a world that no longer felt like home? Would they be able to carry the magic of Cyberia with them, or would it fade away like a distant dream? Mia brushed away her tears, her intense emotions surfacing. With a sense of sadness, she moved closer to the portal, ready to face whatever awaited her on the other side, resolved to carry the spirit of Cyberia wherever she went. Expecting the gatekeeper's appearance, she was bewildered when General Titanous emerged, his presence both startling and commanding. With a firm thrust, the general planted his shining spear into the soft sand, addressing the group with pride.

"I want to take a moment to express how truly inspired I am by each one of you. Your journey has been remarkable, and the challenges you've overcome are nothing short of extraordinary." A warm, encouraging smile illuminated his face, "Yet, there is a flicker of hope. One final possibility remains." His gaze settled on Max, his expression both insightful and reassuring. "Have you overlooked the fact that the sacred Map suggested the existence of another Crystal?"

Amid the swirling chaos, a spark of clarity ignited. "Yes, yes!" Max shouted, frustration evident in his voice. "The map showed me a vision of another crystal, but it vanished before I could fully grasp its meaning. I didn't mention this to Mia since we had just arrived in Cyberia. I dismissed it as irrelevant to our journey."

Mia stared at her brother in disbelief. The others exchanged puzzled looks at the general and Max. The decision to keep this information from her left Mia confused. Frustrated, she demanded, "What is it that you didn't want to reveal to me, and why?

"I will answer your question," the General declared, asserting the newfound authority bestowed upon him by the Pathfinder. "Max was aware of a crystal but not of its capabilities. The Dendritic Agate is genuinely one of a kind among the Crystals of Time. Its remarkable characteristics, with veins resembling delicate fern patterns, give it an unmatched beauty akin to the pristine purity of freshly fallen snow. The information your brother kept secret was the location of the crystal: Malware Island. However, he had no idea that the Dendritic Agate was secured within an impenetrable vault inside the fortress." He paused, allowing the weight of this revelation to sink in. "Mia, I believe your brother acted wisely. He wanted to protect you from unnecessary distress when you arrived in Cyberia. Now, I pose this question to all of you: faced with choosing two remaining crystals but needing only one, where would you have decided—here or on Malware Island? The harsh [truth I must share is that the four crystals in your possession have turned into nothing but artefacts. Their formidable power extinguished with the destruction of the Crystal of Volcanis."

The Princess broke the contemplative silence. "I do not understand. You mentioned that all hope is not lost. What purpose does this Dendritic Agate serve when we require five crystals to rejuvenate the ecosystem?"

"The Dendritic Agate has the collective power of all five crystals. Max, if you look at the sacred map, it would have adjusted itself accordingly."

"Even so, without the sacred Map, how could Malice Malware properly align the Dendritic Agate within the Great White Clock?" said the Princess, confused.

"A question I anticipated, princess. His vault holds the wisdom of an ancient sorcerer who guides this decision. The reason or source of such power is beyond my comprehension."

Isaiah sank to his knees in the sand. "General, are you suggesting there was no need to face the Serpent, the Queen bee, the Dream-Stealer, Arachnida, and the most formidable of them all, Volcanis?" His gaze was distant, and he added, "I found this place the most testing because I cannot swim." Valour, appreciating his honesty and dark humour, touched his shoulder to acknowledge his silent courage.

Arabella's dismay deepened. "Why would the Pathfinder lead us on a treacherous and unnecessary journey, culminating in this moment? What end does it serve?"

"I believe the aim was for you to forge a resilient bond," the General declared. "Your trials were interwoven with trust, an unspoken promise to stand united. You have faced the most daunting challenges and come out stronger, ready to endure any storm in the face of adversity. As I gaze upon all of you, I can confidently assert that the Pathfinder has achieved his goal: to form an unbreakable connection between your hearts."

Arabella processed the information, acknowledging its truth and validity. "Your gracious and eloquent words resonate like the rallying cry of a general whose respect we cherish deeply."

The General smiled in appreciation of the compliment. "The relief from this revelation, following such devastation, is clear on your face. From this moment on, I pledge to stand by your side. Together, we will work to claim the Dendritic Agate from Malice Malware and ensure it is in its rightful home, the Great White Clock in Glimmerhavan."

"I must stress the formidable strength of Malware Island's defences," the Princess stated. "It features a complex network of cutting-edge technology, so sophisticated that it can detect even the slightest intrusion, whether by land, sea, or air." Realising the weight of her impulsive words, she quickly added, "I apologise for my haste. If there is a path forward, you have the wisdom to guide us. However, considering the time it will take to travel from here to Malware Island and to penetrate its defences, our window of opportunity to rejuvenate the ecosystem will have closed."

Mia's eyes widened as she grasped the only conceivable solution. "We use the portal," she whispered aloud.

"The chosen one has excellent insight," smiled the General. "This quest will involve a team of just two: Princess Arabella and myself," he provoked.

"General, I cannot allow this," declared Valour. "I took a personal oath before King Osred to protect the princess at any cost."

"Valour, your commitment to the Princess and her father is admirable. Yet, I, too, have pledged to protect all of you."

Unaware of Valour's promise to her father, Arabella focused on the quest. "Valour, I find myself encircled by numerous protectors. It brings me joy to say that I would willingly sacrifice myself to keep you safe, just as I would for the others," she quickly amended, noticing the curious expression on Isaiah's face.

The general lifted his eyes to the sky. "I can ask the Pathfinder questions and interpret his responses," he said, turning his attention to the

Princess. "You share this gift; it's why your father entrusted you with this quest. As you learn to grasp the Pathfinder's insights, you will understand that his wisdom surpasses all others."

"Princess!" Max recalled. "You once urged me to hold onto those words of cosmic significance—if only I could. In our world, those words are woven into the lyrics of a song, a melody meant to create a better world."

A blush crept across the Princess's cheeks. "I must confess, I wasn't entirely truthful. I didn't read it in the stars; I heard a voice in my head. Who in their 'right' mind would admit to something like that?"

"Touché!" the general laughed heartily. "Once you learn to embrace the guidance of the Pathfinder instead of resisting it, it will become the driving force behind every decision you make against evil. You will also gain the extraordinary gift of communicating with animals."

"Will Max and I be granted this power?" Mia asked, excitedly.

"No Mia. Only those of Cyberian origin." The general redirected their focus. "In my secret lair, a sanctuary awaits you—one that is concealed from royalty and others. You have earned this privilege. You will wait for the Princess and me to return from our mission to retrieve the Dendritic Agate. You have been the focus of relentless pursuit, with spies sent across distant lands, including Argent, who is neither lost nor drowned but remains very much active."

Valour and Mia voiced their mistrust of Argent, each surprised to discover the other's thoughts. "I thought I was the only one who felt this way," Mia admitted, a sense of relief flooding her.

"The sacred map will not reveal the Dendritic Agate's place of insertion within the Great White Clock until we have it in our grasp," said the general. "That task will certainly not be easier with the final battle approaching."

"Final battle?" the Princess asked, confused.

"Cautious of the advancements in your quest, King Kronos' strategist deployed a battalion of 600 warriors to safeguard the Great White Clock. Argent will have conveyed information to Malice Malware regarding the loss of the Crystal of Volcanis. Malware will be uncertain whether you know of the Dendritic Agate. Nevertheless, he will thwart any attempt to retrieve it. However, with the assistance of the Portal, we will reach the island before a Whispering Courier can traverse the provinces to convey that warning."

"Even if we had the Dendritic Agate in our grasp, how can we confront a battalion of Drakonian warriors?" Isaiah asked.

"Let us take this one step at a time, Isaiah," the general advised. "Let's focus our thoughts on gaining the Dendritic Agate. I can transport two companions on each trip to my lair. The last will be the steeds. They will have to be blindfolded to alleviate any fear."

"And Oscar! I refuse to leave him behind," declared Mia. "He has formed a strong bond with Bilko, my WhiteTail." A broad smile graced her face when the general quickly consented. She noted Isaiah's hesitancy, an expression suggesting he might also need a blindfold when stepping into the Portal.

"Who's first?" the general asked.

"Isaiah and me," Mia said, clutching his hand. "If I can do it, so can you," she whispered reassuringly.

Chapter 32

Province of Lumina

The portal manifested in a forest clearing, where towering trees loomed overhead, their canopies reaching out in every direction. General Titanous waved for Mia and Isaiah to follow, directing them to a spot where their steeds could graze on the abundant vegetation. The sound of rushing water grew louder, culminating in the sight of a breathtaking waterfall. Crystalline water flowed from the towering cliff above, splashing into a shimmering pool below. Sunlight filtered through the waterfall, casting a brilliant display of colours. The air was fresh and revitalising, a refreshing change from the humid paths they had journeyed. Unaware of the wonders that lay ahead, they stopped to enjoy the fine mist that brushed against their faces.

They ascended a narrow path that clung to the cliffside, leading them behind the roaring waterfall. They watched as the general stepped through the holographic rock face, entering the expansive cavern beyond and gesturing for them to follow. The walls pulsed with intricate, glowing patterns reminiscent of complex circuitry, their light weaving a captivating interplay of technology. The cavern felt like a convergence of the natural and digital realms. At its centre stood a control hub unlike anything Mia had ever seen. It emitted a calming hum, accompanied by a holographic monitor that could display multiple files across various screens with a simple wave of the hand. The general focused intently on one screen that showcased the Guardian Gazing Orbs, strategically positioned at key vantage points for continuous surveillance beyond the perimeter. Sensor-activated doors slid open, revealing sleeping quarters, a lounge, a dining area, and other amenities.

The portal reemerged, guided by the gatekeeper, as Mia and Isaiah observed the monitor. The general stepped forward to greet his next visitors. Mia noticed that Max and the Princess shared the same awe as they took in the magnificent waterfall. Once inside the high-tech cavern, they marvelled at their surroundings before gathering at the console. They patiently awaited the arrival of everyone from Volcanis and the settling of the steeds, eager to discuss the challenges posed by Malware Island. The general activated a three-dimensional display on the screen. With a wave of his hand, the AI intuitively recognised his preferences and interests. As he navigated the information pages on Malware Island, he zoomed in, resizing and rotating the 3D models of the inner grounds where he intended for the portal to materialise within the fortress.

The control room hummed with a blend of technological wonder and strategic precision as he delved into the intricate details of their mission. Mapping out the journey ahead, he divided the route into distinct phases, outlining a sequential path he and the Princess would follow to reach the vault. The seriousness of his briefing deepened as he highlighted the threat of laser beams that could trigger a lethal crossfire in unauthorised corridors leading to the vault. The significance of the Princess's role in the quest became clear at that moment. Her selection to accompany the general was strategic. Her skin, equipped with optical filters, acted as a defence, allowing it to absorb, obstruct, or redirect laser beams. The general looked starkly at the Princess. "Your courage is indeed priceless, but bear in mind that bravery encompasses more than just fearless deeds, but wisdom, strategy, and resourcefulness."

The Princess frowned. "Your strategy to use my gift to find our way through these passageways is quite logical, but how did you come to possess such detailed knowledge of the fortress and its vault?"

"I must keep the particulars of that knowledge to myself, but I can tell you that I have ventured into the vault and witnessed its concealed secrets. It was there that I first learned of the Dendritic Agate and the corruption of the Five Crystals of Time by Malice Malware."

Max, sure it was the Pathfinder, pondered why the general hesitated to reveal his source, but he made a valid point. "What about the portal's noise when it appears out of nowhere on the fortress grounds? It's sure to alert the guards."

"True, except during a mighty thunderstorm. The storm will be our signal." A cryptic smile played on his lips at how he knew of such a forecast.

Max raised another issue regarding the CCTV surveillance in the general's lair. "Throughout our journey, I haven't noticed any CCTV cameras until now. Why is that?"

"In Cyberia, we refer to this surveillance as Guardian Gazing Orbs. The orbs can only operate in Lumina, Arbitration Land, and Malware's fortress. While the storm rages, the orbs will be the least of our concerns. The main objective is to get as close to the vault as possible before detection. Entrust the task of opening the vault door to me. Are you satisfied with everything you have heard, Princess?"

"Yes! I am, General," she replied without hesitation.

"Good! We leave quite soon."

Bittersweet anticipation enveloped her as her loyal companions prepared to bid her farewell. Arabella took the time to engage with each one individually, cherishing the bonds that had transformed them into her chosen family. Finally, she looked at Valour, the lionhearted warrior whose steadfast loyalty was a cornerstone of strength. In their embrace, gratitude flowed from her lips, her fingers tightly grasping the collar of his cloak. Valour's sturdy arms enveloped her, offering unspoken reassurance that melted her heart. Setting aside her concerns, she realised for the first time that maybe his feelings went beyond guardianship.

The echoes of the general and her footsteps faded, casting an unsettling silence in their absence. The once lively cavern now felt vast and empty. Mia withdrew to the living quarters, finding comfort in Oscar's reassuring presence. Settling on a cushion, she drew strength from the creature's gentle sighs, her mind preoccupied with the safety of the Princess and General Titanous. The others followed suit; each lost in their thoughts.

Valour's gaze was distant, his expression blank. His feelings for the Princess had blossomed from a small acorn into a mighty oak, deeply rooted and steadily growing. Initially, his admiration was a mere seedling, a quiet respect for her strength and grace. As they faced challenges together, that seedling began to sprout, nourished by shared experiences and moments of vulnerability. With each adventure, his affection deepened, transforming into a sturdy trunk that supported his unwavering loyalty. He found himself captivated by her courage and compassion, traits that drew him closer and made his heart swell with pride. The branches of his feelings extended outward, reaching for her in ways he had never anticipated, intertwining their lives in a bond that felt both natural and inevitable. He cherished every smile she offered and every laugh they shared, each moment adding to the richness of his feelings. Yet, beneath the surface, he grappled with the fear of vulnerability, unsure if she could ever see him as more than a guardian.

In the quiet moments, when he watched her from afar, he felt a profound connection that transcended friendship—a longing to protect her, to stand by her side, and to be the one she could rely on. Valour's heart, once a simple acorn, had grown into a powerful force, rooted in loyalty and blossoming with the hope that one day, the Princess might recognise the depth of his love.

Chapter 33

The Royal Palace
Valaria

Post King Kronos departure, Malice Malware organised an intimate dinner for King Golen onboard the Infector against the backdrop of the Royal Gardens. With Scarlet and Slade present, the verdant surroundings created the perfect evening. The absence of Whispering Grass had left a mysterious void. Seated to dine on the deck, they engaged in lively conversation. The tantalising aroma of delectable dishes filled the air, and the glisten of crystal glasses mirrored the stars above.

The conversation veered towards Lord Elric, who, like the Gran-Mother, had vanished from Valaria, leaving Slade feeling disconcerted by being outwitted by someone who appeared less cunning. Malware was pleased with how Golen had casually dismissed his former advisor, deeming him unnecessary baggage. Regardless, Lord Elric continued to be a significant threat and ordered that he be found and eliminated.

The excellent mood took an unforeseen turn when Whispering Grass emerged with a message received by the candlestick maker. With King Golen enthusiastically agreeing to a war pact, Malice Malware nodded his approval in granting Whispering Grass permission to speak openly. They listened intently as his nephew Argent recounted the devastating setback the princess and the humans had encountered. However, it was the extraordinary miracle he had witnessed from a distance—the sudden emergence of the teleportation machine, under the command of General Titanous—that truly captivated him.

Malware, concern etched on his face, said, "I find it perplexing how this mysterious object Argent spoke of could materialise and vanish at Titanous's command. Does it possess the capabilities to move as swiftly as a Whispering Courier or even match the speed of the Infector?"

He pondered whether Titanous's had knowledge of the Dendritic Agate. If so, it could ruin his streak of good fortune. Yet, only some were privy to the Agate's capabilities and concealed location. He shared his inner thoughts, hoping for a curtain of sense to stop this uncharted feeling that he'd never felt before.

"Admiral," said Slade, "not only is the Dendritic Agate safe within your vaults but even if the impossible became possible, there is a battalion of King Kronos' warriors protecting the Great White Clock."

Golen's brow furrowed. "I agree with you, Admiral. While King Kronos has provided reassurance about the formidable defences safeguarding the Dendritic Agate, we must not underestimate General Titanous's unforeseen knowledge or power."

Malware nodded solemnly. "Rest assured; the general's abilities weigh heavily on my mind. However, underestimating him would be a grave mistake we cannot afford."

"What say you, Scarlet, my love?" asked Golen.

"I agree with Slade, Your Highness. Even if the inconceivable were to occur, they would still need to battle 600 Draconian warriors."

"And what of your thoughts?" asked Golen of Whispering Grass.

Whispering Grass conveyed a grave caution in hushed tones, creating an unsettling atmosphere on the top deck. He unveiled the perils of the general possessing such a majestic device until his voice faded to a whisper. With a resonant thud, Malice Malware's hand struck the table, prompting him to speak louder.

"Your reaction," Whispering Grass concluded, "will determine the action needed." Malice Malware rose to his feet, his voice drastically changing from his previous demeanour. He commanded Slade to prepare the crew for the voyage to his fortress on Malware Island. He directed Whispering Grass to send an urgent message to his stronghold and another as a warning to the Drakonian commander in Glimmerhavan. Scarlet was torn between staying aboard and accompanying the king. Aware of her dilemma, Malware signalled his decision with a sharp, cobra-quick gaze for her to remain with the king and then impatiently watched as they disembarked.

The frigate rapidly rose from the royal gardens. Stocked with stored fuel cells for nocturnal scenarios when solar power was not feasible. Malware planned to utilise the slipstream's energy to drive them forward at full speed.

The crew sought refuge inside the protective hull to escape the howling wind. The echoes of the wind and sporadic shudders of the vessel cutting through the atmosphere were their only ties to the external elements. Dark, ominous clouds loomed ahead, stretching across the horizon like a harbinger of a storm of colossal proportions. The ship found itself at the mercy of the maelstrom, posing a formidable test of its structural integrity and the resilience of its crew. The bridge deck, designed with modernity in mind to withstand the elements, stood as a technological marvel against the raw forces of nature.

As the vessel collided with the storm Malware struggled to see the deck. Despite the rapid movement of the bridge-house wipers, they failed to clear the splattered screen. The wind howled like a wild beast while distant lightning added a dramatic touch to the turbulent scene. The distinct smell of salt and seaweed, reverberated through the ship. A wave came crashing down with a thunderous roar engulfing the Infector in a suffocating shroud of darkness. For a heart-stopping moment, it felt as if the vessel would be swallowed whole by the tempest. Yet, amidst the mayhem, Malware stood resolute, his voice cutting through the chaos like a lighthouse guiding lost ships to safety.

The crew, momentarily stunned by the storm's ferocity, moved with purpose, their actions a well-rehearsed dance of survival, each member instinctively knowing their role in the face of adversity. Malware's adrenaline surged as he locked his gaze on the radar, the screen flickering erratically under the strain of the storm's fury. The peculiar storm had appeared without warning, a dark spectre on the horizon that had quickly morphed into a monstrous force. He tracked its movements with a keen eye, calculating their course and the best way to navigate through the chaos.

Thorn opened a hatch and shouted commands to his shipmates below, urging them to double-secure the rigging ropes and sails. Seawater surged in from the seabed, rushing inside the ship, while the wind cruelly snatched away his words. Struggling to maintain his footing and gripping the outer rail, he urgently gestured toward an open sail, warning the deckhands of the imminent danger it posed. In the midst of the turmoil, a rogue rope coiled around a crew member's legs, yanking him overboard into the dark abyss. Thorn fought to reel in the exposed sail, desperate to maintain control and stability against the ferocious storm. The crew scrambled across the deck, grasping anything they could find to steady themselves. Two sailors were thrown overboard as the ship listed sharply.

Following Malware's commands, Slade wrestled with the helm, adjusting the rudder and settings to prevent the ship from turning perilously into the wind. His efforts allowed the crew to secure the furled sail, even as rainwater cascaded down from the rigging like a powerful waterfall, drenching everything in its path. From Malware's standpoint, the ship had transformed into a conduit for the very elements, but with its robust masts, the vessel appeared as a resilient lone warrior confronting the fury of the sky. Inside the bridge, he fought to keep his balance. The ship shuddered as if in the grip of an invisible menace, experiencing tremors it had never known. Malware was straining to see through the intense squall as water pinged across the deck's wooden planks in the deluge.

Unnerved, he aimed to navigate through the maelstrom and emerge on the other side—weathered but undefeated as the thunder provided a dramatic soundtrack to the tempestuous scene. He held onto the radar screen he had designed, determined to overcome the chaos unleashed. The state-of-the-art system, meant to provide precise navigation even in the fiercest of tempests, seemed to have betrayed him. The once-reliable display flickered erratically, its digital contours fracturing into an incomprehensible blur of data.

Over the deafening roar of the storm, Malware shouted, "We're flying blind, Mr. Slade! The radar's gone rogue."

Slade's face reflected the gravity of the situation, as he had never encountered a storm of this magnitude. The ship's compass spun wildly, and the stars' guidance was obscured by the black clouds as he wrestled with the ship's wheel.

Malware adjusted the rudder and aileron controls, directing their joint efforts towards averting the ship from dangerously tilting from side to side, a movement that, if uncontrolled, could escalate into a catastrophic roll. He shouted commands over the ship's external speakers, wondering if the wind carried away his words.

Taking control of the wheel, Slade felt immense relief, knowing they were now in the best possible hands. "Admiral, I've spotted a break in the clouds below!" he yelled, peering out the starboard window. With a swift motion, Malware turned the wheel to the right and pushed the wheel forward, sending the ship hurtling downward at a stomach-churning speed.

Reaching a stable position amidst the light-toned clouds, Malware steadied the ship, having skillfully navigated past the most tumultuous part of the journey. The once-violent winds had softened, transforming into a gentle breeze that whispered calm promises. The sun began to break through the dissipating clouds, casting a warm golden light over the deck and illuminating the faces of the weary crew.

Slade sighed in relief, grateful for his continued existence. The weight of fear lifted from his shoulders like a heavy fog dissipating in the sun. He glanced at Malware, whose unwavering focus had been the anchor in the storm. With poise and reassurance, the Admiral directed, "Take the helm, Mr. Slade."

Chapter 34

The Fortress
Malware Island

The portal descended onto the fortress grounds with an eerie, shimmering hum masked by the continuous thunder. Princess Arabella emerged, instantly enveloped by cascading sheets of rain. Thunder roared and echoed ceaselessly with its overpowering reverberations. Like a vengeful spirit, the wind wailed, challenging her balance on the slippery cobblestones amidst the downpour. She could make out a looming structure with jagged spires and weathered stone walls that seemed to have borne witness to a multitude of sinister acts.

Leading the way, the general set a rapid pace. A bright lightning flash revealed his determination. His boots made a rhythmic splash through the puddles as he zeroed in on a specific doorway. Arabella's heart pounded as his spear struck the locked door. The resounding impact of metal clashing against the wood echoed louder than the thunder. The force of the strike led to the outer stonework of the sturdy oak door ripping off its hinges, crashing inwards. Stepping over the wreckage, the General motioned for the Princess to follow, acutely aware that the guards, seeking shelter from the relentless downpour, would soon emerge. The breach of the oak door had triggered the piercing wail of the klaxons, alerting them to the disturbance.

In the dimly lit corridor, the spectral guards began to materialise, their ranks swelling with each passing moment. Their faces bore the fierce features of predators—sharp eyes glinting with primal intensity and snarling expressions revealing pointed teeth. The intricate designs of their armour resembled the scales of mythical beasts, shimmering in the low light. Each guard wielded steel weapons that emitted a faint, ominous hum as they prepared to strike. The Princess felt a surge of adrenaline coursing through her veins, yet the General's steady presence served as a reassuring anchor amidst the looming danger. He faced the horde of adversaries with his spectral sword, its blade shimmering with an otherworldly light. With each calculated move, he unleashed arcs of electrical energy that disabled his foes without delivering fatal blows. Those ensnared in the web of crackling currents fell to the ground, their bodies twitching as the energy coursed through them. The display of skill surpassed anything the Princess had witnessed in open combat—a mesmerising blend of grace and power that left her breathless.

As the guards fell in a domino effect, more spectral foes continued to pour into the corridor, relentlessly pursuing them. Yet the General remained undeterred; he advanced deeper, becoming an impenetrable shield, defending the Princess from all directions. The blue sparks from his spear illuminated the stone walls, casting a dazzling dance of expertise that highlighted his every movement. The seemingly infinite corridor presented relentless challenges, but Titanous's determination held firm. He fought as if he embodied an entire army, each swing of his sword a testament to his prowess. The guards' desperate assaults became futile against his skill, their snarls of frustration echoing in the confined space. With every clash of steel and crackle of energy, the air thickened with tension, and the Princess could feel the weight of the battle pressing down on them.

In a breathtaking moment, the General spun, his sword arcing through the air like a comet, sending a shockwave of energy that knocked several guards off their feet. The corridor lit up with flashes of blue and white, illuminating the chaos around them. The Princess watched in awe as he moved with a fluidity that seemed almost supernatural, each strike precise and deliberate, a dance that left no room for error. As the last of the guards fell, the General turned to her, his eyes fierce yet calm. "We must keep moving," he urged, his voice steady despite the chaos. The Princess nodded, her heart racing, knowing that with him by her side, they could face whatever lay ahead.

They drew closer to the laser-guarded corridor and the entrance to the stone circular stairwell leading down to the vault. The General gave a warning. Princess Arabella understood this as the pivotal moment of their journey. She studied the intricate laser grid, her keen eye navigating what stood between them and the heart of their objective. Advancing, she momentarily held her breath, purposefully stepping into the first corridor to activate the hidden laser sensors. Like lightning emerging from the shadows, the darkened passage erupted in a blinding brilliance of the lasers' searing intensity upon their target. With a twist of her body, the optical filters in her skin reflected the lethal light towards the lasers, causing the system to short-circuit. Progressing through the corridor, she continued to exploit the lasers' vulnerability, yet the toll on her body became increasingly evident.

The heat from the lasers seared her skin, and the sting of singed hair wafted through the air. The toll on her body became evident upon reaching and conquering the final lasers. Too proud to reveal her discomfort, she masked her pain and trailed behind the General as he moved ahead. "The guards will not pursue us any further because this is a strictly prohibited zone and a dead end," he reassured as they progressed down the winding stone stairwell. In the surrounding darkness, his firewall spear illuminated their path. At the bottom of the steps, the layout revealed the vast steel vault door looming in front of them.

Standing before the vault marked with intricate symbols from a forgotten time, the General and the Princess shared a moment of silent unity. With a reassuring nod, he leaned in, pressing his ear against its circumference as if seeking a heartbeat within the cold, unfeeling metal. In sequence, his fingertips delicately explored the grooves and intricate patterns etched deep into the door. Pinpointing the elusive mechanism vital for unlocking the vault, he withdrew a small magnetic tool from his cloak.

The device emitted a soft yet noticeable hum as it connected to the door. Its digital screen flickered with a flurry of numbers, accompanied by a series of audible clicks as it calibrated the necessary settings. As the tumblers aligned, the main bolts released with a satisfying sound. Gears whirred and shifted, and the door creaked open, revealing the long-hidden secrets. A rich aroma of aged parchment filled the vault, steeped in the essence of knowledge. The expansive room exceeded Arabella's wildest dreams. Its lofty ceiling was adorned with intricate frescoes that illustrated scenes of wisdom and enlightenment. Towering oak shelves lined the walls, filled with rows of extensive and valuable books, each one a testament to history and a treasure trove of information.The meticulously organised leather-bound volumes displayed titles in long-forgotten languages, each representing the enduring pursuit of wisdom.

Priceless paintings and sculptures depicted the great intellects and innovators of bygone eras, capturing their profound insights in brush-strokes and stone. The colours were vibrant, the details intricate, show-casing the remarkable artistic skill behind these masterpieces. Portraits of philosophers, scientists, and innovators gazed down at the visitors, their eyes appearing to track their every move. The centrepiece of the vault captured their gaze: the Dendritic Agate; inside a clear, unbreak-able glass casing, the iridescent marvel of nature was the embodiment of magnificence. Delicate veins of intricate dendrites appeared like ten-drils etched into the very stone.

The General turned to the Princess and cautioned. "Your Highness, step back and shield your eyes!" His spear gleamed with an inner light as he raised it high. A powerful burst of energy erupted from its tip as it lowered like a lance towards the Dendritic Agate. The vault erupted into a blinding spectacle of radiance, illuminating like a thousand stars blazing in the night sky. In an awe-inspiring moment, the glass casing shattered into countless pieces. Freed from its glass prison, the Den-dritic Agate pulsed with a newfound vibrancy as if eager to share its boundless energy with those who dared to seek it. Lowering his spear with a feeling of accomplishment, the General advanced towards the Snow-White crystal, its mesmerising glow appearing to cast a captivat-ing charm. Resting on a crimson soft velvet cushion, the Agate seemed to pull him closer with each step eagerly. He extended his gloved hand, holding his breath in admiration as he grasped the precious gem. Feel-ing the surface sent a shiver through his arm as he pivoted to present the radiant prize to the Princess. His elation swiftly turned to dread as she collapsed to the floor.

The shock of seeing Arabella's face pale and non-existent struck him deeply. He presumed the lasers she had bravely faced had left their treacherous mark. Panic gripped as he knelt by her side. The charred, cracked skin surrounding the optical lenses caught his eye, particularly the severe damage to the sclera of her open eyes, now veiled in a yellowish film.

Recognising the Princess's existence teetered on a fragile edge, he stowed the Agate in a sturdy pouch and strapped it beneath his cloak. With no other option, he lifted the Princess and deftly swung her over his shoulder. The weight of his precious cargo made his muscles flex and ripple as he ascended the stone stairwell. The steady thud of footsteps alerted the guards of the warrior's return. As he reached the upper corridor, their spectral eyes flickered with an eerie intensity. Impatient and enraged, the general struck the floor with the butt of his spear. The ground quaked as a brilliant flash of light enveloped all who approached, rendering them vulnerable to his potent strikes as he battled through the long line of chaos.

Each passageway turned into a battlefield as he moved with unmatched speed, his spear a flurry of motion as he weaved through the spectral-infested maze. His breath synchronised with the pulsing tempo of his strikes, too rapid for the eye to follow. Warding off wave after wave of enemies, their cries of torment were music to his ears. Striding over the shattered door, he gained ground to the courtyard's centre. The downpour had lessened as he looked upon the shimmering portal, the gateway to freedom, yet barricaded by the last line of guards intent on preventing his escape. Fuelled by a primal thirst for victory, they closed their expanding ranks around him. Despite the weight of the Princess on his shoulder and the overwhelming odds against him, he clenched his free fist, steeling himself for the final confrontation, and charged into their ranks toward the portal, unleashing a fierce battle cry.

The General's spear became a twirling conductor's baton, orchestrating destruction and salvation in movements blurred by speed. His enemies became desperate, their attacks growing more chaotic as they failed to halt his advance. With a fluid, sweeping action, the General rotated, spear thrust outward at waist height, unleashing a formidable surge of power that toppled the guards like scattered defeated skittles. He boarded the portal unscathed, untied the pouch containing the Dendritic Agate, pushed the crystal aside, and waited for the portal to reemerge at his lair.

Chapter 35

The Waterfall Cavern

In an effort to push aside her concerns for the Princess and the General, Mia chose to spend time with Bilko as he grazed. Her brief moment of peace was shattered by the unmistakable sound of the portal reappearing. Shock coursed through her as she stood frozen, watching the General pass by, holding the Princess in his arms and moving toward the shimmering pool at the foot of the waterfall. The General stepped into the water, wading until he was directly beneath the roaring fall. Mia stood motionless, struggling to make sense of the bizarre scene. The alerts from the Gazing Orbs prompted the others to gather around her. Isaiah, preventing Valour from rushing into the water, pleaded, "Valour, please, whatever has happened, you must trust the General's judgment."

Max stood nearby, his face pale and troubled. "I pray she's going to be okay," he whispered, his voice barely audible over the waterfall's roar.

With his strong arms outstretched, the General turned the Princess from her front to her back, intending for the waterfall's pressure to help cleanse her clouded optical lenses, vital for her to breathe freely. As he emerged from the pool, he spoke of her courageous deeds, including securing the Agate, while highlighting the waterfall's restorative qualities as he carried her to his quarters. Gently, he placed her in his hammock and, without another word, slipped away into the forest. The General's watchful eyes swept the area, hunting for the delicate Frostleaf Petals blooming in the woods' sequestered corners.

In a secluded clearing illuminated by dappled sunlight, he found the icy blue-coloured Petals nestled among moss-covered rocks and ferns. He plucked the petals from a cluster of delicate stems, handling them gently to preserve their fragile beauty and honour their mystical power.

Tracing his path back along a faint trail of crushed leaves and broken twigs, he emerged from the forest with a grave expression. Valour watched intently as the General arranged a handful of the petals in a crystal chalice with water from the pool. Adding a solitary Moonstone Fern to the concoction, he poured the blended elements over a silk cloth, allowing it to absorb the soothing elixir. He delicately placed the chilled compress on the Princess's closed eyelids, infusing her with its healing essence.

With no more he could do, the General asked the group to join him in the control room. Valour and Mia refused to leave the Princess unattended, standing vigil by her side, each clasping one of her hands. Max unfurled the sacred map at the General's request, his eyes widening in utter disbelief. Gone were the familiar outlines of Cyberia's seven provinces, replaced instead by the imposing image of The Great White Clock, its intricate design dominating the parchment. The clock looked a marvel of intricate design, showcasing elaborate details from its deepest foundations to its dial. It displayed a vibrant, colour-coded representation that closely resembled the complex circulatory system of a living organism. It was like the clock had its own lifeblood, an elaborate network of veins and arteries.

At the heart of the clock rested the essential missing element—the Dendritic Agate. To Max, it was clear that the crystal functioned as the clock's life force. It channelled precious energy through every part of the timepiece, bringing its gears to life and setting its intricate mechanisms in motion with a grace that felt almost alive. The map chose to reveal its long-guarded secrets through a collective vision, enabling the entire group to unfold their shared destiny by focusing on the exact location where Mia needed to place the Dendritic Agate.

The map suddenly shifted into an unusual format, unveiling intricately arranged mirrors scattered across countless mountains in the five provinces. This unexpected element of power surprised everyone except the General, who pointed out that these mirrors were designed to capture the first rays of sunlight. "These mirrors reflect the light in a precise, invisible direction, ensuring that the solar fountains stay replenished until the sun sets below the horizon. The solar fountains play a harmonious balance with the elements of rain, wind and light, prompting the release of a mist rich in moisture that fosters the growth of vibrant plants and flowers." The General preempted the question that Isaiah was about to ask.

"Unlike the Great White Clock, these mirrors are impervious to damage. No laser beam can penetrate their protective shield, and no outside interference can alter their projection. Hence, the Great White Clock was the perfect target for Malice Malware's assault. I have now implemented an antivirus program to safeguard against any future breaches of the system." The map again reconfigured, prompting the General to continue.

"This design reveals the intricate roots of the Great White Clock. They intertwine with the vast network of roots belonging to the tree species across the five provinces. These roots extend deep into the earth, branching out to form a complex web of connection. This allows the trees to communicate, sharing vital resources and information that support their growth and survival. This reliance gives a unique sense of unity, creating a resilient ecosystem where each tree significantly supports the others. The roots serve as conduits for water flow and nutrients, allowing the trees to adapt to the changing seasons. During a drought, the roots would reach deeper into the earth, tapping into hidden aquifers to ensure every tree receives the moisture needed to thrive." The general finished by pointing out that the Great White Clock not only marked the passage of time but also functioned as the land's heartbeat.

Mia entered the room with a contagious excitement in her step, her eyes sparkling with relief and joy. "Princess Arabella has opened her eyes!" she announced, the words ringing through the room like a joyous bell. Gathering around the hammock, the Princess, full of gratitude, met their worried expressions with a warm smile. Valour addressed the General. "General Titanous, thank you," he whispered with appreciation. "You have preserved my Princess's existence, and I will always hold your actions and bravery in the highest regard."

The General nodded solemnly and looked at the Princess. "I shall ensure that all zenizens of Cyberia remember your courage forever."

"Is the Dendritic Agate safe?" she asked.

The General departed and reappeared, cradling the glistening Snow White gem. "This accomplishment owes a huge thanks to each of you; even in apparent failure, your contributions were indispensable." He held the Dendritic Agate across the hammock for Princess Arabella to touch, and a sense of shared purpose took hold. As if by instinct, the others followed suit. With everyone touching the mystical gem, a tingling power emitted from it, connecting them all in a tangible and electrifying unity.

In a genuine and touching moment, Mia made a solemn vow. She declared her pride in the responsibility of inserting the Dendritic Agate, stressing, "I will carry out this task on behalf of every one of you. None more so than you, Princess," she added tearfully. The depth of her words revealed a potent and unselfish commitment to their collective cause.

"We will leave you to rest for a while," said the General, understanding the need for a respite but realising a plan had to be formed among the group. The General faced the daunting challenge of preparing for the impending confrontation with the Drakonian Battalion, wrestling with worries beyond conventional battle strategies. His apprehensions were not solely about engaging the enemy directly but centred on the pivotal role Mia had to fulfil. Their mission extended beyond combat; it involved safeguarding Mia's secure ascent to the highest branch of the Great White Clock, a mission laden with both danger and importance. Their strategy would require a solid front line to engage the Drakonians to ensure Mia's success in her climb and the critical insertion of the Dendritic Agate. But the General knew climbing the intricately woven branches was complex considering the weight she had to bear of the bulky crystal. His foremost worry centred around Drakonian archers and their poison-tipped arrows, a concern he privately conveyed to Max, whose ashen-coloured expression said it all. Additionally, the general carried the solemn task of informing Mia of the imminent danger, a conversation that demanded careful consideration and tact.

Alone, the Princess guided her thoughts back to the vision that straddled the boundary between reality and the subconscious state she had experienced. In her vision, she vividly saw Scarlet the Deceitful guiding General Titanous through the intricate security measures of Malice Malware's fortress. Scarlet moved gracefully and confidently, navigating the labyrinthine passages and disarming the lethal lasers. The vision felt like she was an unseen observer, witnessing a secret alliance between Scarlet and the General. Like other prominent figures, she had struggled with the General's choice to release Scarlet the Deceitful from captivity after her capture for manipulating the dreams of influential individuals. Had he bargained for her freedom? She believed the vision had revealed a hidden truth, a secret too delicate to share with anyone but the General.

Eager to join the others, she rose unsteadily to her feet. The group paused their conversation, their attention drawn to her entrance. The General, showing concern, politeness, and appreciation for her unique viewpoint, stood up and motioned for her to take his place at the centre of the hub. The Princess settled into the cushioned expanse of the majestic chair, hewn from a felled tree. Her brow creased as she surveyed the intricate holographic displays. "General," she began tentatively, her voice a blend of curiosity and concern. "Do you have a plan for integrating the Dendritic Agate?"

The General, adopting a composed posture against the console, spoke with a tone tinged with concern and a serious expression. "Unfortunately not. Our focus has been Malice Malware's reaction to our possession of the crystal."

A smile of contentment graced the Princess's features. "The thought of his loss of the Dendritic Agate fills me with a joy that words cannot convey. That thought alone will motivate us to craft a successful plan, no matter our challenges."

After a thorough discussion on how Mia could scale the towering clock, Isaiah proposed a particularly intriguing idea that shifted the entire direction of their strategy. His suggestion, filled with unexpected possibilities, sparked a renewed sense of hope among the group. The General, recognising the potential of this new approach, expressed his appreciation by giving Isaiah a reassuring pat on the shoulder, a gesture that conveyed both trust and camaraderie. Despite her initial reservations, Mia felt a flutter of anticipation mixed with anxiety as she considered the implications of this plan. With a deep breath, she nervously nodded in agreement, ready to embrace the challenge ahead.

Chapter 36

The Fortress
Malware Island

The Battleship Infector began its descent. Slade realised that the stabilising rudders were malfunctioning. Urgently, he shouted, "Admiral, the landing rudders are unresponsive. I have no control of our descent."

The Admiral's face tightened as he processed Slade's words. "Divert all power to the emergency thrusters!" he barked, his voice steady despite the chaos around them.

Slade gripped the controls, his knuckles white as he fought against the ship's erratic movements. "Power diverted, but it's not enough! We're coming in too fast!" He could feel the ship shudder beneath him, the timbers groaning as it fought against the pull of gravity.

Malware regained control of the helm, and in a desperate attempt to decelerate, he extended the flaps to their full stretch, but it was too little, too late. He shouted to Slade to warn the crew of the impending rough landing.

"Brace for impact!" Slade commanded, his eyes fixed on the rapidly approaching surface.

Malware made the critical decision to let the ship take the brunt of the force in the water rather than on the beachhead to minimise the impact. With a final effort, he slammed his hand down on the emergency thruster controls. "Come on, come on!" he muttered under his breath. The ship jolted violently but struggled to slow its descent. The sea rushed to meet them, a blur of colours and waves. The serene calm was violently disrupted as the ship crashed into the sea. The thunderous impact surging a massive wave outward. With a resounding crack, the main mast splintered, sending ropes and rigging whipping across the deck. Crew members were hurled like rag dolls, their frantic attempts to hold on drowned out by cries of agony and alarm.

Thrown forcefully across the bridge deck, Slade crashed into the door, his head taking a brutal hit. Regaining his composure, he was surprised to see the Admiral still gripping the wheel as the vessel emitted a loud wooden groan while floundering; amid shouts of water seeping beneath the hull's waterline.

Malware stepped out onto the bridge deck, bellowing his orders on what was needed to address the leaks. Deckhands rushed below to manually operate the bilge pumps while others fetched the oakum and tar. Slade supervised as the crew hammered the oakum pegs, crafted from old ropes, into the gaps between the wooden planks of the hull and readied the tar to cover the oakum and seal the cracks. Divers were ordered overboard to examine the damage, but their feedback was bleak. They reported that splintrills were essential for repairing the waterline and stabilisers for flight. Understanding that replacing the ship's mast would also take considerable time, Malware shook his head in despair.

A rider emerged as a dark silhouette against the horizon, galloping away from the fort. A rowboat was lowered with Malware standing while rowed ashore. Absorbing the messenger's words, it was the news he had dreaded. His face darkened with anger as he yanked the rider from the saddle, mounted the horse, and galloped down the shoreline. Slade watched from the bridge deck, sensing that something was gravely amiss in the Admiral's frantic return to the fortress.

Malware's mind churned with a storm of fury, driven by an insatiable urge to reclaim what had been ruthlessly stolen from him. Outside the fortress, the vigilant guards of Triad Trojans, Rootkits, and Botnets stepped aside to allow their master passage, relieved that the breach was not their doing. Within the fortress, his protectors, a diverse assembly of Spectral guards, trembled in the presence of his wrath as Malware leapt off the horse. He strode through the corridor, and all who stood in his path cowered in submission. He disdained those who had not promptly retreated, delivering swift kicks.

Upon passing the burned-out lasers, he entered the vault, and a sight of devastation met his eyes. The once-pristine glass showcase that had housed his precious Dendritic Agate lay shattered, its shards scattered across the floor like a constellation of broken dreams. The intruder's breach had marred his personal space and the sanctity of what lay within.

In the operation centre, intricate data streams buzzed with the soft hum of advanced technology as he gestured for the holographic projection to materialise. This triggered the surveillance playback on the Guardian Gazing Orbs. As the playback commenced, he observed with a blend of anticipation and apprehension. The orbs unveiled the scene through the bad weather: the portal's emergence and General Titanous disembarking from the mysterious craft with Princess Arabella. He wondered how such a brilliant craft came into being, but the overriding question was how they had managed to find their way to their objective through the maze of corridors.

Watching the general affix a device to the vault door, he puzzled over the action. The sequence continued with the shattering of the impenetrable glass containing the Agate, followed by the orbs' lenses obliterated by a bright white flash, similar to the fate of the other orbs lining the corridors. A mix of anguish and joy filled him as the outer orbs unveiled the general shouldering the princess back to the mysterious craft, only to witness the general pivot, a sudden white flash, and then nothing.

Malware concluded that the optical lenses within the princess's body had deactivated the lethal lasers, indicating that she was either injured or deceased. The question troubled him: how did the general possess not only the knowledge of the vault's location and the concealed lasers but, more crucially, the vault's combination? It was evident that Titanous had utilised the princess's abilities for this precise task, leading the telltale signs to suggest a traitor lurking within his inner circle.

Malware's emotions swirled in frustration and anger as he vowed to uncover the traitor's identity who had ruined his carefully laid plans. With his Battleship Infector incapacitated and stranded, unable to thrive on the havoc it sowed until repaired, he experienced a profound sense of isolation and helplessness.

In this vulnerable moment, Malware's thoughts turned to the last resort: King Kronos' formidable battalion of guards protecting the Great White Clock. The guardians were the final bastion against the clock's rejuvenation, an event that, if the Dendritic Agate was inserted, would reset the digital world, erasing his corruption.

While reflecting, a realisation dawned on him. He grasped that the humans were the root cause of his predicament. In retrospect, he recognised that he should have prioritised disregarding the princess's safety and eradicating their existence on the podium in Glimmerhavan. A different decision at that pivotal moment could have averted this humiliation. His mind circled back to the traitor.

Chapter 37

The Royal Palace
Valaria

Alone in her secluded chamber, Scarlet sat deep in contemplation, her thoughts consumed by the Dendritic Agate. It had taken her this long to realise that General Titanous's fixation was on the elusive crystal, not on her, nor even Malice Malware. Memories of their encounters flooded her mind as she reflected on her connection to the enigmatic gem. The general had disrupted her carefully laid plans, emerging as the only person ever to provoke a blush and awaken emotions she thought long buried. His presence sent shockwaves through her, stirring feelings she believed were securely locked away.

Scarlet's first encounter with the general occurred in the grim setting of a Lumanian dungeon, where their eyes met in a moment that felt magnetic. His penetrating gaze seemed to pierce her soul, crumbling the defences she had so painstakingly constructed. In that instant, her heart fluttered, and her cheeks flushed—a vivid betrayal of the stoic façade she had maintained.

In the dungeon's shadowed nook, the general had leaned in, whispering an ominous offer. In exchange for her cooperation in gaining access to the vault on Malware Island, he vowed to protect her most precious asset—her beauty. But beneath the surface of this enticing proposition lay a dark threat. If she dared to betray him, he warned, she would no longer be known as Scarlet the Beautiful by the time she emerged from her imprisonment.

The thought of becoming a withered shadow of herself filled her with profound dread. For someone who had always relied on her beauty and mystique, such a fate was even more terrifying than facing Malice Malware if caught. The general's allure was both irresistible and dangerous, leaving Scarlet's heart torn between her loyalty to Malice Malware, her vanity, and her inexplicable attraction toward him.

Her heart still raced from General Titanous's chilling proposition as she carefully weighed her options. She understood the gravity of the situation—any misstep could lead to disastrous consequences. After a tense moment of contemplation, tinged with vulnerability, she agreed to his terms but added her own condition. She would assist him in gaining access to the vault, but on the condition that the treasures within remained untouched. Her terms reflected her cunning and understanding of the dangers lurking within the vault. The tension in the alcove grew palpable as she awaited his response, hoping he would concede to her demands.

The general fastened a peculiar bracelet around her ankle to seal their pact and guarantee her cooperation. The accessory, intricately engraved and set with a mysterious gemstone, was no ordinary piece of jewellery. It was a binding contract imbued with dark magic. If Scarlet betrayed and lured him into a trap, the bracelet's magic would be activated, robbing her of her youthful appearance by rapidly advancing her age. With Admiral Malware away aboard his battleship, the timing was perfect for their plot to unfold. The general's ability to appear in the courtyard of Malware Island on that stormy night, bypassing all the fortress's security measures, was beyond her comprehension. Had he employed the same enigmatic method Argent had reported to his uncle, Whispering Grass?

The general's subterfuge had been crucial to the success of their covert operation. Disguised as a spectral guard, he had moved unnoticed, showcasing his cunning and mastery in manipulating appearances to his advantage. As for Scarlet, her expertise in navigating the fortress's labyrinthine corridors ensured their passage went unquestioned. She confidently led him past the unsuspecting guards, fully aware of the dangerous game they played. Her confusion stemmed from the general's brief visit to the vault. His uncharacteristic haste had driven him to depart quickly without thoroughly exploring the hidden treasures. The speed of his actions raised numerous questions. What hidden truths were concealed in the depths of his mind? It left her wondering if the Agate was his sole objective or merely a test to gauge the security measures he needed to overcome. One thing was certain: the admiral would be too late to thwart General Titanous. His swift, calculated approach had given him a considerable head start.

Scarlet's mind raced, acutely aware that the admiral would likely suspect betrayal from a close confidant, making her a prime target. The looming threat compelled her to devise an escape plan. Her thoughts turned to King Golen, the only one who might offer salvation in these dire times. Scarlet realised that her survival depended on forging an alliance with Golen and unravelling the tangled web of deceit that now ensnared her. With her fate hanging in the balance, she had no choice but to navigate a difficult path toward safety, with Golen as her beacon of hope amid the gathering storm.

Her thoughts shifted to Lord Elric and Slade. Slade had underestimated the cunning, seasoned old fox. She firmly believed that while he shadowed Elric, the lord's network of spies was equally vigilant, tracking Slade's every move. There had to be a compelling reason for Elric's departure from Valaria, and she found herself pondering what that reason could be—and where he might be now. Amid the chaos, she felt a quiet amusement at the thought of willingly joining him to escape her troubles.

Scarlet viewed Whispering Grass as a formidable threat, having learned of him before their initial meeting when the admiral summoned him to the fortress. The person she encountered, however, was far from the image she had envisioned. His most notable feature was his huge feet. Yet, despite this, he had cleverly outmanoeuvred Lord Elric and earned the favour of both Golen and the admiral with his exceptional powers of persuasion. This rendered him a dangerous opponent for anyone on the opposing side.

Scarlet also suspected, though she downplayed the notion, that Whispering Grass might have been the mastermind behind King Osred's demise. While the act would have required Malice Malware's approval, it seemed implausible that such a significant act—taking the existence of a royal—was solely motivated by the promise of gold. Scarlet was convinced that Whispering Grass had far more ambitious goals, though the exact nature of those ambitions remained a mystery. She admired his skill in deception but wondered if it would lead to even deeper and more lasting consequences than those already at play.

Chapter 38

The Great White Clock
Glimmerhavan

Once a flourishing town nestled amidst rolling hills and verdant forests, Glimmerhavan had long represented tranquillity and prosperity. Yet, a dark shadow loomed over its picturesque charm as the Drakonians, an influential group of hybrid beasts, launched their invasion. With their scaled bodies and thunderous footfalls, the imposing creatures shattered the once-peaceful ambience. Leading the fearsome Drakonians was Theron Ironclaw, a commander renowned for his unmatched skill and raw physical strength. His directive was clear: safeguard the town's most treasured possession, the Great White Clock, and prevent infiltration attempts by Princess Arabella and the humans. The clock, revered by the townsfolk, held mysterious powers that influenced the environment across five chosen regions. The once-open square, where children had played and merchants traded, had been transformed into a heavily fortified stronghold, with 600 Drakonians arranged in a tight, formidable perimeter.

Theron Ironclaw's formidable physique was clad in resilient scales that shimmered in midnight grey and olive green shades. The sheer power of his warriors mirrored his fearsome presence. Some among his battalion bore sharp, curved horns reminiscent of regal crowns, adding to their already intimidating appearance. Their sinewy muscles stood as a testament to their rigorous training and enhancements, evolving them into the pinnacle of warriors. As they patrolled the perimeter around the Great White Clock, the ground beneath their boots trembled with each step, underscoring their immense stature and might.

Commander Ironclaw surveyed his surroundings with sinister satisfaction. Though unflyable, his membranous wings stretched majestically from his back, casting an ominous shadow over the cobbled streets. His piercing eyes glowed with dark intelligence. Under his command, the town was transformed into a fortress, seemingly impervious to any potential threat. Skilled archers were strategically stationed in concealed, elevated positions atop trees, buildings, and towers. They could rain arrows upon advancing forces from these vantage points, targeting key adversaries and disrupting any potential confrontation. Ironclaw reinforced the key entry points into the town with electrified gates to withstand even the most brutal assaults. He positioned chicanes outside these gates, creating bottlenecks that would slow down attackers and allow his forces time for a focused defence.

The Treetop Inn became both Ironclaw's residence and his headquarters. Its elevated position gave him a commanding view of the town and allowed him to reorganise his warriors efficiently. The Inn served not only as a dwelling but also as a strategic hub, where he could maintain control and make decisions that would influence the outcome of any emerging threat. His presence in this elevated abode symbolised his authority and tactical edge over his enemies.

The zenizens of Glimmerhavan were compelled to retreat into hiding, yet they did so with a quiet resilience. Even in the face of overwhelming darkness, they nurtured the belief that change was on the horizon. Their faith was rewarded when General Titanous discreetly called for a meeting at a specific location, rallying them on a mission to win back their town and protect their treasured ecosystem.

Chapter 39

The Gathering

The General's call to arms spread like wildfire. Determined to reach their destination, winged rabbits and glowing squirrels raced through the foliage like a miniature stampede. Flocks of birds with crest-like crowns and ribbon-like tails took flight to follow. From the town of Glimmerhavan, zenizens of all ages, both big and small, were followed by swarms of fireflies. GiggleSprites, riding their majestic deer, raced towards the secretive meeting point like a strong wind before a raging storm.

United as an imposing legion, the Earveers commanded such a formidable presence that tree branches swayed and leaves rustled noisily under the weight of their passing. Matching the spirit of beavers, they moved through the woodland with remarkable finesse, leaping from one tree to the next, with the expanse becoming their aerial highway, reflecting the graceful flight of hummingbirds with their elongated ears. The thunderous thuds of the Bulwarkodon herd reverberated across the plain. Their colossal hooves harmonised with a series of trumpeting sounds that varied in pitch and intensity, orchestrated by the nasal calls of their long trunks, echoing through the grasslands. Their versatile appendage, capable of gentle and forceful actions, was lifted high, almost as if to acknowledge its strength.

At twelve feet, the Bulwarkodon stood with its front half cloaked in a dense, ebony-hued carapace, from its massive head to its sturdy legs, rendering it nearly impervious to harm. Its ears, resembling giant sails, fluttered energetically, acting as dynamic regulators of its body temperature as it accelerated. In full stride, the Bulwarkodon defied its enormous size. Dust and debris kicked up in its wake, creating a temporary whirlwind of earth and vegetation. Their eyes gleamed with a compelling focus, their intelligence and wisdom evident as the crowd in the meeting place parted to allow them their space.

Late to arrive were the Nano TalonHawks. Sized comparably to swans, the TalonHawks, within their murmuration, embodied the ultimate birds of prey, demonstrating unparalleled precision in identifying minute objects from significant distances and executing attacks with pinpoint accuracy. Their digitally enhanced eyes comprehended the vastness of the environment; with their razor-sharp talons, they presented a formidable combatant of the skies. With fascination, the siblings witnessed the TalonHawks occupying all available spaces, from the Bulwarkodon's backs and heads to the backs of horses and deer. General Titanous stood with great pride, overlooking the gathering army he had summoned to the clearing. With each glitchmark, their numbers swelled, creating an inspiring sight. Elevated on a broad, flat stone that jutted out from the mountainside like a stage, he stood alongside the princess, the siblings, Valour and Isaiah. Like the General, their expressions exuded an overwhelming pride in their commitment and readiness to confront the formidable battalion of 600 Drakonian warriors.

General Titanous steel-blue eyes were capable of dispelling any doubt. With a firm grip on his spear, his presence inspired those around him as he spoke of the imminent peril overshadowing the heart of the Never-Ending Forest. "Listen, all ye who dwell in this sacred realm," his voice billowing and resonating with authority. "Those standing alongside me have succeeded in a quest of the utmost importance. They have obtained the Dendritic Agate, a crystal of unparalleled power that can rejuvenate your dying ecosystem." The gathering stirred, a murmur of hope and curiosity spreading among them." The snow season will soon be upon us, with it, the looming danger of no return. But fear not, for the Dendritic Agate can change your fate." He set aside his spear, took the shimmering Dendritic Agate from Max, and held it aloft for all to see. Like a potent magic, its brilliance cast a majestic glow that caused the onlookers to gasp.

"Mia, the chosen one among us, can insert the Dendritic Agate into the heart of the Great White Clock. Only she can channel its power to restore balance, but she cannot do it alone." The General's eyes scanned the crowd, his gaze piercing. "She needs our protection. We must unite, regardless of any differences, to ensure the success of this quest. We must ally to safeguard your home," he declared, his voice carrying a weight that resonated with each listening ear. "I acknowledge the extreme challenge you would face against the battalion of Drakonians. The red code of battle may stain the ground, but our cause is just. We fight not for conquest but for the survival of all who call this place home. Let the might of our unity overcome the challenges ahead. Together, we shall face the coming storm and emerge victorious. The fate of Mia rests in our hands, and we shall not falter."

The General's impactful declaration echoed in the hush, and he paused, not expecting the enthusiastic response from the gathered crowd. The sudden eruption of thunderous cheers and the chant of his name caught him off guard. The princess stepped forward, reaching out to clasp his hand, her affection for him mirroring her love and respect for her father. Waiting for calm, the General requested an audience with the leaders of each faction, urging them to gather and discuss a plan.

In the cool night air, fire sticks illuminated the ground around the war council, with each member standing for a different faction gathered for the meeting. The General's eyes turned towards Mia, a beacon of hope in the gathering. He stated, "The Drakonians have fortified the Great White Tree to a degree where any daring attempt to climb it would result in self-destruction." When he explained how she was to be lifted by the Earveers in a harness solid and resilient enough to bear both her and the weight of the crystal, he noted not a flicker of resistance to the idea. Not wanting to take the credit, he instantly gestured towards Isaiah, acknowledging him as the architect.

The General outlined the plan etched into the earth by a broken twig. "Our objective is clear: to divert the attention of the enemy forces, preventing them from impeding Mia's flight to reach the face of the great clock." He invited Elder MossFoot, the esteemed Mayor of Glimmerhavan, to speak.

The mayor recounted the harrowing tale of the once-thriving town centre turned into a spectral wasteland upon the ominous arrival of the Drakonian Battalion. With profound insight, he outlined their strategic defences. He divulged the nerve centre of their command—the Treetop Inn, presided over by their Commander, Theron Ironclaw. He added, "One mysterious night, a shipment arrived under the cloak of darkness. The guards took the delivery to an outhouse hidden from prying eyes. The only witnesses to this operation were the fireflies. Unaware of the contents of the delivery, the fireflies unwittingly became the bearers of crucial information. Flickering inside the outhouse, they uncovered many crates, each housing oxygen tanks. These tanks were earmarked for the battalion's use during an ecosystem collapse."

The General thanked the mayor for his valuable input and remarked, "The vision I see indicates that after their mission in the town is complete, they will march back to Drakonia, sustained by the oxygen tanks until they are outside the ecosystem's zone. It would point to the strategic planning of Tarries Gorgarim, a renowned Drakonian tactician."

Once the overall plan was settled, a unit of Earveers was summoned, and a harness was brought forth. Mia cautiously stepped into the intricately crafted apparatus, woven from the sturdiest vines by skilled weavers. The Earveers arrived, with three positioned on either side of the harness. Another stood behind to provide stability and direction during flight. The General passed Mia the weight of the Dendritic Agate to hold. She readied herself for takeoff as the Earveer's large ears pulsed gently in anticipation of their precious cargo.

The weavers carefully adjusted the vine lengths connecting the loops on the Earveer's brace to the harness, ensuring a secure and comfortable fit. With a final signal from Mia, the Earveer's ears began to pulse with increasing intensity, emitting a humming sound that filled the air. The vibrations grew more vigorous, lifting her steadily off the ground. As they ascended, Mia marvelled at the sensation, feeling the wind rush past her as they lifted her effortlessly. The Earveer's movements were precise. Below, onlookers craned their necks in awe at the spectacle unfolding above them.

The vines held firm, cradling the weight with ease. Suspended high in mid-air, Mia's anxiety was tempered by a smile—a smile of the trust bestowed upon her youthful shoulders, particularly by Isaiah, who had contemplated the idea of the Earveers. Arabella's initial delight at watching Mia descend quickly morphed into dismay when the General announced that neither she nor Max would play any role in the impending battle. He addressed the princess first, his voice steady and authoritative. "A royal goes into combat only to face their equal in rank, and no king or prince is leading this battalion." He then turned to Max, his expression softening slightly. "There may come a time when we all stand shoulder to shoulder, but this is not that moment. Rest assured, I alone bear the responsibility for your sister's safety. Neither she nor I will fail either of you."

The General then shifted his focus to the council, his demeanour shifting to one of urgency. "We have much to arrange. When the next moon rises, we shall launch our attack. There will be no second chance. Time is ticking on a razor's edge." His words hung in the air, heavy with the weight of impending conflict, as the council members exchanged anxious glances, fully aware of the stakes involved. The atmosphere crackled with tension, each acutely aware that the fate of many rested on their shoulders.

Chapter 40

The Battle of Glimmerhavan

The moment to advance to the front line arrived. Max, displaying visible emotion, struggled to find the right words while helping his sister onto Bilko's saddle. The Princess, equally moved, tearfully implored Isaiah and Valour to exercise care. In a solemn interaction, Isaiah and Valour assure Max that they are prepared to sacrifice their existence to protect his sister. Max and the Princess could only look on as the General-led army vanished into the woods like shadows weaving through the darkness.

The dense foliage afforded them concealment, their footfalls and hooves scarcely audible on the moist forest floor, progressing stealthily toward the outskirts of Glimmerhavan. Amid the dusky atmosphere, the elegant and incandescent fireflies flitted purposefully to and fro, coordinating messages with each flicker of their luminescence, signalling a silent confirmation that every contingent had assumed their designated positions. Halting, the General turned his full attention to Mia as she dismounted. The Earveers moved into position as the General secured her in the specialised harness. His eyes met the Earveers and issued his directive, "Mia is our key to victory; at all costs, she must reach the clock face. Fly her high. The Drakonians will not expect the primary source of their troubles to originate from above."

Ascending, Mia felt the gaze of a thousand eyes as she dwindled into nothing more than a polka dot in the sky. With a decisive gesture, the General directed the Nano TalonHawks to take flight. Their ultimate mission was to protect Mia and the Earveers from the archers' arrows. The General mounted the commanding Bulwarkodon, positioning himself at the forefront to spearhead the charge through the enemy's chicanes and electrical barriers. Valour and Isaiah, the elected leaders of their formations, stood at the rearguard. Valour commanded the GiggleSprites who sat proudly on his majestic WhiteTail, poised to follow the General's directive. The GiggleSprites maintained a disciplined formation behind the Zenturion. Armed with swords, and bows on their shoulders, their quivers overflowed with glowing arrows that could pierce through the darkness to find their mark.

Isaiah led the residents of Glimmerhavan, whose horse restlessly scraped at the earth. Some wielded bows made from the sturdy wood of ancient trees. Others held makeshift swords and daggers, whereas farmers gripped their pitchforks. Elder MoosFoot, who traditionally displayed signs of a nervous disposition, wore a determined expression, benevolently befitting his position as mayor.

Titanous knew that this moment would define not only their fate but the fate of the entire realm. He took a deep breath, steeling himself for what lay ahead. His towering figure gleamed in the dim light as he ordered the Bulwarkodon forward by pressing his heels into her side. She lifted her trunk in response, echoing a call that marked the advance. The commotion that followed shattered the night's tranquillity. The war bugle had sounded, a decisive moment that would shape Glimmerhavan's future.

The alarm horn blared, igniting a coordinated drumbeat of readiness along the Drakonian front lines. Flaming arrows arced through the air, unleashed in a rapid flurry of action, exposing the concealed enemy as they charged toward the first line of defence. In the treetop inn high above the forest floor, the Drakonian commander awoke abruptly to the battle drumbeat that shattered the tranquillity of the early morning darkness. Theron Ironclaw leapt from his makeshift bed. His long, curved tail trailed behind him as he moved quickly to the window. The surrounding treetops swayed with his archers' hurried movements, cocking their bows alongside those positioned on rooftops and the towering clock.

The General's firewall spear emitted a brilliance that lit up his presence with its spotlight glow. His symbolic cloak billowed in the wind, representing his mystique. Observing from above, Mia watched the selflessness of his courageous progression with a sense of awe and admiration. To her, it was unmistakable that the General had drawn the enemy's foreboding gaze and anger upon himself more than anyone else. Inspired by reaching the chicanes, the Bulwarkodons shrugged off the stream of the enemy's arrows that struck the ground or ricocheted off their protective hides. With a display of sheer power, the herd worked in unison. The sound of their tusks scraping against the heavy chicanes was calculated and precise as the giant felled trees were tossed aside.

Theron Ironclaw concentrated on the vanguard of the assault and on the brilliant white glow emanating around the leader as he guided a herd of Bulwarkodon through the chicanes. He dismissed the caution after being warned that General Titanous had a majestic crystal that could replace the five needed. He believed travelling from Volcanis to The Never-Ending Forest was impossible before the snow season had begun. How he did so bewildered him: his thoughts would have differed if he had known about a mysterious teleportation device. The ultimate barrier the General faced was the solar-powered electrified fencing, which tapped into the boundless energy of the sun's rays. Each section glistened with photovoltaic cells, absorbing and converting sunlight into its electrical grid, ready to unleash a sense of dread against any approaching intruder.

The herd thundered forward, their ivory tusks crafted from dentin—a dense, non-conductive element—breaking through the fencing, demonstrating their strength and resilience against any obstacle. The mesh crackled with fiery arcs, leaving a path of short, smoking circuits in their trampling wake. Valour and Isaiah charged toward the openings with the barriers down as their signal. The GiggleSprites rose in their stirrups, unleashing flaming arrowheads aimed at their target. The General's eyes attentively traced the arrows' trail of smoke as the missiles soared overhead, successfully striking their intended mark.

Although visibly shocked by the incursion, Theron Ironclaw's foresight into the possible repercussions of storing oxygen tanks in a timber-framed warehouse proved prophetic as he visualised the enemy's objective. The threat became imminent as a relentless wave of flaming arrowheads, coated in pine resin for sustained combustion, set ablaze the thatched roof. At that moment, he grasped the peril to his battalion's escape route, recognising that even if he successfully repelled the attack, the danger persisted in an airless environment with the snow period fast approaching. Ironclaw rushed out onto the walkway and ordered his captain to redeploy 30 warriors to quell the flames by any means necessary. The battle-hardened captain reissued the order, his voice cutting through the clamour like a war horn. The commander nodded approvingly at his captain's decisiveness to form a chain from the watering hole to the fire.

Without warning, squadrons of white-crested birds carrying hefty stones gripped in their talons unleashed their cargo, propelling the stones downward toward the firefighters; some found their mark, while others peppered the ground with a staccato rhythm, leaving punctures in the surface. Drakonian archers instantly released a volley of arrows, striking the white-crested targets precisely. Ironclaw's expression hardened as he witnessed dozens of the birds plummeting to the ground. Those who managed to survive received no quarter as they fell inside the battalion's perimeter. Ironclaw was alerted to another aerial assault by a piercing screech. Nano TalonHawks attacked his concealed archers in the trees. He looked on despairingly as a fierce struggle erupted amidst the flurry of feathers, talons, and claws. Amid the pecking frenzy, archers protecting the clock face spiralled to the ground below. Other TalonHawks appeared to be shielding a harnessed figure, hurtling toward the clock tower's façade by Earveers.

Theron Ironclaw adjusted his helmet securely over his horns. Pulling his sword from its sheath, he hastened along the walkway. In his mind, the attackers would falter at the sight of the General's defeat in battle. Whether it was too late or not, his courage, more than anything else, would earn him the highest praise from King Kronos and all Drakonians, establishing an everlasting legacy.

Mia's keen eyes found the outline of an entrance on the side of the clock's face. She gestured for the Earveers to hover closer. She examined the door's intricate carvings, her brow furrowed in concentration. She reached out, frantically tracing the delicate patterns with her fingertips, searching for a hidden latch. As the door swung inward, her heart raced as she cagily unfastened the harness. Clutching the Dendritic Agate, she awkwardly scrambled into the grand structure, her way lit by the soft glow of luminous moss that clung to the interior walls. She trod lightly along a narrow walkway surrounding the clock's intricate mechanical wonders. Glimmer and Havan, the creators of the grand clock, were the two figurines suspended above on running rails. They stood in an unsettling sense of animation. Crafted from wood, they appeared on the brink of awakening to break free from their enforced slumber and start their customary walk along the narrow rails encircling the outer face of the clock.

The clock's inner workings resembled a delicate dance of gears and cogs, each meticulously interlocked in various shapes and sizes. Designed to function in perfect harmony, the teeth of the gears facilitated a smooth transfer of power, which governed the release of energy from a coiled spring, delivering precise, rhythmic pulses—a set of heavyweights provided power through a complex system of pulleys and chains. The hands and dials were affixed to rotating shafts intricately connected to the clock's inner machinery, faithfully marking the passage of time. Within the clock's core, a resplendent golden pendulum had once swung with precise regularity into the abyss below, serving as the conductor of the clock and the guardian of its accuracy.

Concealed optical lenses, made of polymers and crystalline substances, cannoned and interlinked across vast distances, which harnessed and amplified the sun's radiant rays, creating 'Solar Fountains' that infused warmth and light into the coldest and darkest corners of the regions. But at the heart of the clock, its extraordinary mechanisms wielded the ability, through its vast network of 'underground roots,' to sculpt the landscape, adjusting terrain and flora to optimise oxygen production, distribution, and preservation. The ingenious system for supplying oxygen to the provinces offered a dependable and unceasing source, enhancing the well-being and vitality of the province's inhabitants.

Mia was jolted by a series of explosions that threw her off balance. She grasped the catwalk tightly on her knees as dust cascaded from the tower's ceiling. It struck her that their plan was unfolding as intended—

the storage area containing the oxygen tanks were being effectively destroyed by fire. Gaining her feet, she began locating and removing the shattered five crystals from their Coombs before finding where the Dendritic Agate would fit into its ultimate resting place. Following the sacred map's markings, her fingers traced the path of arrowed metallic carvings. Within a circular hollow she discovered the niche where the vibrant Agate crystal would be positioned. Its design mirrored the precise contours, creating a natural socket made for the very moment. Her hands quivered, and in an unexpected moment of reverence, she pressed her lips to the crystal, offering a silent prayer of gratitude for what might be the most significant event to ever unfold in her life. The noise of the ongoing battle outside jolted her back to reality and aligned the Dendritic Agate into its niche.

General Titanous surveyed the battlefield; his gaze locked onto the ranks of Drakonian warriors. Unfazed by their daunting appearance, he spurred his enormous mount onward, and with a tremendous leap, landed among the crowd of scaled adversaries, launching himself into the battle with an unexpected ferocity. The clash of steel reverberated across the battlefield as the General felt adrenaline coursing through his veins, sharpening his senses for the fight ahead. The Drakonian warriors, momentarily stunned by the audacity of his leap, quickly regrouped. With each swing of his firewall spear, the General carved a path through their ranks, his movements a seamless blend of grace and raw power. A Drakonian warrior lunged at him, claws poised to strike. Titanous evaded the attack with a swift sidestep and countered with a powerful thrust, driving his spear deep into the creature's side. It let out a guttural roar before collapsing to the ground. The General radiated confidence like a protective shield. His firewall spear cracked with illuminating energy as warriors converged upon him like a swarm of predators. Each swing of his spear seemed to slice through the very fabric of reality. To his watching troops, he was a force of nature, and with every strike, he inspired them to rally behind him.

Valour and Isaiah's swords struck true and fast, but the Drakonian warriors surged forward with a ferocity that seemed to draw strength from the very fear they instilled. Each swing of a Drakonian blade felt relentless as the ground beneath their feet transformed into a red canvas painted with combat struggles. The scales shimmered ominously, and their roars echoed like thunder, drowning out the cries of the fallen. Valour's heart sank as he watched the GiggleSprites and farmers fall in alarming numbers to the relentless onslaught. Once joyful and mischievous, the GiggleSprites were embroiled in a desperate fight for their existence, their laughter giving way to cries of panic. The farmers, who sought only to protect their land and loved ones, were falling one by one against the superior might of the warriors.

"Isaiah!" Valour cried, his voice hoarse and barely audible over the uproar. "We can't let this continue!" Isaiah let out a fierce battle cry as he joined Valour. Unexpectedly the winged rabbits and glowing squirrels turned the tide. From nowhere, they appeared in great numbers in and around the Drakonian legs, biting and clawing up to their faces. Frustration welled as the warriors sought to regain control, but the unending tide hindered their ability to concentrate and fight effectively as they desperately tried to fend off the furry attackers.

Isaiah urged the zenizens of Glimmerhavan to follow. With renewed determination, they pressed on, knowing that the battle was far from over as they fought back as one against the tide of darkness. The sudden periodic explosions from oxygen tanks disrupted the fighting rhythm, catching the Drakonian warriors off guard. The General seized a momentary advantage to assess the situation. The fight had spilled over into the town centre, where the clash had unfolded like a theatre of war. In narrow alleyways, the struggle intensified as warriors from each side engaged in close combat. The clashing of blades, shouts, and the occasional roar of a wounded beast echoed off the walls. Amid the chaos, the General observed as Valour and Isaiah fought side by side. He couldn't help but marvel at the display as the duo defended each other's backs, their weapons moving with fluid grace. It was a testament to the bond forged on the battlefield and the unyielding spirit that fuelled their resistance. The smoke of battle swirled around them as the General locked eyes with the Drakonian commander, a formidable figure clad in intimidating armour. The intensity of their gaze served as a prelude to the impending confrontation.

Mia carefully positioned the crystal into its designated slot, her heart pounding with a mix of excitement and trepidation. As she completed the task, a thunderous chime erupted from the colossal cast bells, resonating through the air like a declaration of war. Instinctively, she covered her ears, bracing against the overwhelming sound that vibrated through her very core. As the chime rang out, the ground beneath the tower began to shake and tremble, sending powerful shockwaves that would ripple across the entire five provinces. Feeling dizzy and unsteady, she struggled against the tremors as she made her way to the exit door, her heart pounding with uncertainty about what lay ahead. She struggled but managed to fasten her harness to the hovering Earveers, closed her eyes, and leapt into the void. A wave of fear washed over her as she felt the drop, her stomach twisting in knots. Just as panic began to grip her, the Earveers regained their balance, lifting her smoothly upward and onward to the safety of the clearing, where her brother and Princess Arabella awaited her arrival. In that moment, Mia understood that she had unleashed a force of monumental significance, one that would alter the very fabric of Cyberia.

The General backed away from the commander to listen to the triumphant call from the Bulwarkodons, signalling Mia's success and serving as a predetermined cue for everyone to retreat. Mia looked down at the town centre and wished that she hadn't as she witnessed the carnage of the battle raging below. Not knowing who was alive, dead, or injured, her joy turned to horror.

Undeterred, Theron Ironclaw surged forward, his sword raised high. The sleek, obsidian blade was crafted from a rare celestial alloy, shimmering with a silver light. It was designed for both thrusting and throwing, capable of piercing through the most formidable armour. General Titanous met the challenge head-on, his spear gleaming with an ethereal light. The clash of their weapons reverberated through the town centre, marking the epicentre of the struggle. Their battle unfolded like a fierce maelstrom, a symphony of clashes and strikes.Their skills were matched only by the intensity of their determination. The town's fate hung in the balance as they engaged in a duel that would echo through the annals of history. The clash of their swords sent sparks flying in all directions. A deep-seated rage fuelled the commander's attacks, his movements aggressive and unrelenting as he sought to overpower his opponent through sheer force.

The General's swift footwork and precise counters showcased his finesse, a masterclass in combat. As the commander charged forward, swinging his sword with ferocious intent, the General feigned a retreat, drawing Ironclaw into a false sense of superiority. Just as the commander committed to a powerful downward strike, the General executed a well-timed sidestep, allowing the blade to slice through the air where he had just stood. In that instant, he seized the opportunity, stepping in close and using the hilt of his sword to strike the commander's wrist with precision. The impact jolted Ironclaw's grip, causing his sword to slip from his hand and clatter to the ground. With Ironclaw momentarily disarmed and off balance, the General swiftly followed up with a fluid motion, sweeping his leg behind the commander's ankles. The formidable warrior stumbled, crashing to the earth in a heap.

Theron Ironclaw lay defeated, gasping for breath as the General kicked his weapon beyond reach. The General stood victorious with a heavy boot pressed firmly across Ironclaw's neck. Another emotional sight seized the attention of the General's army. Once frozen in eerie stillness, the clock's four dials began to stir with newfound life. The two figurines, Glimmer and Havan, freed from their dormancy, commenced their routine walk along the narrow walkway surrounding the outer clock's fascia. The precision of their movements resonated with a harmony that reached the depths of the warriors' hearts. Emotions ran the gamut from astonishment to a profound connection with something more significant than the immediate battlefield. It was a moment of unexpected beauty amid the chaos, stirring a shared sentiment of unity among the army. In that fleeting instance, the commander knew all was lost, leaving an indelible mark of disgrace.

The General drove the stump of his spectral spear into the ground, the impact creating a resonant echo that demanded attention. The cacophony of battle was replaced by the sporadic explosions of oxygen tanks in the background. "Hear ye all," he bellowed, "there can be no winner in this battle that has pained so many. I will allow your commander to have his existence, but on condition my army withdraws peacefully." He released his foothold and looked down at the commander. "By offering this withdrawal, I want you to inform King Kronos that this will be the only withdrawal that I will ever make."

"I give my word that I will allow you to withdraw," Theron Ironclaw answered through gritted teeth.

Faced with the uncertainty of a Drakonian's trustworthiness, the General stood firm. His penetrating gaze remained locked on the commander as he declared, "Trust is not forged in the heat of battle; it is built during times of peace." He gestured skyward, asserting, "This is my assurance that you will honour your word." The ominous presence of the Nano TalonHawks, circling above, added weight to his statement. "I will return to collect the fallen. If you choose to stay in Glimmerhavan, what remains of your battalion will fade into insignificance." He allowed the commander to rise back onto his feet.

The General ordered a retreat, his voice resolute as he stressed the importance of prioritising the wounded. Valour approached, his expression grave as he delivered the news: Isaiah had been injured by shrapnel from an exploding oxygen tank. The weight of the revelation hit the General like a physical blow, and his heart sank at the thought of his comrade's pain.

Max and the Princess stood at the edge of the clearing, their eyes fixed on the horizon. In the distance, a figure emerged, carried by the weary wings of the Earveers. "It's Mia," the Princess exclaimed excitedly. The Earveers descended with a grace that belied their exhaustion. The rising sun bathed them in a sweaty glow, emphasising the weariness etched into their faces. Mia landed on ground, her face tinged with relief and grief. She unclasped herself from the harness and turned to the Earveers, acknowledging their role in her journey with heartfelt gratitude: "Thank you, my faithful friends. Your loyalty and courage will forever be my guiding light." The Nano TalonHawks, swirling in murmuration, commenced their descent, with a percentage of their formation missing. Mia, visibly upset, declared that they had sacrificed their 'exsistence' for the greater good.

Max felt a deep ache in his heart as he thought of the heartbreaking things his sister must have witnessed. The weight of her struggles was evident in her eyes, a mix of resilience and sorrow that spoke of lost innocence. He knew this day would forever remain in his heart as the moment his sister matured and said goodbye to her childhood, forever marked by the challenges she had faced.

The Princess took Mia's hand and guided her toward Bilko and Oscar, who were tethered to a sapling, barking and bleating with excitement at her arrival. "These precious creatures are just a small part of why sacrifices must be made," she said.

Mia, caught in a moment of indecision about whom to embrace first, unexpectedly chose the Princess. "One day, you will become a remarkable queen, and on that day, I believe peace will return to Cyberia."

The Princess was momentarily at a loss for words by the weary procession of GiggleSprites and farmers making their way back into the clearing. Among them, Isaiah, bearing serious injuries, clung to his horse's neck for support. Valour held the reins, guiding their steeds through the tired group of strays. The Princess, Max, and Mia rushed to help. Valour leapt from his WhiteTail and carefully lowered his injured friend into his arms. Cradling Isaiah, he made his way beneath the protective canopy of a nearby tree.

Valour examined Isaiah's wound which he had hastily bandaged with torn clothing on the battlefield. The severity of his injury was evident in the amount of the red code he had lost. Turning towards his Princess, Valour shook his head solemnly, signalling that Isaiah's exsistence was fast coming to its end. Overwhelmed with the realisation, the Princess and Mia sank to their knees, shock and tears intertwining in their expressions. Max looked on with the moment's gravity etched across his face with tear-filled eyes.

A sudden rush of cold air swept through the clearing. It was a chill that penetrated their jackets, wrapping around them like a brisk embrace. The air was sharp and refreshing, carrying with it the scent of pine and the promise of winter. They exchanged brief words of surprise, their breath visible in the frosty mist. The sky began to shift, dark clouds gathering like a thick blanket. Slowly, delicate snowflakes started to fall, drifting lazily at first as if unsure of their descent. Max and Mia watched in awe as the first few flakes landed softly on their outstretched hands, melting almost instantly. The snowfall quickened, transforming into a flurry of shimmering white.

The Princess knelt and held Isaiah's hand. "If you can hear me, my brave Isaiah, we have won. We did it."

General Titanous strode into the clearing, flanked by the Bulwarkodons, the last remnants of his army> Max's anger ignited, emotions raw and unrestrained as the General approached. Snowflakes dusted his hair, contrasting sharply with the fire burning within him. He pleaded with the General, desperation lacing his voice as he urged for action to save Isaiah's life or he would never return to Cyberia. Mia, caught in a whirlwind of feelings, stepped forward, her voice trembling as she agreed with her brother. The haunting prospect of losing Isaiah forever was a weight too heavy to bear.

Kneeling beside Isaiah, General Titanous felt the burden of uncertainty pressing down on him as he reached out to touch the gaping wound that marred Isaiah's side. Princess Arabella rose, placing a reassuring hand on the General's shoulder. In that moment, a silent understanding passed between them, and they both closed their eyes, entering a profound state of meditation.Together, they focused their thoughts and emotions, channeling their collective strength toward the Pathfinder. An inexplicable surge of energy coursed through their bodies, creating a connection that transcended the digital realm. An unseen force, both mysterious and ethereal, swirled around them, weaving a tapestry of healing that embraced their hearts. Their eyes opened in astonishment as they witnessed a remarkable sight: Isaiah's red code, the undeniable evidence of conflict began to dissipate, fading like a distant memory.

The colour slowly returned to Isaiah's ashen face. The jubilant General declared, "The love and affection you've all shown has restored Isaiah's existence. However, I was told that this intervention will be a singular occurrence."

"I have the power, too," said the Princess emotionally. "I heard the Pathfinders words. The Pathfinder truly exists!"

"Max. Mia. The Pathfinder has expressed his gratitude for everything you've done for Cyberia. He mentioned that you've earned the right to receive your digital amulets upon your return," said the General.

"Return?" Max asked, puzzled.

"Yes. You will go back to your world to rest before the amulet ceremony in Arbitration Land, which I will oversee," he explained.

"But what about the Drakonians? We can't just leave you here," Mia said, her concern for their safety outweighing her interest in the amulets.

"The Drakonians will retreat in embarrassment. However, King Kronos and Malice Malware will continue their scheming, preparing for an all-out war. The five provinces must brace for an unprecedented challenge that will far exceed today's injuries and losses. Glimmerhavan must now confront the aftermath of the battle and honour the fallen."

"Can I take Oscar with me?" Mia asked.

"You know the answer to that. In your world, Oscar wouldn't exist."

"Could you ask the Pathfinder or the Gatekeeper to hold off until we see Isaiah recover from his injuries?"

"You've accomplished more than I ever thought possible in saving Isaiah's life. You will see him upon your return," the General replied.

When the dreaded moment arrived and the portal materialized with a loud noise, Mia knelt down to gently kiss Isaiah's forehead. They both said their goodbyes to the Princess and Valour, embracing them tightly. Mia exchanged heartfelt farewells with Oscar and Bilko, their final expressions of gratitude directed at General Titanous. Max began, "General, your guidance and support have been our guiding light. Without you, our journey would have been impossible. Your wisdom has served as our compass, and your courage has been our strength."

Mia added, her voice filled with emotion, "You haven't just defended us against threats; you've shown us the true power of unity. Your dedication to protecting Cyberia has left a lasting impression on our hearts. We owe our success to you and are deeply grateful for everything you are."

With a nod of unusual emotion, General Titanous replied, "It has been an honour to stand alongside you both. Remember, the strength of Cyberia lies in its defenders, and you have proven yourselves to be its champions. Go forth knowing that you have protected and inspired change. Until we meet again, I bid you a fond farewell." Max and Mia stepped into the portal. As it began to close, Mia turned to form a heart shape with her fingers, blowing a loving kiss in their direction as the portal—vanished.

Epilogue

The Pursuit of Lord Elric

Lord Elric's spies alerted him that his name was being whispered in the clandestine circles of assassins as someone marked for elimination. He understood his time as a royal adviser to the new king was over before it truly began and made plans to leave Valaria. He recognised that his best opportunity to outwit the enemy who had outsmarted his king rested in the relatively safe refuge of Arbitration Land.

The sole companion he trusted was the horse he rode out on through the palace gates. Cloaked in a garment woven from digital ether, it masked his scent from the SablePaw hounds that could track him down. Moving through the woods and diverse landscapes, he utilised the survival skills he had learned in his youth and was pleased with how swiftly those treasured memories came flooding back when he needed them the most.

He could sense the proximity of his pursuers. At times, their dark laughter would resound through the stillness of the forest night, chilling him to the bone. He forged on to cross over into the province of Verdantis. Fatigued and weary, he settled down for the night, only to be jolted awake by a deep rumbling beneath him. The rumbling escalated into a fierce quake as if the land was awakening from a long, deep slumber. The trees around him swayed violently in the brisk wind, their branches groaning and leaves rustling in a wild dance. This sudden disturbance created tangible energy, leaving him disoriented as he struggled to rise unsteadily to his feet.

The intensity of the moment suddenly struck him. This was no mere disturbance; it was a profound sign, a powerful testament to the Princess's successful effort to restore the fragile ecosystem balance across the five provinces. In that instant, he understood the significance of what he was witnessing—the land was alive and thriving once more, a reflection of the Princess's unwavering dedication and courage.

Overwhelmed, he dropped to his knees. Tears flowed down his cheeks as he witnessed the beginning of snow falling into a blanket of joyful heaviness. Memories of past winters flooded his mind, each tinged with nostalgia as the snow settled softly on the ground. It was as if nature was painting a masterpiece, the white canvas inviting new beginnings. But this snowfall felt different, a reminder that beauty could emerge from even the darkest times. As he stood there, he felt the weight of his worries begin to lift, replaced by a sense of possibility. It reignited the resolve within him that had been gradually fading into despair and defeat.

Lord Elric continued his journey with newfound strength, knowing the true battle against his king, Malice Malware, and King Kronos had only just begun.

Cyberian Chronicles
The Pathfinder

Set to debut in June 2025, the conclusion promises to be an epic culmination of the intense conflict that has unfolded. As tensions reach a fever pitch, heroes and villains will confront their most formidable fears and challenges. Alliances will be tested, destinies unveiled, and emotional farewells will resonate with unexpected twists. The stakes have never been higher; the fate of Cyberia hangs precariously in the balance as the final showdown approaches. The finale is destined to leave a profound impact, lingering in the minds of readers long after the last page is turned.

The Pathfinder

Website:
MaliceMalware.com

For film or educational inquiries, please forward messages to:
malicemalware@yahoo.com

Printed in Great Britain
by Amazon

51804177R00148